THE VALUE
OF KINDNESS

Winner of the 1992 Willa Cather Fiction Prize

The Willa Cather Fiction Prize was established in 1991 by
Helicon Nine Editions, and will be awarded annually to a previously
unpublished manuscript chosen by a distinguished writer through
an open nationwide competition.

The judge for 1992 was James Byron Hall.

THE VALUE
OF
KINDNESS

Stories
ELLYN BACHE

HELICON NINE EDITIONS
KANSAS CITY, MISSOURI

Certain of these stories first appeared in: *Ascent, O. Henry Festival Stories,
Craszyquilt, Writer's Forum 12, Southern Magazine, The MacGuffin, Virginia
Country, Southern Humanities Review In-Print, and Pennsylvania English.*
Book Design: Tim Barnhart.

Cover: Philip Evergood, *Lily and the Sparrows*, 1939.
Oil on composition board, 30"x 49".
Collection Whitney Museum of American Art, New York. Purchase 41.42.

Partial funding for this project has been provided by
the Kansas Arts Commission and the Missouri Arts Council, state agencies;
and by the N. W. Dible Foundation.

Library of Congress Cataloging-in-Publication Data

Bache, Ellyn.
    The value of kindness / by Ellyn Bache. -- 1st ed.
        p.   cm.
    ISBN: 0-9627460-8-8   :   (on acid-free paper) $11.95
    I. Title.
PS3563.A845V35   1993
813' .54--dc20
                                                            93-10820
                                                            CIP

This book is printed in the United States of America.

FIRST EDITION

HELICON NINE EDITIONS • P. O. Box 22412 • Kansas City, MO 64113

For my Family:
Terry, Beth, Matt, James, and Ben

CONTENTS

PIGEONS

AT THE AGE OF EIGHTY, Esther DuBois was sued by her neighbors, the Fines, for feeding the pigeons in her back yard.

"There are hundreds of them," Harold Fine claimed.

"Hundreds nothing," Esther replied. "There are maybe twenty."

"He's counting the other birds, too, Ma," Esther' s daughter, Barbara, told her. "You know it's not just the pigeons ."

"Frankly, I'm afraid for my son," Louise Fine said. "A two-year-old has no defense against those filthy things. I can't keep him indoors all the time. Bird droppings everywhere. The place is a sewer."

"Sewer! Ha! The birds come, they eat, and they go. What droppings? Show me."

"Do you realize there's a fatal blood disease they carry?"

"Listen. When I was a child in Brussels my mother fed birds every day," Esther said. "Never once did I get sick or die from a fatal blood disease."

Face-to-face confrontations quickly reached an impasse. Esther received a summons to appear in court at the end of July.

"Do you really need this aggravation, Ma?" Barbara asked. "What would be so terrible if you just stopped feeding them?" Barbara had two teenagers home from school for the summer, so life wasn't easy for her, but still Esther meant to hold her own.

"People would be better off if they would concentrate on being generous to helpless things instead of making an issue," she said.

"Ma, you can't afford to have this thing land in court, you know you can't."

"I'm an old woman. The court will take that into consideration."

"No it won't. You know who'll end up paying for it? Don and me. The shoe business is in a major recession, Lisa's getting braces on her teeth, and all we need is a court case to worry about right now."

3

"I'll pay you back," Esther said aloud. But even at eighty, Esther was not above a small glimmering of malice. She had adopted Barbara under very trying circumstances, about which Barbara had never been told, and in the back of her mind Esther was thinking: *you owe me.*

Barbara visited her mother every morning. This was so Esther could continue to live on her own, without a paid companion. Barbara took Esther to the store, now that she no longer drove, and ran her daily errands—a matter of half an hour. After the summons arrived, Harold Fine stopped speaking to Esther directly. Instead he cornered Barbara on her arrival to convey any message he might have.

"Listen, Harold," Barbara told him. "My mother is eighty years old, she's not in wonderful health, and she doesn't have all that many hobbies. Don and I haven't had a vacation for two years because I have to check up on her every day. But when someone reaches that age, you do those things. Most neighbors would take that into consideration."

"It's not that I'm in the business of hassling eighty-year-old people," Harold said, holding his hands out in an assertion of innocence. "But when the well-being of a child is involved, you take it as far as you have to."

Esther heard this. "In Brussels there was a statue of a woman feeding pigeons," she told her daughter. "If they make statues of such a thing, how terrible can it be? No judge is going to rule against helpless birds."

"Wait and see," Barbara said.

It had been Esther's habit, even before this trouble, to have a light lunch after Barbara's departure, and then retire to her air-conditioned bedroom for a nap. The heat of Southern summers had never agreed with her. Her first forty-two summers in Belgium had been seasons of rain and breeze, which she still recalled with fondness. After the summons arrived, her old body moved more slowly than ever. In the dense humidity it was all she could do to keep her eyes open through lunch. When she hit her bed, the whir of machine-cooled air floated above her and she slept right away. Her dreams, which she had always remembered, became vivid scenes from her past (re-livings, almost), as exhausting as the tension with the Fines.

At one moment Barbara would appear before her as she was now, a nervously thin woman of forty, dry skin beginning to line, speaking at length about the depressed shoe business. At the next Barbara would be a dark-haired teenager, laughing at her parents for their old-world ways, teasing that she might not be their daughter after all, given that she was so dark and they were so light. Then Esther's late husband Edgar would appear: first as an old man sitting in this very bedroom, troubled by heart disease, and then just as suddenly healthy and young, talking with her in their apartment in Brussels early in their marriage.

"The rooms are too dark," Edgar would say. And Esther would laugh and tell him it didn't matter, she would fix it up. It was what they could afford, after all, on his government salary.

Always she woke with a start, past and present jumbled in her mind, the scenes not overlapping so much as seeming all of a piece, dots on a continuum. And she, possessing the whole, could pluck portions of her life at will: her youth, her marriage to Edgar when she was thirty, their voyage to America when Barbara was a toddler, and everything that had happened since.

Then her moment of clarity departed, the images dimmed, and she was a drained old woman, chilled by the air-conditioning, staring at the red numbers on her digital clock. Often several hours had passed. She forced herself up into the kitchen and prepared her evening feeding for the birds. Seed. Bread crusts. Whatever leftovers she thought suited a pigeon's digestive system. When the sun dropped low in the sky, she ventured into the yard and began to sprinkle her offerings on the ground. At her appearance, the pigeons dipped from their roosting places by the score, a flap of gray wings.

Esther held some of the bread in her hand. Several of the birds ate from her fingertips—birds she had nursed from skeletons into balls of luxurious feather. The air in the yard was still except for their motion. She was sweating when they had finished. Back in the house she prepared her own meal slowly, watching as she ate, the pigeons flying away and the smaller birds coming to scrounge for what was left. Lately, after she finished the dishes, if the Fines were not in their yard, she would go outside again to retrieve any bird droppings that had been left behind. It had never been her intention to present a health hazard to two-year-olds.

"Histoplasmosis," Barbara told her one day. "Histoplasmosis and psittacosis."

"What are you talking about?" Esther asked.

"The Fines are right. Pigeons do spread disease. Histoplasmosis is a fungus that attacks the lungs. Usually it's not serious, but if it spreads out of the lungs to other parts of the body, it can be fatal."

"Who told you that?"

"I looked it up in the encyclopedia. Pigeons can also spread parrot fever. Psittacosis."

"Show me one person who ever had it."

"You get it by handling diseased birds."

"I don't handle diseased birds," Esther said flatly. "You think diseased birds would have the energy to fly down here every day to eat?"

"What I'm saying, Ma, is that he does have a case."

"Oh—a case. *Birds.* If you could remember the war, you'd know about cases. Cases to knock your socks off."

"Oh mother." Barbara laughed. "When you try to use slang you sound so—*European.*"

"So? What's so terrible about being European?"

Esther felt a little ill when Barbara left. She went to the bedroom without lunch. She was suddenly ashamed of her Europeanness. She dreamed about her apartment in Brussels. Edgar was at work and her mother was visiting her. It was at the beginning of the war.

"You married too late," her mother was saying.

"That's nonsense, mother. Lots of women have children in

their thirties."

Her mother sighed. "You'll soon be forty."

"Then maybe I should leave well enough alone. Edgar and I are happy, the two of us." But she did not feel happy. She woke to the sound of her own voice and knew she'd been talking in her sleep.

One day Harold Fine left his house early and returned with a load of lumber in his car. He brought the wood into the yard, stacked it into a pile. Esther watched him from her kitchen window. By noon sweat was dripping into his eyes and the beginnings of a stockade fence had taken shape between the yards. Fine's face was intent and full of anger. He pounded on the wood with muted fury. Such hate. For the first time in thirty-five years Esther thought of the political refugees. She could not eat her lunch. She went to her bedroom and lay down.

When she slept, she dreamed the political refugees were in her apartment in Brussels. The shades were drawn and the rooms were so stuffy she could hardly breathe. She and Edgar had harbored the young couple for several months during the war. The husband was dark and wild-eyed. The wife was pregnant. Esther always insisted on calling them political refugees, though actually they were Jewish. In the dream Esther was wearing her coat, as if to go out, but instead she and Edgar were sitting in their bedroom, away from the refugees, arguing in hoarse whispers.

"What are you—crazy?"

"I'm going out for a short walk, Edgar. How much harm could it do? I haven't been outside for months. How long can one person do without sunlight?"

"Yes. And I've spent two months telling everyone how sick you are, how you're having such a difficult confinement."

"It's one thing for you," she said. "You go out every day. But for *me...*"

"What? You want to be the one buying meat for us on the black market? If I didn't go out every day, four of us would be eating rations meant for two," he said. His voice was bitter.

He gestured with his head toward the next room. "Think how it must be for *them*," he hissed.

Then time shifted and she was sitting in her Brussels living room, couched in the brownish light that filtered in through the lowered shades. She had been crying for some time. The refugee man was sitting beside her, trying to offer comfort.

"Don't be upset," he said. "We know what will happen sooner or later. We've accepted that. Who knows, maybe we even have a plan. If we can just hold off until the baby comes. . . . "

But Esther was crying for herself, not for them—for her confinement to small spaces and low voices and dearth of sunlight. She cried harder. When she was finished she sat for a long moment ashamed: that he, not she, should be kind.

Harold Fine was still hammering, hammering when she woke, building his wall. Esther gathered scraps for the evening feeding and went out into the yard. Fine looked at her but didn't speak. She heard the flapping of wings and turned toward them. Hate or no hate, she meant to feed her birds.

Two days later Barbara made Esther an appointment with Legal Aid. Esther was not receptive. "I'm telling you, any sane judge will throw it out."

"Ma, don't be such a stubborn mule."

"I don't like to make appointments in this heat."

"The appointment's at nine in the morning. The building is air-conditioned."

"Barbara. . . no."

"You know what could happen if you lose this thing?"

"What?"

"It could cost you the house." So Esther went. The air-conditioning in the county office building was set to seventy-eight degrees for energy conservation purposes, and the lawyer could not have been more than twenty-five. "He's one of those ones who think you're stupid if you have an accent," Esther said afterwards. He spoke slowly, as if to make sure she understood, and said he thought Fine's argument was pretty solid. By the time the appointment was over the day was yellow with hazy heat. Esther felt slightly lightheaded. She could hardly wait to get home to her own air-conditioner by her bed, which kept the room at a pleasant sixty-seven degrees.

She dreamed about the birth. A mattress from her mother's house had been set up in the dining room of the dim apartment, where now the refugee woman lay gripping her husband's arm, biting on a towel so as not to scream.

"When the next pain comes, push," Esther's mother was saying. Esther's mother had been brought in because there was no question of a doctor, and because Esther knew nothing of childbirth. "Besides, no one will question your mother coming for a visit," Edgar had said.

A low groan escaped from the woman's mouth. Esther, too, wanted to scream. This birth seemed to have been going on for days, for years. For months they had breathed this stale air, had walked barefoot on the dark wood floors, hushed and afraid of sounds outside in the hallway. For months they had been polite to these strangers. She had never understood how the young woman, clumsy with pregnancy, remained content, somehow, like a cow. She understood the husband's wild eyes better. And now the woman's calm was gone. She clung to her husband's arm and groaned. The scream rose in Esther's throat, high and wild and free. She swallowed it back. She smoothed the woman's hair from her forehead until the woman's sweat was on her hands, but she didn't make a sound. There were things she wanted more than screaming.

The woman tensed, her whole body a taut muscle. "Push now," Esther's mother said in a fierce whisper. "*Push.*"

The woman pushed, a slight grunt escaping through the towel. And pushed more, pushed longer. A wet head emerged, capped in dark hair, slowly, slowly, into Esther's mother's hands. A surprised expression on the little face. And the body, slippery, covered with blood and slime. The woman relaxed.

"A girl," someone said. The baby cried. Esther's mother

held it up, a cold wet thing with dark hair, angry and red.

"You have a daughter," Esther whispered into the woman's ear. But the woman held it only briefly, tears flowing down her cheeks, and pushed the infant toward Esther. "Your daughter," she said.

She woke to the ringing of the doorbell. The police? She sat bolt upright, alarmed. After all that, to be caught? Then she looked down at her trembling, wrinkled hands. The air conditioner whirred in her ear. Had so much time passed? Could she be old? She smoothed her dress and stood up, propelling her thick slow body toward the door. It was Fine.

"Mrs. DuBois, the trial is next week," he said with forced calm, forced patience. "I'm willing to drop the charges if we can come to some kind of an agreement. This is my last offer. You stop feeding the birds and it's forgotten. I won't even charge you for the fence. What do you say?"

Charge her for the fence! "I say nothing doing," Esther said.

It was a bad week, a heat wave, humidity above fifty percent every day. Barbara checked on Esther at odd hours, sometimes twice a day. "You don't need to sleep so much, Ma," she said once, startling Esther awake from a nap. For a moment Esther could not decide which Barbara was talking, the teenaged Barbara of her dream, or the nervous, fortyish Barbara. It seemed really not to matter.

"So much sleep makes you sluggish," Barbara said. "You heard what the doctor said."

"I have to get up my strength to feed the birds."

"After today you might get a long vacation. I'll pick you up at nine tomorrow to go to court. Frankly I hate to see this fiasco."

"Fiasco nothing," Esther said. "This is a matter of principle."

That night she was awake until after two. Maybe Barbara was right she should limit her naps to an hour. When she finally dozed she dreamed that the stockade fence had enclosed her, shutting the birds outside.

• • •

The Legal Aid lawyer moved for dismissal, but the judge decided to hear the case. The testimony took less than an hour. The judge ruled in favor of the Fines—a hundred dollars.

"For nuisance value," the Legal Aid lawyer said. Fine had asked for damages and payment for the fence, but these were denied. Esther was ordered to stop feeding the birds.

"See? All that trouble for nothing," Barbara said on the way home. "There's something to be said for appeasement, you know. Living with conditions as they exist. The Fines aren't going to be satisfied with a lousy hundred dollars. They'll make your life miserable."

Esther was very tired. She felt in herself that afternoon a sort of drawing coldness, though the temperature was above ninety. She knew it was the beginning of her death. She had no wish to fight it, but she sensed that it was to come on her slowly, and in the meantime she must go on as usual, prepare her bowl of bread, take her naps. She knew she would dream of the political refugees, and perhaps wonder what had happened to them after they left her apartment, leaving Barbara to her care. She would dream of her mother, who had died before the end of the war. It couldn't be helped. When she woke she would have some soup and then go into her yard, Fines or no Fines.

"The birds are just helpless, but the Fines are troublemakers," Esther said. "I'm not much for appeasement."

"If you were, you'd be a whole lot happier, Ma."

Esther was silent for a time. Her eyes were drifting shut. "And where would you be?" she asked at last.

"Now what's that supposed to mean?"

"Did you know that during the war pigeons carried Allied messages through enemy lines?" Her voice was heavy. Perhaps she would doze for just a minute. If her death was to be leisurely, she had to conserve her strength .

"Oh, honestly. Do you really believe that makes any difference now?"

"It doesn't hurt to bestow a little honor," Esther said.

"Bestow a little honor! You tell more war stories, Ma."

Esther's eyes were just a slit beneath heavy lids, but she no longer wanted to sleep. "I'm about to tell you a war story," she said, "that will knock your socks off."

ANDREA'S MOTHER IS
A VERY SICK WOMAN

THIS IS HOW MUCH ANDREA HATES HER MOTHER: when Dolores goes into the hospital for her surgery, Andrea wishes her dead.

She does.

She finds her father in the kitchen, hidden behind the newspaper, weeping. In the nineteen years of Andrea's life, her mother has never before entered a hospital. Seven hundred diseases and never an admission. Andrea is mortified to see her father in tears, proving himself slight and spineless.

"What time's the operation?" she asks, giving him opportunity to compose himself. Retrieving a white cotton handkerchief from his pocket, he blows his nose loudly. "Eight tomorrow morning," he replies, sniffing.

"She's just in for hemorrhoids," Andrea says. "Nobody dies from hemorrhoids."

If they are going to mourn her, Andrea thinks, she ought at least to have cancer or heart disease. Something terminal.

"We'll get a bite of supper and then stay with her through visiting hours," Andrea's father says. "Andrea, this isn't optional."

The story is that Andrea's mother wanted to be a nurse but couldn't afford the schooling. The truth is, Dolores has been in love with illness all her life.

Andrea was five when Dolores sat down on a curb in front of a department store full of Saturday shoppers and said she could go no farther. "You stay with her," Andrea's father ordered. "I'll get the car." Andrea's mother put her head in her hands and her feet in the street—a huge, sprawling woman camped on the sidewalk like a beggar. "Do you need help?" a stranger asked. Dolores didn't speak. "No," Andrea said. "My father went to get the car." Humiliated, terrified, Andrea stood guard on the curb, wishing her mother were normal. She wishes it still.

Dolores took to her bed for nearly a month then, claiming a nervous breakdown. Andrea's Aunt Sheila brought

13

casseroles, and her Uncle Leo, the doctor, came every day. In Dolores's family the boys went to medical school and the girls, to capture their brothers' attention, had interesting diseases. They didn't know then Leo would die at forty from a melanoma he diagnosed himself, leaving Dolores forever thwarted in her yearning to make medical history under his care.

Three weeks after she sat down in the street, Dolores finally got herself up and dressed. "I knew when I saw dustballs under the bed and didn't care, I was getting better," she said triumphantly. At that time, Dolores's energies went mainly to cleaning.

So why, a few months later, on a winter day so dark that all the lights were on, so dark that the navy-and-gray somberness of the outdoors permeated the apartment nevertheless, was Andrea's mother back to ferreting out every fingerprint and speck of dust? Rubbing the furniture raw, lugging the vacuum from room to room? And why, once the roaring motor stopped, was the vacuum's sound and energy replaced by heaviness and darkness—not the effect of diminished outside light, but of Dolores's mood? As young children do, Andrea sensed her mother's heaviness as surely as she did heat or cold. She knew Dolores felt this emotion whenever she prepared Andrea's meals or cleaned the apartment or shopped for food: this heaviness that was boredom.

Why?

At the hospital, Andrea's father buys a pot of tulips in the gift shop, which seems premature since the surgery is twelve hours away. Andrea hates hospitals and feels sick just entering one. She has a slight pain in her right side—the sort her mother would immediately diagnose as appendicitis but Andrea dismisses as ovulation cramps. Upstairs, in a double room occupied for the moment only by a single person, Dolores perches atop a bed rolled to sitting position, arranging newly permed hair cut short in case she can't attend it. She wears an almost-sheer gown that reveals large breasts sagging onto her stomach, thin flabby arms, an ex-fat-person's body, embarrassing. Andrea's father, oblivious, hands her the tulips.

"Oh Richard, they're lovely!"

"My God, mother, what do you have on?" Andrea asks.

"Do you like it?" Dolores moves her shoulders to model. "Better than that backless nightshirt the hospital gives you," she says. As long as a person is ill, Dolores believes, it's appropriate to go around naked.

"Here, put on your robe." Andrea commands, lifting it from a corner of the bed and thrusting it toward her mother. "You'll freeze." Andrea doesn't actually believe her mother is susceptible to freezing. She recalls the night in high school when Dolores flung the front door open to wind and snow and Andrea saying goodnight to a date, and stood in front of them for ten minutes, in a gown reminiscent of this one, scolding, oblivious of the cold, while the boy contemplated the horrors of Dolores's flabby body.

"Where have you been?" Dolores shouted then. "I've been having heart palpitations! I almost called the police." And on and on until the boy left shamed and flustered, never to return.

Now Dolores puts on the robe so dutifully that it's clear her thoughts are elsewhere. "They made me take off my nail polish in case I don't get enough oxygen on the operating table," she says, lifting long fingers for Andrea's father to see. "They want to be able to see in case my fingers turn blue."

"How comforting," Andrea mutters.

"I hate to look at naked nails," Dolores complains. The nails do look naked. Dolores is never without red and garish polish. Andrea's father engulfs Dolores's hand with his own, as if to hide whatever offends her. "My nails are my only vanity," Dolores sighs.

At this, Andrea imagines herself four years old again, inhaling the acrid scent of polish remover as Dolores sat at the kitchen table, industriously eradicating last week's manicure. Out with the old, in with the new! Dolores filed her nails, pushed back cuticles. The dark heaviness of boredom gave way to stillness and serenity. Base coat, then a pause for drying. Two coats of red—never pink, never peach, always red.

Another wait. Top coat. Dolores was the soul of patience. Often she polished Andrea's nails, too. Two females in league together.

And then. Nails dry, orange sticks and files zipped away, cotton balls swept into the trash, Dolores wiggled red-tipped fingers in Andrea's direction. She grabbed her, hugged her, began to tickle Andrea's arms and chest. Tickled to bring merriment and excitement to the room—to ward off the dark heaviness that might otherwise return. She tickled Andrea's ribs, under her arms. Too small to escape, Andrea squirmed and laughed. After a while she hated her mother because the poking fingers were a kind of pain, and she was laughing, laughing, and could neither breathe nor stop.

The drawing cramp in Andrea's side now takes her breath away, too. Unlike her mother, she won't announce her discomfort to the world. Rather, she examines her own nails with satisfaction, unpolished and bitten to the quick.

A white-clad nurse's aide sweeps in, holding a thermometer and blood pressure cuff. Pleased, Dolores sinks back into her pillow. She opens her mouth, extends her arm, submits like someone at a weight-loss spa, about to get what she's paid for, however unpleasant. When the aide bustles out, Dolores says ruefully, "Even after all these years I still think it was a mistake not to go to nursing school."

"You could still do it if you want to," Andrea replies, picturing Dolores's spiky nails poking into someone's right side, producing pain identical to Andrea's. "A lot of women go back to school."

"It wouldn't be the same."

"It hasn't been easy for her," Andrea's father tells her. "Your grandparents could afford to give each child only one thing. Medical school for Leo and piano lessons for Aunt Sheila. With your mother's underbite, she didn't have a choice." He contorts his face, showing the lower teeth protruding in front of the uppers, monsterlike. "It was braces or nothing."

Dolores smiles heroically. "Richard, don't. She's heard this."

"It's true, Dad. I have." Although the braces were successful, they loosened Dolores's teeth. Now she wears dentures and has ended up with nothing. On the other hand, for all his medical training, Uncle Leo, being dead, is hardly better off.

"So. What did they give you for dinner?" Andrea's father asks, changing the subject.

"Soup and more soup." Now it's Dolores's turn to contort her face. Her liquid diet will help her after surgery, when for a time she won't be able to go to the bathroom easily. Dolores discusses this at length with friends on the phone. In Dolores's view, the functions and malfunctions of the body are public. Hearing it, some of the callers grow uneasy. Dolores doesn't understand. Why so squeamish?

But Andrea knows. Discussing the aging of the body with the now-retired postman whose feet were ailing, Dolores once said, "My arms I can see getting weak with age. But not my feet or legs. I've always had strong legs—as strong as yours, I bet. Calf muscles like a rock."

The postman cleared his throat, a gesture Andrea took for embarrassment and Dolores read as disbelief.

"Really—like a rock. Here, feel," she insisted, reaching for his hand.

"No, no, that's all right," the postman muttered, drawing back.

Dolores pursed her lips, hurt. She did have strong calves. Shouldn't she be proud? The body is a shrine.

Or else Dolores was holding up the x-ray of an ulcer that ate away at her stomach twelve years ago, holding it like a portrait, up to the light, to the curious eyes of a neighbor. "You see why I'm not someone who can go six hours between meals." She jabbed at the black and gray shadows with red nails, sipped slowly from a glass of milk and cream. "Six hours and the lining of my stomach would be raw. Dripping with blood." *Blood.* The neighbor blanched. Andrea, seven years old, knew the x-ray didn't actually show the ulcer, though Dolores pointed to a specific spot as if it did. "Often these tests aren't definitive," Uncle Leo had said. So Dolores gulped Maalox and sipped her milk and cream, conscripted to ignorance. Above the blood-colored nails, rolls of fat lined Dolores's upper arms, her neck, her chins. Milk and cream and crackers, whenever the pain began. "What else can I do?"

Then Andrea was eight, thin and wiry, expecting the cookies Dolores set out after school—Vienna fingers, always the same. Dolores's presence when Andrea came in was perfectly reliable, even if Dolores had been out shopping or lunching and might have preferred to stay. There were no sitters, no notes on the door.

In this sense, Andrea felt superior to her friends, more cherished. Each day she separated the halves of the cookies, licked the icing from inside, spoke briefly of school. But no cookies greeted her that day, only an apple. "I think the fruit is better for you," Dolores said, examining Andrea as if her eight-year-old flesh were massive and hanging, enormous as Dolores's own. Andrea burned under her gaze. She ate the apple, and in the months after that, Dolores began to lose weight. No more milk and cream for the ulcer, only a new drug. From that moment on, there was never a moment when Andrea didn't want a cookie.

"You know what Dr. Fellows said?" Dolores offers now. "He said surgery is always easier on a person like me, who's kept herself thin." She smiles knowingly, hugging the remains of her former huge body to herself, pockets of loose skin invisible under the robe.

"Then you have something to be proud of," Andrea's father says.

A loudspeaker intervenes, announcing the end of visiting hours.

"You have to go," Andrea's mother whispers, as if it's just dawned on her what this means.

"Come on, walk us to the elevator," her father almost bellows in his effort to be cheerful. "Getting out of this room will do you good."

"Not without my face on," Dolores says. As if it were removable, Andrea thinks.

"You look fine," Andrea's father tells her.

But Dolores pulls the bedside tray toward her, lifts the top, examines herself in the pop-up mirror. "Fine? Just look!" She takes makeup from the compartment beneath the mirror and paints a clown face, bright lipstick against pale skin. Andrea's side hurts. She wishes her mother would hurry. Her first knowledge was of this same large red mouth, talking incessantly, laughing too much, unseemly in a woman so incessantly sick. Dolores rolls the lipstick down, blots her lips on a tissue. She turns with a face completely different from the one a moment ago, vibrant and healthier, as if she's come alive. "There," she says. "Just let me get my slippers."

"Let me," Andrea's father says. The slippers are in the suitcase in a little closet by the door. Dolores reaches the closet first, lifting the case like a longshoreman, then freezing as she holds it in mid-air. "Oh. My bursitis." Paralyzed, immobile, she stands with the suitcase locked in her fist.

"Her bursitis," Andrea's father echoes, grabbing the case, setting it on the floor. Dolores sighs, grateful. She massages her afflicted shoulder. Andrea rolls her eyes. At home Dolores often stops with the full hot kettle in her hand, allowing Andrea and her father to rescue her from scorching water. Sometimes she gets cortisone shots in the joint—very painful—which ease the pain but don't effect a cure.

"I assume they'll biopsy the hemorrhoids," her mother says mournfully as the three of them walk down the hall toward the elevator, her father's hand beneath her mother's elbow as if she requires support.

"What for? I thought hemorrhoids were just veins," Andrea replies.

"They start out that way, but in case they've become something more serious. . . . " Dolores reduces each step to a slow shuffle, as if she's already post-operative and frail. She purses her lips so as not to show emotion—fear or pleasure, Andrea isn't sure which.

Is there such a thing as malignant hemorrhoids? As an ulcer that refuses to show on an x-ray? Bursitis that can't be x-rayed at all? They reach the elevator, and Andrea pushes the button, pushes away the ache in her side—another fantasy, a hypochondria, a reaction to stress. She will not let her mother invent a sick life for her. Never again! This is an old grievance. Maybe the worst.

Andrea was six, trusting. "You're allergic to high protein, probably," Dolores said. Andrea had sampled an oyster from her mother's plate and later threw up. It could have been coincidence.

"What's high protein?"

"Seafood and stuff."

For the moment Andrea didn't mind. Dolores put her to bed, placed a thermometer under her tongue. She loved her unquestioningly when Andrea was sick. When her stomach settled, her mother brought her toast and tea. She spoke in a gentle voice. Then—only then—Andrea's mother was a nurse.

But Andrea recovered. Always! Soon she was in a restaurant with other girls—a birthday celebration. They sat in the circle of a cool red leather booth, four girls and two mothers. Not Andrea's mother. Each girl wore a party dress and patent shoes. Each held a lavish menu, a printed page on parchment, covered in velvety red, bound with a golden tassel. They could just barely read it.

"I'll take the fried shrimp," the birthday girl announced.

"Me, too," another agreed.

The birthday girl's mother looked to Andrea, eyebrows raised.

"I'd like shrimp, but I better not."

"Oh? Why?"

"I'm allergic to high protein."

The two mothers exchanged glances. They grinned, lifted fingers to cover their mouths. Grown women giggling. "Allergic to high protein!" They laughed so much they had to dab their eyes.

Embarrassed, Andrea lowered her gaze and ordered a hamburger. She watched the others hold shrimp by batter-coated tails, take delicate bites of meat. Years later she told her Aunt Sheila, who said, "Eventually you got over it, didn't you?" No. Never. You never got over what your parents did to you when you were young. There is no such thing as high protein. No hemorrhoids that turn into something more serious. No ovulation cramps strong enough to masquerade as appendicitis, ovarian cysts, ruptures, cancer. Andrea will never be sick again.

"Good luck," her father says, kissing Dolores on the cheek. The elevator yawns open in front of them. "We'll be here in the morning before you go up."

Andrea's side aches in earnest now. She slips into the elevator while her mother looks on. Andrea knows it hasn't been easy for her, getting braces instead of music lessons or nursing school. Cleaning the house instead of healing patients. Tickling Andrea to bring laughter into the house, scolding her to ward off ill-intentioned boys, a boring fate. Andrea feels sorry for Dolores—of course she does—but her side hurts, and the most she can bring herself to do is give her mother a little wave. She doesn't offer a hug.

Andrea is still in pain the next morning when Dolores comes down from surgery. Usually these cramps are gone in a day. Dolores doesn't have her face on as they move her from the stretcher to her bed. No: the person before them is someone else altogether, without polish, without lipstick, without even her dentures, making her face look as if it has collapsed. She is hooked to an IV, older and uglier than Andrea imagined.

Andrea's father strokes Dolores's hair, the perm turned to frizz, lustreless and sticky. Dolores moans again. Andrea knows that two days later her mother will lie in that hospital bed in a sheer nightgown, the hospital sheet hugging her waist, her breasts flowing onto her stomach, talking on the phone, telling all the details. Triumphant. Anyone else would cover herself up.

So why does Andrea feel so lightheaded? The cramps pull at her, sharp and defined. She tells her father she'll be back in a while and makes her way to the car. She has to press her hand to her side in order to walk.

She sits in the passenger seat perhaps twenty minutes, hunched against the aching. She begins to shiver, feverish now. A little nauseated. This is not "nothing." By the time she lets herself out of the car, hand digging into her side to subdue the pain, she judges she has just enough strength to make it to the emergency room.

The next twenty-four hours are a blur. Blood tests, hands poking at her middle, white-coated interns making pronouncements about her elevated white count, the examining room ceiling as she lies there interminably, looking up. And hours later a rush of walls and faces floating by above her as she is wheeled to surgery on a stretcher.

She doesn't remember waking up in recovery, although they tell her she did. What she remembers is much later, her father saying, "All over now." Her father patting her hand.

Then she dreams in and out of herself, weaving through nausea and pain. She isn't awake, really, until sometime the next day. What wakes her is thirst. Her mouth, dry and cottony, tastes vaguely of vomit. Her side hurts—differently—and her stomach is full of gas. She is in a normal hospital room, hooked to tubes. Another woman lies in a bed beside her. Her eyes focus. The woman on the other bed is Dolores.

"Oh good. You're awake," her mother says. "You were lucky. It was nothing."

"It doesn't feel like nothing," Andrea croaks. Her mouth is so dry, it's amazing the words come out.

"*Mittleschmertz*," her mother says.

"What?"

"German. *Mittle* means middle. *Schmertz* means pain. Ovulation cramps."

Andrea groans. Her fear exactly. Hypochondria.

"Don't worry, Dr. Fellows says it happens all the time. They take out the appendix just for good measure."

Of course. To appease the patient's neurosis. She is racked by humiliation. "I wish I had something to drink," she says.

Dolores shifts her position and motions weakly toward the nightstand. "I think there's ice over there. You could have ice chips."

Andrea is not focused enough to do anything constructive about ice chips.

"I'd get them for you myself if I could," Dolores says, her voice growing coarse and low as if wrenched from unspeakable depths. "Maybe if you ring for the nurse."

Andrea feels herself sinking back into her fog. Her mouth sticks to itself. If she sleeps, everything will go away.

"Here, I'll push the button for the nurse myself," Dolores says.

Andrea is drifting now. But dry. She hears Dolores move again, then tell her comfortingly, "Dr. Fellows says you'll feel a hundred percent better in a day or so."

Andrea doesn't believe it.

"You will," Dolores continues. "You'll be up and around in no time. You'll be out of here before I will."

Andrea pictures herself drinking from a waterfall. A lake.

"Maybe if you get some rest," her mother tells her.

After a while she opens her eyes. Her mother is still watching her. Dolores rolls closer, puts her hand to her butt, the site of her pain, and grimaces. "You know I'd help you if I could—if I weren't sicker than you are," she says.

Despite the dryness and fog, Andrea hears this with some clarity. Her stomach rumbles, her mouth feels stuffed with cotton, but she thinks—"sicker than you are"—and feels almost grateful, almost comforted, knowing that in some way, even now, her mother is.

STAR

STEVEN SIMPLE (NEE GINSBURG) was sitting in the living room of his suite at the Book Cadillac Hotel in Detroit. He'd been flown there to tape a segment of *The Sonya Show* for USA Cable that evening. He would get five minutes to talk about his life, and then he would sing. Tomorrow morning he would fly back to L.A. In the meantime he was waiting to interview a girl named Kimberly O'Connor, who aspired to become one of his *shiksa* princesses. This was a term borrowed from Neil Sedaka, who'd used it to refer to his backup singers during a stage show in Las Vegas. It was then that Steve had decided to model himself after Sedaka instead of John Lennon, and also to drop his last name, Ginsburg. Steven Simple: it was a joke. While he was growing up, everyone except a neighbor lady named Elmira Birnbaum and a couple of girlfriends had believed he was stupid. So he'd call himself Simple, what the hell? He was thirty when he changed his name and maybe acknowledging it would change his luck. That was ten years ago. On *The Sonya Show*, he would confess to psychologist Sonya Friedman (as he had confessed to other talk show hosts, with varying degrees of emotion) that he had never been good in school and so had turned to music. That wasn't the whole story, but it would do.

There was a knock on the door—shy, a little fragile. He did not know anything about the O'Connor girl except that his agent, Waldman, thought she might be all right. Steve was going to be in Detroit anyway; he might as well take a look at her. He always selected the princesses himself. He chose them leggy (like Sedaka's) and fair enough to contrast with his own darkness. Usually he picked blondes.

This one was a redhead. "Mr. Simple?" She was long, white-skinned, very bright around the face. Hair wilder than he liked. A looker, though. He sensed that the hair was not the result of a too-tight perm, but of natural curl.

"I appreciate your seeing me," she said, more humbly than her appearance warranted.

24

He motioned toward the living room. She walked like a dancer: graceful, just the right motion of the hips. Tan slacks, not too tight; a brown sweater, ditto. In the show the princesses were understated, in neutral jumpsuits, sometimes sequined, but neutral. She had the sense to know that.

But still she looked flamboyant. Her hair wasn't carroty but a true red. A neon sign, a focus. One thing he didn't need was a princess who upstaged him. Stick to blondes, Waldman had once said. Blondes were safe, even when they were stunning: a chain of daisies on pale wallpaper.

"Sit down." He pointed to the sofa, took the chair for himself. She handed him a résumé. He hadn't expected that and it threw him; she'd already sent her credentials to Waldman. He put the piece of paper on the coffee table. "I'd rather hear you sing." Really he'd only wanted to get a look at her, talk to her. If she was good enough, he'd set up a session with the other princesses later. Now she'd backed him into a corner. If Waldman were here, he'd smooth it over. Waldman would read parts of the résumé aloud. He'd let people see that Steve Simple's time was too valuable to be wasted on details. Good agents did such things. But Steve sometimes thought Waldman had figured out the truth—that Steve couldn't read the résumés himself. He didn't let himself dwell on that. No one else knew; why should Waldman?

The girl was nervous, actually trembling, as if she knew the résumé was a mistake. Steve shifted over to the piano and motioned her to stand beside him. Her hands shook, a pulse beat in her neck. She glanced at the closed door to the bedroom. Maybe she expected a come-on? He never messed with the princesses. Either she'd be all right when she sang or she'd fold completely.

"Let's do 'Bus Ride'," he said, naming one of the old songs from his *Roo* album. It was a classic; everybody knew it. He started playing. The minute she opened her mouth he saw how much she reminded him of Roo Weinberg herself: the red hair, the shaking hands, everything but the voice. Roo had never been able to carry a tune. Suddenly he couldn't draw air. Roo was dead twenty years and her double had walked into a Detroit hotel room. He stopped playing.

"I'm sorry," the girl said. "I guess I'm not good enough."

"No, it's me, I made a mistake," he said. "Let's start over."

He put his hands back on the keyboard. She sang, but shakily. He didn't want her to break down here in front of him. He knew something about breakdowns from the original Roo: how they could suck you in. He smiled at her, reassuringly. "Now I'll sing," he said. "Here's what I want you to do." He told her where he wanted the words and where the ah's and where the doo-be doo-be-doos. Her voice got stronger as they went along. There was nothing wrong with her voice.

"Mr. Waldman will get back to you," he said afterwards.

"Don't call us, we'll call you," she said. Tears in her eyes now. What the hell did she expect? "It was nice of you to see me, anyway." Jesus. Roo had had blue eyes and Kimberly O'Connor had hazel, but the tears were identical.

"I'll tell you what," he said. "Let me hear you one time with the others."

She looked at him, frozen, a spotlighted animal.

"We're having a rehearsal over at the studio at six, before the taping. I'll hear you then."

Usually he was not a sucker for tears. You didn't get this far if you were. When you could barely read, you learned all the tricks early. You could do them better than anyone else. You weren't fooled by cheap imitations. One year in high school, he'd gotten three different girls to tape textbooks for him—one for each of his subjects. He told each one he liked the sound of her voice and wanted to hear it as he went to sleep at night. He was in love with Roo at the time and did not sleep with these other girls, but he was charming. He committed each taped book to memory (he could always remember everything he heard) and not one of the girls ever found out about the others. A few tears? Nothing to him.

He was no fool. Every year during standardized tests, he sat next to Bernie Levitan, a brain who had a quirky way of holding his paper so Steve could see it. Bernie never knew.

Steve could read well enough to copy answers when they were only a, b, c or d. The teachers believed Steve was one of those intelligent students whose lack of motivation left them in danger of failing. After he started his band, he traded off singing spots for term papers. It was a wonder he ever made any money. He was not a con man by choice; he was charming because he had to be.

His only mistake was taking the SATs in twelfth grade. His father wanted him to. They scattered people around the cafeteria so many seats apart that he couldn't see Bernie Levitan's pen, much less his paper. His parents were devastated by his scores. Later it was guilt that made him go to the University of West Virginia, after his father arranged it. His parents hadn't been to college and wanted it badly for their children. He could no more have told them he couldn't read than strip in public. They didn't know to this day—and he believed if word got out his star status would count for nothing, and the few people who loved him would be ashamed.

He'd even been afraid to tell the neighbor lady, Elmira Birnbaum, about his reading—and Elmira believed in him absolutely. She knew he'd heard music in his head since childhood and had always been able to play any instrument that happened to be around. She never refused to listen to him sing; she never told him it would come to nothing. Years later she told him: "See, all that time you sweated your grades, I always said in the end it wouldn't matter. It's a good thing you turned out a star because otherwise I never would have lived you down." For a long time she was the only one who supported him, and still he never told her about his reading.

Not that she oohed and ahed. In his early days, Elmira said his stuff wasn't bad. Her idea of "not bad" was that it reminded her of soap commercials.

"God, soap commercials," he'd said.

"That's so terrible? They pay people good money to write soap commercials."

"No, it's great. I barely pass the year, everybody looks at me and thinks, there's Ginsburg, the walking disaster. And you have me writing soap commercials." This was at a period when his life caused him something close to physical pain.

Elmira was drying a glass. "Artistically," she said, "it doesn't hurt you later to have spent some time as a walking disaster."

A few years later she said to him: "Competent, yes. Talent, yes. Staying power, that's another story. We might not know for a decade." So he went to college, even though Roo begged him to remain in D.C. When he decided he'd better drop out before he failed everything, he consulted Elmira first. He said he wanted to concentrate on his music.

"You won't be satisfied with just good, it's genius you want?" she said. She tried to stare him down but he knew a few things by then and stared back at her. "Well then, you better be strong for it," she told him. "Genius has a black bottom to it."

He thought of a colored person's black bottom. He scratched a pimple on the end of his nose. He was twenty years old and still had pimples. They never covered his whole face, just appeared large and red in strategic places. He thought: red nose, black bottom—the lyrical possibilities. But coming from Elmira, a black bottom was a dark, eerie, unfathomable place, and maybe he better not take it lightly.

Elmira told him she had visited the Black Bottom of Her Soul once as a young woman. "Believe you me, it was no pleasure, even thinking back on it now. It still gives me the shivers." The inside of her head had felt like a vise pressing on it; she had worried about going insane. This seemed very strange for Elmira, who stood before him six feet tall, sun-tanned, chewing a piece of gum. She started talking again. Even the simplest things afforded her no pleasure at that black bottom, she said—even the spider web she found across the.grass in front of her house one morning, glistening with drops of dew.

"When those small moments don't give you the least bit of joy, when you see through them in a second and down to the dark pit at the bottom of them, then you know you're in trouble. You want genius? That's what you're in for."

Steve didn't have the faintest idea what she was talking

about, or what personal experience might have provoked such terror in her, or what any of it had to do with genius. She didn't offer any details. He didn't know any more now than he had then, except that the discussion had armed him for everything. Having recovered from her own experience, Elmira said, she was in a position to warn Steve. Imagination could take its flights; did he think the trip was always into the stratosphere? It could with equal ease dip into the depths of blackness, and only the very strong would recover. She was utterly serious. Steve remembered nodding, baffled, wondering what the hell was going on.

Then she had said, "So sing your songs, Steve. With your grades...you think God has some other plan in mind for you?"

Sonya Friedman was a pleasant-looking blonde who came into the dressing room while they were doing his makeup. He recognized her from watching her show the week before— or rather, tapes of her show that Waldman had sent while Steve was working in Atlanta. The tapes were Steve's idea; before he made a TV appearance, he always liked to get a feel for the tone of a show. The truth was, he got a lot of his information from television. It was from a TV talk show that he first learned he couldn't read because he had a condition known as dyslexia. He sat, transfixed, hearing a psychology professor explain exactly what happened every time he looked at a page of words. The professor explained the dislocation of letters and words, and Steve's frustration, so matter-of-factly and calmly that it might have been a common experience many people shared, when for more than thirty years Steve had thought he was the only one. "It's very frightening," the professor said, "looking at a puzzle everyone else seems to be able to figure out and not be able to make heads or tails of it."

No shit, Steve had thought. The professor had gone on to outline most of the details of Steve's life. "They almost always try to cover up. Whether it's by becoming troublesome or charming— that seems to be a matter of personality. Either way, it's painful to live your life as a freak." Steve was drinking coffee and raised his cup in toast to the TV. "Hear, hear," he said. Dyxlexia research was just beginning to unravel some of the tricks that could be played by the human brain. "Some of them *can* learn to read and others can't—easily— but even then there's a lot that can be done to help." Ah. . . help. He was beyond it. Roo had been too confused to care if he could read, but she was dead and his parents and fans and maybe even Waldman believed he was normal. He wasn't going to spoil it by getting help. He'd turned on the shower and stood under it for thirty minutes, trying to get himself back together.

As to *The Sonya Show* he'd seen last week—he had liked it. Sonya Friedman was cool, attractive, bright—a psychologist—but she had a no-nonsense approach that reminded him of Elmira. Walking into the makeup room now, she looked brisk and capable and, physically, much the same as she had on tape. That was in her favor. So many of them looked worse. She was wearing a red blouse and dark skirt that accented her thinness. She smiled, all confidence. "I'm Sonya Friedman," she said. The hand that she offered him was cold as ice.

So were Kimberly O'Connor's hands, when she showed up ten minutes early for the rehearsal, looking beautiful but terrified, as if she'd never set foot on stage before. She calmed down a little when he sat at the piano—having gone through that part of the routine in his hotel room a few hours ago, he supposed. Roo, too, had always calmed down when he started playing. What was wrong with these beauties? In high school Roo Weinberg was so good-looking you'd have thought she'd go through life secure as a nursing kitten, what with him staring at her all the time, ready to do battle to keep her out of danger. When his sister Lois brought her home, he babbled constantly just to keep her in hearing range. Or else he'd play the piano to keep himself from running out of words. He'd heard the stories about Roo's reputation, but was beyond caring by then. He hoped she was loose; he hoped she'd let him touch her. He knew Kimberly O'Connor must have had her own share of admirers. And still she stood by the piano practically trembling, rubbing her hands together for warmth.

Then she started to sing. Her voice was stronger than before, and her voice was sweet. But her looks were too flashy for a backup singer, there was that jittery quality about her that drew your eye. She was a dead ringer for Roo— looks and manner both. She made Carole and Francie look dim; she was like a fire burning between the two of them. He saw no possibility of toning her down; it had been the same way with Roo. Both women had the whitest skin, the longest legs, the roundest breasts—and hands as cold as ice.

The routine ended. Kimberly O'Connor kept standing there by the piano. There was no way he could use her, considering.

"You know we're traveling the next couple of weeks and interviewing some other girls," he said. She stood stock still, catatonic, until he put a hand on her shoulder to guide her off of the sound stage. He decided to let her down easy, let Waldman give her the definite no. She walked with him to the waiting room at the end of the hall.

No windows here, just intense fluorescent lights and bright modern furniture. TV monitors sat on both end tables, showing what was being taped outside on the sound stage. Francie and Carole stayed outside drinking Cokes, but Steve motioned O'Connor in. She sat on the royal blue couch he indicated, following the motion of his hand like an obedient animal. It frightened him. He thought of Roo in her passive mode, waiting for instruction.

He began talking to her as idiotically as he once had to Roo, saying inconsequential things about his tour. Next to him, Kimberly O'Connor was a knot. "We won't make an immediate decision on another backup," he said finally. "Not for a couple of weeks."

"A couple of weeks... I see." Thinking—wasn't she?—why don't you just lay it out straight, you bastard. She stood up, a wooden soldier, ready to go.

"You might as well stay for the taping, now that you're

here. You could stay back here with us or go up front with the studio audience." It would be easier if she left, but he couldn't make himself stop talking. "You ever see this show taped before?"

"No." She sat back down, but stiffly.

"We're on last," he said. Sonya's audience would wait for Steve Simple, hang on through a diet expert, a couple of commercials, a *Reader's Digest* author. He was grateful. A month from now, a year from now, they might not give him the spot reserved for the star.

"Detroit your home?" he asked.

"No. Chicago. I've only been here a year."

"A cold-weather junkie."

She held out an arm, to demonstrate its whiteness. "I can't handle the sun."

"So I see." Roo had also hated sun; had hated freckles the way only a madwoman can, scrubbing them at times like Lady Macbeth, and obliterating them at last with sleeping pills, which obliterated the rest of her, too. But O'Connor seemed complacent about her skin. That, at least, was reassuring.

"I saw you a long time ago in Chicago," she said. "It was before you got so famous." She was watching him, sidelong, deciding what to say. Not at all unfocused now. "You had a whole different kind of style."

"I was America's answer to the Beatles."

She laughed. Loosening up. He felt better.

"You must have been a little kid," he said.

"No. I'm twenty-eight." Her eyes narrowed. Puzzled that he hadn't picked up the age from her résumé? No matter, he wasn't going to hire her, he'd never see her again. He noticed tiny lines around her eyes. Redheads aged young. He was relieved that she was older than he'd thought. Roo had been twenty-two when she died.

"Don't knock it; I wrote a lot of my songs as a Beatle. Unfortunately, nobody heard of them until later." When cornered, always change the subject. "They didn't get an audience until I went solo, with just the piano. Did you know that?"

"Yes." She looked at him straight on now, smiling, mischievous: "I do my research."

Animated now. . . a relief.

Francie and Carole came back in, gave him glances, wondered why he'd invited the girl to stay. Good mannered, they talked to her and at the same time watched the show on the monitor, which had started a few minutes before. "You married?" Francie asked. "Was." A wry smile. Steve kept his eyes on the TV, but he was listening to O'Connor. Went to Northwestern, majored in drama. Then the marriage. No kids. The divorce. "I didn't get a chance to do much with singing until late." She spoke to Francie, to Carole, but kept her eyes on Steve. The girls were princesses and he was the king, the power source. He knew the look well.

"You're up next," an assistant producer said, sticking her head into the door.

"Come watch us from out front," Steve told Kimberly. It would be more prudent to leave and come back to find her gone, but he couldn't bear it. "See how we look out there—the style."

He was leading her on. He wasn't going to hire her.

"After the show we're all going to get something to eat," he said. "You can come with us."

"Thanks."

The princesses stared at him. He never did this. He always had a regular woman and didn't fool around. The woman never traveled with him and was never the sort reporters wanted to interview for *People* magazine. The current one was a computer expert for Hewlett-Packard in Fort Collins, Colorado. She met him once a month for a weekend, spent her vacations at his house in L.A. It was a kind of stability. The arrangement left no possibility of a permanence that would allow her to notice he didn't read even the morning paper. He accepted that. Maybe that was the black bottom of stardom Elmira had warned him about. He'd expected to pay a price.

But walking down the hall to the sound stage, he was tired

of it. Kimberly O'Connor had fallen into step beside him. He wasn't touching her, but he sensed the muscles in her legs and stomach unknotting—white, long legs, and not much of a stomach: smooth, flat. He wanted to touch her. He wanted to feel her relax to tell her all his secrets. Tomorrow morning he'd be gone.

He liked the sensation of standing backstage in a TV studio, on cold concrete, anticipating what would come next. The curtain in front of him hung from two stories high, cool to the touch because of the air-conditioning that kept the cameras cool. In a moment, on cue, he'd step into light of the stage, into heat, into brightness, and it would be like being born.

"Tell us about Steve Simple the person," Sonya Friedman was saying. Usually in his mind it was clear what he'd say, but Kimberly O'Connor was sitting in the studio audience and he felt reckless. He could give them more than the dumb-kid-who-made-it good story. He could tell them about his dyslexia. The story would set them on their asses. Possibly it would set him on his ass, too. His black bottom. Waldman would smile knowingly, his parents would be afraid to face their friends at bridge. God. Sonya was talking about the *Roo* album. A singer who'd gotten famous writing about a beautiful young suicide made good patter. But Roo had died twenty years ago and Steve had been talking about her for ten, and the talk show hosts had covered most of the angles.

He figured Sonya would go the sympathy route. The love affair. The sad past history. Of the *Roo* album, he always said, "Well, she was a nice Jewish girl and I was a nice Jewish boy, but it didn't work out, except that I wrote a lot of songs about her." The audiences loved it. He never said she slept with almost every male who asked her, or that she had instant, genuine amnesia about the acts she might have performed. He told her it was unwise to bed down with strange men, but logic held little sway against insanity. The Weinberg family still lived near D.C., so he never hinted that Roo was not just disturbed but literally mad. He also never admitted that he finally ran away from her with his band because the demands of her illness threatened to suck the music right out of him.

The talk show hosts believed Roo killed herself because she was lonely. He didn't argue. They believed he wrote his songs out of grief. Once, one suggested he'd never married because he was still suffering from Roo's death. "No one grieves, in that sense, for twenty years," he'd replied. What was he supposed to do—say he didn't marry because he didn't want some woman to find out he couldn't read? But as soon as he'd gone off camera that day, Waldman called to scold him. "For godsake, Steve, don't deny it," he'd said. "Just let them assume." So now he let them assume.

But Sonya Friedman was after the shock tactic. "It's not many people who turn a suicide note into a song," she said.

"And not many people who write such a lyrical suicide note." His voice sounded stringy, sarcastic. He did not say he could never help the songs he wrote; he wrote what he heard in his head. He was sorry Roo's suicide note had set itself to music, but it had.

I'm falling through the hole
At the bottom of my soul
And there ain't nobody to catch me.

Their friends had thought it a mystery note, but Elmira Birnbaum had understood at once. "You told her what I said to you that day, about the black bottom. I recognized it right away."

"Yeah, I did."

"I knew you might tell her. But who could predict she would find a hole at the bottom of her soul and not a pit?"

Elmira put her hand on his hair—the only time she ever touched him—and said: "Steve, a pit you can climb out of. A hole you can only fall through. It's not your fault."

But it was. If he'd stayed in D.C., Roo might have lived. It was he who'd snipped the hole—wasn't it?—and let her fly through blackness alone. For the next ten years, on the road with his various bands, nothing good happened to Steve Ginsburg.

Except that he wrote his remaining songs about her. A purge. After a time there was no Roo the person, only Roo the myth—young girl kills herself for love. He began to think about her coldly, from a distance, the same way he thought about the other bald fact—that, for all his posturing, he still couldn't read. About the time all the heat was drawn out of him, he got his chance to make the *Roo* album. The *Roo* album made him famous. And that was that.

The O'Connor girl was looking at him. She was staring worshipfully, as if he possessed something transcendent and had the power to impart it. Roo had given him that same look when she asked him to stay in D.C. and make her sane. He was tired of being worshiped. The truth was, all he could actually give O'Connor was a job. If he were going to start something more, she would have to know all about him.

"Steve Simple the human being," Sonya was saying, stalling for time. "What makes Steven Simple run?" He thought again of making a clean breast of it. *I could never read.* Think of the youngsters he could save. His parents would get over it. Elmira would certainly approve. Or maybe people would laugh.

He opened his mouth, because Kimberly O'Connor's eyes were bearing down on him and Sonya Friedman was wishing the hell he'd get on with it. He wasn't sure he had the courage. He only knew that the music he had heard all these years had been of substance, and the rest—the fame, and even the power it had given him—was all gloss.

BELLYFLOP

IF THERE IS ONE THING MARY LOU PAYNTER wishes she were right now, it is a stewardess like her roommates Angie and Jill instead of a receptionist home from work early, sitting beside an apartment-complex swimming pool so upset she can hardly think. Being a stewardess is never going to happen because Mary Lou is too short. It's 1968, and the airlines require you to be at least five feet two inches tall. Mary Lou is barely five one.

Even if she had her wish of being taller, she wouldn't be able to fly overseas like Angie, whose perfect Spanish meets Pan Am's requirement of fluency in two languages. But surely she could find a job with Eastern like Jill, who's just finished stew school and is working her first flights. She'd get to travel and see all the things she wants to see. She'd bring home miniature bottles of airline whiskey like Angie does, and tell stories about the passengers. But above all, on a regular basis, she'd feel the way she always does whenever a plane lifts her above the earth and the clouds—as if she's leaving her small life and small worries on the ground, and starting all over again in the sky.

Having that feeling on a regular basis, Mary Lou believes, would have defended her against her current predicament. She'd never have fallen so fast when she met Glenn McAdams at a party in Miami Springs, or been so impressed when he looked at her through slanty gray eyes and said he flew for Eastern. She wouldn't have started thinking how pilots' wives flew free any time they wanted, anywhere in the world. When Glenn said, "Honey, you need to relax some if you want to make it in Miami," Mary Lou might have laughed instead of feeling insulted. Certainly she wouldn't have felt the need to spend an hour with him in the bedroom of that Miami Springs apartment, proving just how relaxed she could be. And right now she wouldn't be reeling from the two pieces of information she's received since yesterday: one, that Glenn isn't a pilot after all, and two, that she, Mary Lou Paynter, is pregnant with his child.

A curl of water rises from the pool and hits Mary Lou's lawn chair, soaking her legs to the thigh. The sole swimmer is Bettina, the six-year-old niece of the apartment's manager, Mrs. Alvarez, practicing her dives. Officially, no children are allowed, but Bettina swims better than most adults and is so little trouble that no one objects. It's just that every dive she makes turns into a bellyflop. Every one. She bellyflops into the water, swims the length of the pool, gets out, walks to the deep end, and bellyflops again. Sometimes she does this a dozen times in a row. Mary Lou's stomach hurts just watching it.

"Sorry," Bettina murmurs, surfacing, pushing black hair out of her eyes.

"No problem," Mary Lou says. But she drags her chair out of range before she lets herself sink back into her thoughts.

Ever since she got out of the doctor's office, Mary Lou has been half stunned and—unaccountably—half angry with her friend, Lucas, for revealing Glenn's true identity. Lucas, who teaches math at Miami-Dade Junior College and lives in a houseboat at Dinner Key, broke the news last night while spooning rice into a steaming bowl of black bean soup at Centro Vasco, their favorite Cuban restaurant. Looking down at his bowl, deeply absorbed in activity, he said, "How do you know for sure Glenn is a pilot?"

"Because he told me," Mary Lou said. "Why wouldn't he be?"

Lucas shrugged. Mary Lou had taken Glenn to a party on Lucas's houseboat once, during which they sailed around the Biscayne Bay, looking up at the stars and drinking beer. Mary Lou got drunk enough to tell Glenn she was of the opinion that there were more stars over Miami than over Washington, D.C., where she'd lived all her life until last April.

"Baby doll, it's twelve hundred miles between D.C. and Miami, but compared to the Milky Way, that's not much mileage," Glenn had whispered, making his breath tickle her ear. "The stars you can see are the same."

"I know that. What I'm saying is it *seems* like more stars. Because of the tropical sky."

Glenn raised his eyebrows as if Mary Lou were stupid,

which she hadn't liked.

Anyway, that was the night Glenn and Lucas met.

In the restaurant, Lucas sprinkled chopped onions on top of the soup and rice and stirred the mixture for all eternity. "I don't want to hurt your feelings," he said finally, "but today the phones were on the blink at the college and one of the people up on the pole fixing them looked an awful lot like Glenn."

"I guess a lot of people look like him," Mary Lou replied, deciding Lucas was jealous. Mary Lou first met Lucas when he opened a savings account at the bank where she works. A week earlier, she might have felt differently about him, but she'd just had her first dates with Glenn and was receptive only to Platonic friendship. In appearance, Lucas is more the math teacher than the boating enthusiast—dark and scholarly—where Glenn is blond and athletic. Though Mary Lou senses Lucas would like their relationship to be more serious than it is, she knows it never will be. "Glenn's not all that unusual looking," she told him in the restaurant, deliberately tasting her soup to show she wasn't upset. Black bean soup was something she'd never had before Lucas introduced her to Centro Vasco. It was the kind of thing she once would have thought disgusting. Beans! But they were tasty. And Lucas always paid.

Lucas raised his own spoon toward his face without putting it in his mouth. "I went down and talked to him. I asked if he wasn't Glenn McAdams who'd brought you to that party."

That's when the thick black liquid landed in Mary Lou's stomach in a lump. "Maybe he works for the phone company part time when he's not flying," she managed. "For extra money."

"I don't think so," Lucas said. "Pilots get paid pretty well."

So there was nothing left for Mary Lou but to confront Glenn. She did it on the phone. By the time she hung up she'd fallen out of love. She'd said to Angie, "I wonder what he was doing all those times he told me he had a layover out of town."

Bettina slams into the water again. The splash barely misses Mary Lou, even in her new position. Reaching the edge, Bettina smiles sheepishly. "Someday I'll get it."

"Someday," Mary Lou replies. She imagines herself six years from now, supervising a child of her own this size, whose absent father is not even a pilot but only a telephone lineman. Her neck and arms are slick with sweat, but nevertheless she starts to shiver.

In her apartment, the hum of the air conditioner coats everything with a chilly blue silence. Angie is on her way to Barcelona, and Jill is either out running errands or not back from the flight she worked last night. With no seniority, Jill has to fly odd hours and fill in for absentees at the last minute. The apartment is abnormally neat—the carpet freshly vacuumed, the formica-topped kitchen table wiped down. The white plastic coffee and end tables have been dusted, as has the white formica dresser in the bedroom—all the indestructible shiny white pieces that fill every unit. Even the pillows on the blue and green couch (some of the units have orange and brown) have been straightened. This is Angie's doing. She never leaves for a long trip without first going on a cleaning binge. Mary Lou doesn't know why. Outside, the August sun is a high wicked yellow, but the filter of air-conditioning and curtains turns the light cold and white. Mary Lou gets into the shower and runs the water as hot as she can stand it until she hears Jill come in.

"They've scalped me," Jill wails when Mary Lou emerges. Jill stands in front of the bedroom mirror violently brushing a new haircut. She's wearing a tiny pink sundress from which long arms protrude, all angles and motion. It's hard to imagine her walking gracefully down the aisle of a 727, statuesque and elegant in her Eastern uniform. She shakes her head, pulls the ends of her hair out as far as they'll go. Before she became a stewardess, Jill let her hair hang straight to her shoulders, light brown and tomboyish, streaked from the sun. Now, because the airlines require it to be no longer than chin length, it's cut into a teased bubble.

"It looks like a hat," Jill mutters.

It does, Mary Lou thinks. "It's fine," she says. Jill can't stand not looking pretty. In Mary Lou's opinion, half the reason Jill became a stewardess is because stews are universally regarded as good-looking. Because you can't become one if you're not. In Jill's position, Mary Lou wouldn't care about that. She wouldn't care if they required you to shave your head. "I wish hair was my only problem," Mary Lou says.

"What's wrong?" Jill abandons the brush and touches Mary Lou's shoulder, bathing her with attention. As Mary Lou speaks, Jill lowers herself onto her blue and green bedspread as if unable to continue standing. Her face tightens with concern, her lips part slightly with concentration.

"What will you do?" she asks finally.

"I don't know."

"God, Mary Lou." Jill draws a Chapstick from the pocket of her sundress, uncaps it, runs it over her lips.

"If it were me, I'd go home," she manages.

"You, maybe, but not me." Jill's been in Miami two years and plans to marry her boyfriend in upstate New York when she feels ready. But Mary Lou escaped to Miami only five months ago and can't imagine leaving.

"Then your choices," Jill says, sounding stricken, "are to have the baby or. . . not."

"I know."

Jill turns the Chapstick over and over in her hand. "You could get rid of it," she says.

"I don't know anything about that."

"Angie does." Giving this practical advice seems to settle Jill for a moment. Then she sinks into gloom. "I should have known Glenn didn't fly for Eastern."

"You haven't been working there long enough to know all the pilots," Mary Lou reassures her. "Even the ones based in Miami."

"I could have asked around." Jill rubs the Chapstick on her lips again. Mary Lou sighs. It occurs to her that Glenn's identity might have been an issue yesterday, but today is completely irrelevant.

41

• • •

Lucas is of a different opinion. "You have to tell him," he says with more authority than he usually commands. Mary Lou stands beside the kitchen table on his houseboat watching Lucas cook dinner—Dinty Moore beef stew improved with canned tomatoes and an assortment of spices. It looks disgusting but smells good.

"It's none of Glenn's business," Mary Lou says.

"None of his business!"

"You know what I mean."

Wearing a potholder glove, Lucas removes a pan of rolls from his tiny oven and sets it on the table. "Whatever you decide to do, it's going to cost money. Especially if you decide to keep it."

She can't imagine keeping it. She can't imagine *it*. "I don't want Glenn's money," she says.

"That's very noble."

"Please, Lucas."

He's about to pour the stew into a serving dish when he reconsiders, moves toward her, encircles her with his arm. "Hey, I'm sorry. I know it's tough."

Mary Lou lets him hold her. Being small, she's used to people comforting her. "An eternal child," one of her boyfriends once said, circling her wrist with his thumb and forefinger. But she isn't a child, and she doesn't always want comfort, even from Lucas, whose heart comes to the level of her ear and beats a soothing cadence underneath his ribs. Glenn's chest, by contrast, was thick and muscular. She lets Lucas embrace her as long as she can without relaxing against his heartbeat, then makes herself move away.

"I wish I could help," he says.

She tries a laugh. "You're cooking for me, aren't you?"

He sets the food out and motions her into the booth that circles the table. Like all the furniture on the houseboat, these are built in, bolted to the floor. Closets and cabinets lock shut, lamps jut from the walls, everything is designed so as not to come loose when the boat is under way. Sliding into the booth next to her, Lucas traps her against the wall. She's too hungry to care, though given all that's happened, she doesn't expect to want food. She and Lucas don't talk much, just eat until they're stuffed.

"I could lend you some money," he says afterwards.

"No. I have some savings." He knows she lived at home from the time she graduated high school until the time she came here— eight years—saving money, getting bored. But she's too full to say more, lethargic and sluggish. Lucas switches on a lamp. In the yellow circle of light, the wood paneling gleams, as do the tiny perfect cabinets, the locked compartments secured against the rocking of the boat. The room is warm, cozy, claustrophobic. It reminds her of her mother's house, and how glad she was to escape it.

"First you make an appointment with this doctor on Miami Beach," Angie tells her, handing Mary Lou a scrap of paper. "He's the one who puts you in touch with the Cubans." Though Angie speaks airily, a single vertical line etches itself between her dark brows, a surprise in the porcelain-skinned face.

The Cubans. Real doctors, not hacks, Angie keeps assuring her, refugees who came with no papers. "They have to go through U.S. residencies in order to get licensed here. So of course they pay them next to nothing," Angie says, sliding her underwear drawer out of the bureau, dumping its contents on her bed. "They do abortions on the side for the money."

She begins refolding underpants and bras and stacking them in place as Mary Lou and Jill sit on the floor and watch. "I know three different stews who've done this, so I wouldn't worry if I were you. Nobody had any problems. The only thing is, you have to dicker about the price."

Jill chews anxiously on her chapped lips. Mary Lou feels mesmerized by the sight of Angie's fingers folding silk and cotton. At the bank, the Cubans she sees are respectable, intelligent. Not at all the criminal type. Outside, a hard rain beats against the building. Another rainy spell is due next month, maybe all through September. Remembering June when it rained a couple of hours every afternoon, Mary Lou hopes not. She didn't come here for rain, she came for sunshine. She came to see flowers with names like hibiscus and allamanda. She came to be free, not to be pregnant with a telephone lineman's baby.

"I still think you should go home," Jill says.

"If I go home, I'll never come back."

Jill laughs. "Of course you will."

But Mary Lou knows better. She discovered Miami the week her cousin Paul, who worked for *The Miami Herald*, came to Washington to cover a story. Mary Lou was sick of living at home, sick of selling dresses at the Hecht Company. She was twenty-five years old and had just broken her third engagement. She said to Paul, "How about lending me your apartment while you're in D.C.? I really need a vacation." Since Mary Lou's mother was putting him up, Paul could hardly refuse. Her mother thought Mary Lou was crazy, but Mary Lou bought a plane ticket, using the student half-fare card she'd gotten illegally, and flew south.

The minute the plane took off, her broken engagements and the Hecht Company seemed as tiny as the cars rapidly shrinking below them on the ground, so insignificant she couldn't bring herself to worry about them. By the time they landed, she felt cured. It was April and still chilly in Washington, but Miami was bathed in such fierce golden sunlight that Mary Lou couldn't help cheering up. Driving around town in her rented car, she noted that all the colors seemed brighter than they were up north. Some of the tropical evergreen bushes were so lush that their greenness seemed more of a philosophical concept than a color, though she couldn't have defined it exactly. A law student next door to Paul's apartment invited her to the party where she met Jill and Angie. By the time the week was up she'd found a job at First Federal. Ironically, Paul moved to Richmond less than a month later. If she hadn't borrowed his apartment when she did, she'd never have had another chance. The only time she used her half-fare card since was to fly to D.C. for a weekend to tell her mother moving to Miami was the best thing she'd ever done.

"Going home is really not an option," she says to Jill. She studies the scrap of paper Angie's given her. Moving toward the phone, she's aware that both roommates are watching. She's aware of the dramatic possibilities. She lifts the receiver, studies the numbers on the scrap of paper, and dials.

"I don't do abortions," the doctor tells her when she finally gets inside his office. She's waited for the appointment for a week and sat in his waiting room over an hour, studying the fish in his aquarium and the steady stream of old people coming and going—men with knotty bowed calves, women trying to disguise the odor of illness with cologne. Mary Lou was the only one under sixty on the nicked green leather chairs, oozing stuffing.

Ordinarily, waiting in these surroundings would upset Mary Lou, but today it didn't. The dark colors and bright fish were soothing; the place was a cool cave against the glut of sun outside. An odd thing has happened to make her so patient. She's begun to swell up this past week—breasts and belly, the water-bloat of early pregnancy, she supposes. She doesn't feel sick, just caught up in herself. "You're so calm," Jill tells her, filled with admiration. But it's just the opposite. Mary Lou's bodily processes seem to have become more urgent, the blood rushing through her veins with greater speed and vitality than usual, as if trying to impress important company. Mary Lou can't help turning in on herself, listening to the hubbub. Her insides are humming, singing a tune. She doesn't try to explain this. Not to Jill or Angie, and certainly not to Lucas, who in the last few days has taken her to the Studio for chocolate mousse, to Shorty's for barbecued ribs and to the Italian restaurant at 27th and Flagler for pasta, as if now, more than ever, she needs to be fed.

The doctor—who isn't Cuban—sits behind his desk, wearing his white lab coat, writing something on her chart. "I'm putting down that you have a cold," he says. He removes his reading glasses and looks up at her. "As I say, I don't have anything to do with abortions, but I may be able to put you in touch with somebody who does."

In case I'm a cop, Mary Lou thinks. He hands her the chart to give to the receptionist, and charges only five dollars. She assumes he doesn't charge the old people much, either, but makes his money from referrals for abortions.

Emerging into the sunlight, Mary Lou feels suddenly shaky and weak. For the first time in her life, she's about to participate in a crime. Unprecedented. Riskier than flying. It occurs to her that until now, the only illegal thing she's ever knowingly done is buy a half-fare card from an airline.

Since she's already taken off the whole morning, Mary Lou intends to drive right to the bank. But halfway across the causeway between Miami Beach and Miami, her shakiness gives way to an almost unbearable lassitude—half sleepiness and half inertia—and she decides she'd better stop at home for lunch. The heat is so fierce when she gets out of the car that it makes her feel disconnected, dreamy. Walking toward the apartment, she sees that even the the pool is deserted except for Bettina. The girl is perched at the deep end, eyes closed, looking intent. She stretches out her arms, curls her toes over the edge of the pool, squeezes her eyes shut tighter. Apparently some new plan to perfect the dive by not looking. Mary Lou moves out of splashing range. When Bettina springs forward, she sails horizontally above the pool a foot or two farther than usual. She lands harder, too. Smack on her stomach, even before her arms hit the water. Whop.

Mary Lou feels rather than hears the breath go out of her. Without thinking, she springs across the deck. Plunges a hand into the water, pulls the girl up.

Bettina gasps for air but doesn't find any. Mary Lou lifts her onto the concrete. Bettina slumps.

"It's okay. You got the wind knocked out of you. It'll come back in a second."

Opening her mouth, Bettina tries for another breath. A rattling sound, like dying. The next one comes easier. Mary Lou lets go of her. Bettina lies at the edge of the pool, gulping air. "I'm okay now," she says.

That's when Mary Lou notices that her own clothes are soaked. Dress, shoes, underwear. Who's watching this kid? Mrs. Alvarez, the apartment manager? The girl's mother? She's never seen the mother. She's going to have to change her whole outfit. She's going to miss three quarters of the day.

"Where's your aunt?" she demands.

"Inside. Working." The girl's eyes suddenly register fear. "You won't tell her, will you?"

"I should," Mary Lou says. She would if she had the time.

"If you tell her she might not let me swim anymore," Bettina whispers. She slicks her hair back—skinny, scared, an urchin.

"I won't this time. But be careful."

The girl grins. "Hey—thanks."

"It's nothing." It isn't. Since when is she the lifeguard? She heads back toward the apartment to change.

The woman who calls the next evening speaks in a thick Cuban accent. "I can help you," she says. "I help many girl. It will cost you *one*."

For a minute Mary Lou doesn't understand. Then she does.

"A thousand? I don't have that much," she lies.

"No?" A pause. "How much you can get?"

"Maybe five hundred."

"Eight. You can get eight," the woman says.

"I don't see how. No. I couldn't get that much."

They settle on seven. She might be buying a gown, a TV set. Her body hums, building its hive, unaware of her arrangements. She feels unaccountably drowsy—bowl-of-oatmeal and flannel pajamas drowsy, here inside the air conditioning.

A key in the lock startles her. "Talk about the unfriendly skies!" Jill says, coming in. Her face is pale, the spot of rouge high on her cheekbone like a circle of fever. "It was so bumpy we couldn't serve the meal. We spent the flight strapped in our seats."

"Better than walking back and forth, isn't it?" It's a cliche that stewardesses walk coast to coast, or up and down the seaboard.

"Lord, no. I'd rather walk any day." Jill often comes in flustered from these rough flights. Mary Lou suspects most stewardesses don't. *She* wouldn't. Angie is amused by Jill's nervousness. "You're lucky to get assigned to jets so far," she says. "Those 727s don't bounce like the prop planes do. Wait till you have to work a prop." Jill rummages in her purse for Chapstick, greases down her lips. Then she remembers.

"Did they call you?"

"A little while ago."

"Did you dicker? Angie said to dicker."

"I did."

Jill caps the Chapstick and drops it back in her purse. "If it was me, I wouldn't have the presence of mind. I'd pay whatever they asked." Mary Lou discounts this because Jill would never get pregnant by anyone except the hometown boyfriend she'll eventually marry. She's in Miami to let people pay homage to her prettiness before she settles down, to be a stewardess so she'll have a little blip to remember on the straight line of life she'll live for the next fifty years. She looks pensive on Mary Lou's behalf, as if trying to decipher what Mary Lou must be thinking. "I bet this makes you think about Glenn." And then tentatively, "Are you sorry you didn't tell him?"

"Are you kidding? If he wouldn't tell me what he did for a living, what do you think he'd say to *this?*" Mary Lou honestly hasn't given Glenn a thought except that one time when Lucas put his arms around her. It's as if Glenn had nothing to do with it. As if the situation—the way her body feels, the humming—has only to do with itself.

"When is it?" Jill asks.

"Tuesday. Eleven in the morning."

"I'm scheduled to fly then but I'll take off," Jill offers. "I'll go with you."

"You have to go alone," Mary Lou says.

"Then I'll wait here for you to come back."

"No. There's no telling how long I'll be gone."

They both consider this. Then Mary Lou says, "I'm supposed to bring the money in cash."

Jill shakes her head. "God. You have the whole weekend to wait. How are you going to stand it?"

The way she stands it is this: Lucas has a friend, Art, with a speedboat, and Jill agrees to date Art, and on Saturday the four of them go out on the Biscayne Bay. They take turns water-skiing, each one taking off in the shallows near a tangle of mangroves jutting into the bay. Jill is by far the best athlete of the group. She gets up on her first try and stays up longer than anyone. She can ski on one ski or two; she can jump the wakes of other boats. Letting go, swimming toward the boat, her hair slicked down around her face, she looks prettier than she does with her hair teased into a bubble and her body corseted into uniforms of straight skirts and high-heeled shoes.

Mary Lou tries three or four times to ski, but for some reason she can't get up. It's as if her center of gravity has already shifted. Also, the boat is making her queasy. She never gets motion sick, so she knows it's morning sickness in disguise.

When it's Jill's turn, Mary Lou slides off into the shallows and says she wants to get out of the sun a couple of minutes. She'll wait here under the mangroves—gnarled trees with thick roots reaching out of the water, braiding themselves into each other, creating a solid island.

"Then I better stay with her," Lucas says.

Although it's thoughtful of Lucas to stay, Mary Lou can't help resenting his presence. After the boat takes off, they sit on the mat of roots, watching a storm far in the distance, a purple stripe welding sky and water the way Miami storms do, so you can always tell where it's raining. At least Lucas doesn't try to talk to her. Soon the dark area dissolves back into the sunshine and everything becomes colorful and over-bright beyond the mangrove shade. By then Mary Lou's sick feeling has given way to her usual swollenness and bloat. When she hears the humming in her blood, she knows she's recovered.

"Better now?" Lucas asks.

"Fine." She's not sure she likes him knowing how she feels almost as soon as she does.

"Having second thoughts?"

"No. Why would I?"

"I just thought. Maybe you should be."

"Why?"

In the distance, the boat comes around the edge of the mangroves, Jill bouncing along as if she could do it forever.

"How well do you know Angie, anyway?" Lucas asks. He fixes her with a you've-failed-the-math-test gaze.

"I live with Angie," Mary Lou says.

"Yes, the one day a week she's there. How do you know whether to trust her?"

"Oh Lucas, really." She doesn't look him in the eye because the truth is, she *doesn't* know Angie very well. Angie is twenty-eight, three years older than Mary Lou and Jill. Angie's gone most of the time. Angie goes on cleaning binges. Angie steals a lot of Pan Am's liquor.

"What I'm saying is, if these people aren't who Angie says they are, you could end up dead."

"That's ridiculous." To sound convincing, she forces herself to look deeply into his eyes—brown with little yellow flecks. "Besides, there isn't really any alternative."

"There is," Lucas tells her.

"Oh, right. What?"

"We could get married."

Mary Lou is so startled and touched and thrown off balance that tears spring to her eyes. To hide them, she puts her hand in the water and splashes her face as if to cool herself. Married! Lucas keeps looking at her while she goes through this routine, but she can't meet his gaze at all, she has to stare down at the mangroves, the water, Lucas's long tan legs peppered with thousands of black hairs.

"That's very generous of you," she says finally.

"It is," Lucas agrees. When she looks up, he's grinning. "Kind of took you by surprise, didn't it? But I mean it."

He does. She knows he does.

"It wouldn't have to be a permanent arrangement. Just

something so you could have the baby. Without going home."

He knows she doesn't want to go home even though she never mentioned it once. He knows all this while her own family is completely ignorant. This thought brings yet more tears to her eyes. She doesn't know what's wrong with her. She splashes her face again, not at all concerned that Lucas might think she's having heat stroke, only certain she doesn't want him to see her crying.

"I couldn't do that to you," she says.

"Less than a year from now the baby would be born. It would be over. Everything would be back to normal."

For a second she imagines lying next to Lucas's cool tanned skin, listening to his heart beat as the water rocks the houseboat and the air conditioning hums. Then she imagines actually living in the houseboat day after day, getting toothpaste from the little locked medicine chest, tucking covers into the bunk bed, stepping back one step and bumping into the opposite wall. She needs more space than that.

"I couldn't. Really," she says softly, touching his wrist.

"Plenty of people would want the baby."

Mary Lou doesn't expect Lucas to keep arguing. "I think it'll be okay this way," she says.

"It's insane," Lucas tells her, face taut with anger now. "Having it would be a hell of a lot safer. Nine months isn't that much time out of your life."

"Two years wouldn't have been that much time out of *your* life," she says, referring to the fact that Lucas went to graduate school to become a math teacher so he wouldn't be drafted and sent to Vietnam.

Why does he think it's his business?

"I'm not doing this with an eye to personal safety," she says. Cruelly, she knows.

They hear the speedboat again, gearing down, coming into the cove. Lucas and Mary Lou exchange one last glance. She'd placate him if she could, but Lucas moves away.

"Your turn!" Jill shouts.

"Let Art ski. Lucas can drive the boat. I'll wait here a little longer." Mary Lou's voice sounds normal although she feels anything but. Art slogs around in the shallows, adjusting the skis on his feet while Lucas takes the wheel. As the boat zooms off, Mary Lou feels unsteady, as if her whole new life is peeling away from her at the same dizzying speed as the boat.

She forces herself up and tiptoes across the mangrove roots, inspecting the great braid of trees. She's so wobbly that she finally puts a hand out to steady herself on a trunk. The tree doesn't feel solid. The bark is alive, writhing, moving under her palm. She jumps back. Where her hand was, a swarm of tree crabs scurry back and forth—dozens of them, each no bigger than her thumbnail, each hard and spiny and repulsive. Abundant, unwanted lives spawned in the tropics. Bile rises in her throat so bitter that she leans over and throws up into the water. She feels like she's been waiting to do this all day.

"I'll call you when I get to New York," Jill says on Tuesday morning. Mary Lou is too distracted to keep Jill's schedule in mind exactly, but she knows she ends up in New York. In the middle of the night she'll deadhead back to Miami, which means she'll fly as a passenger rather than having to work, and she'll be home early tomorrow morning.

"I bet you're a wreck right now," Jill says. "I would be."

"I guess so," Mary Lou replies. Actually she feels almost numb. She had trouble waking up this morning. Every move she makes feels slow and deliberate. Absurdly, she's trying to decide what to do with the seven hundred dollars she withdrew from her savings yesterday. She doesn't think she should carry them in her purse. If the Cubans turn out to be dishonest, they could steal her purse and dump her before they ever do what they're supposed to. If she keeps the money close to her body, maybe she'll be safer. Finally she stuffs it into her bra.

After Jill leaves, she sits under one of the palmettos near the pool deck waiting for the Cuban woman to come get her. The pool is a flat shimmering surface of turquoise except for a black dot at the shallow end, which turns out to be a water spider the pool man hasn't discovered. Even Bettina is nowhere in sight. Finally a dark-haired woman in black slacks and a mannish white shirt walks into the courtyard.

"Meesus Williams?" the woman asks. Mary Lou gave a false name to the doctor, a false name to the Cubans. She doesn't know why. All her ID is in her purse.

"Yes."

The woman leads Mary Lou into the parking lot and motions her into the back seat of an old Chevy. It's in Mary Lou's mind to memorize the license number just in case, but she forgets.

"We pick up some other people first," the woman says, driving off, leaving Mary Lou to study the back of her head. Although the car isn't air-conditioned, the open windows let in a hot damp wind. Any other time, Mary Lou would fall asleep.

Across Dixie Highway, toward the Tamiami Trail, into the neighborhood known as Little Havana. On a street of small pastel houses of concrete block stucco, the driver honks her horn. A second Cuban woman comes out, hair bleached a brassy red, dressed in white—pants, shirt, shoes.

"She's a nurse," the driver says. The nurse gets into the front, cranes her neck around to smile at Mary Lou. She and the driver speak to each other in rapid Spanish.

A few blocks away they stop at a second pastel house. The driver goes to the door, returns with a third Cuban woman, fat and thirtyish, wearing a formal black church dress. Another helper? Not likely. The woman climbs in next to Mary Lou and studies her hands, which aren't fat like the rest of her, but long-fingered and elegant.

Across 27th Avenue, right turn, through a maze of streets. Mary Lou means to notice the street names, but she doesn't.

Finally they park, and the driver leads them around to the side of an old two-story house, into a jalousied door covered with cloth. Inside, a dark hallway is lined with chairs, a sort of waiting room. The driver motions Mary Lou and the fat woman to sit. The fat woman must also be having an abortion.

Voices come from another room. Laughter. The clank of silverware. Everything smells of corned beef and pickles. When her eyes adjust to the dimness, Mary Lou sees that a dining room is separated from the hallway by an arch. Five or six people are seated at a table. The driver and the nurse join them. There's laughter, the sound of delicatessen bags being opened, the rat-a-tat of Spanish. Mary Lou's stomach contracts. She might be nauseated or she might be hungry. They told her not to eat breakfast. Why are they eating in front of her? She tries to catch the fat woman's eye, but the woman is still studying her hands.

Soon the nurse and the driver return to the hall. "Do you have the money?" the driver asks. Her breath is sharp like cheese.

"Yes." Mary Lou pulls the wad of bills out of her bra. The driver doesn't count them. The Cuban woman holds out a packet of money folded into a rectangle. It seems a smaller packet than Mary Lou's. The driver takes the money into the dining room.

The nurse touches Mary Lou's shoulder. "Come with me." She leads Mary Lou into a dim bedroom off the hall. It's furnished with a double bed and an old mahogany bureau, the wood so dark it seems to drink the little light that comes in through a yellowing shade. Adjacent to the bed is a makeshift examining table—a high cot with shiny metal stirrups bolted to the end.

"Take off your panties and lie down there," says the nurse. Mary Lou thinks an American nurse would say "hop up there." When Mary Lou is settled, the nurse goes out to get the doctor. Between that and the nurse's white clothes, it's exactly like being in someone's office.

From Mary Lou's position on the cot, the doctor seems very tall. His hair is graying, and he looks tired. Serving a residency, probably, staying up nights.

"How far along are you?" he asks.

"Eight weeks."

He slips on a pair of surgical gloves. "Let your knees relax." He feels inside her. He nods, as if to affirm he believes she's telling the truth.

"Now we give you something to put you to sleep," he says. "When you wake up, it's all over."

The nurse is already putting a tourniquet on her arm, then loosening it. She smiles at Mary Lou. The brassiness is erased from her hair by the dim light.

"Tell me what is happening," the doctor says. A pinprick.

"Nothing yet." Slowly black dots begin to dance before Mary Lou's eyes. Larger, filling her whole mind, oblivion made visible.

"Now I'm conking out. No. Conking in." This thought strikes her as very profound. You don't go out of yourself at all, but into it. You fold *in*.

She comes back from far away, up through liquid too dense to swim through quickly. Not on the examining table now but on the bed, part of a white chenille spread thrown over her. The fat Cuban woman sits on a chair against a wall.

"Time to get up now. Ready to get up?" The nurse's voice is loud. It comes from all over the room. Mary Lou closes her eyes.

"Time to get up," the nurse says, louder. She shakes Mary Lou's shoulder. Mary Lou opens her eyes again. She must have slept too long. The Cuban woman had her operation second, but she woke up first. Maybe they gave Mary Lou too much anesthetic. She doesn't care. She wants to sleep.

The nurse puts a hand under Mary Lou's shoulders, helps her sit. She feels a sanitary pad beneath her. She looks. Slightly bloody, not much. The nurse helps her put her underwear on, stands her up. They walk out into malevolent bright sunshine and get into the car.

"Here, put this under your tongue." The nurse hands Mary Lou a white lozenge. It's violently bitter; it wakes her up. At the apartment the driver gets out and sees her to the door. She goes in, falls into bed. She doesn't know how long she sleeps. The phone rings. She picks it up automatically, still not really awake.

"Mary Lou? Why didn't you say anything? Are you all right?"

It's Lucas.

"Just sleepy," she manages.

"I'll come over," Lucas says.

"No. Too sleepy. Really."

"Are you bleeding?"

She doesn't answer.

"Listen to me, Mary Lou. Are you bleeding? Tell me how much you're bleeding."

"Not much," she says. "I'm all right. Really." She hangs up the phone, then lifts it off the hook, covers it with a pillow, and falls back to sleep.

When she opens her eyes again, late afternoon sun pours into the window. Someone is moving around the apartment. Lucas? No. Jill is rummaging in the closet. Suitcases line her bed. Several, not just the overnight bag for flights with a layover.

"What's going on? Why are you home?" Mary Lou's voice comes from far off. "I thought you were in New York."

"We never got there," Jill says from the closet. "The plane bellyflopped."

When Mary Lou hears the word, *bellyflop*, she pictures Bettina bellyflopping into the pool.

Jill comes out of the closet. There's a bruise on her cheekbone. Her uniform is dirty. "A woman died," she says.

Mary Lou's head is fuzzy, but she makes herself sit. The way she finally knows she's awake is this: the humming is gone from her veins.

"What are you talking about?"

Jill pushes a suitcase off the bed, sits down.

"What do you mean—bellyflopped?" Mary Lou feels drugged.

"It started to lift and didn't have the power and flopped down on its belly," Jill says without expression.

"God," Mary Lou says.

"It was lucky only one person died," Jill says woodenly.

Most of Jill's clothes are folded into the suitcases. "Where are you going?"

"Home," Jill tells her.

"Home?"

Jill stands and spreads her arms out to the side. "Look at me!" she yells. "I walked away from a plane crash! Look at me!" Mary Lou does. In addition to the bruise on her face, she has a swollen lip and ripped stockings, maybe from sliding down the chute. But otherwise she looks okay.

"The plane took off. But it wasn't right!" Jill screams. "You could tell it wasn't right!"

Mary Lou knows she's hysterical. You're supposed to slap an hysterical person in the face, but she can't, her head is too swimmy, she wouldn't connect.

"It was like. . . " Jill makes a slapping motion, as if of a hand slapping the plane out of the sky. "And then. . . whap." She claps her hands together.

Her face crumples. She sits on the bed and cries with big heaving sobs. Mary Lou thinks: I have to be clearheaded now, I have to say the right thing. "I guess it was lucky only one person died," she manages.

Jill sniffs and keeps sobbing. Mary Lou lets her.

"What happened to that one lady?" she asks after a while. "How did everybody else get out and only one lady die?"

Jill looks up with a blotchy tear-stained face. "She didn't have her seat belt on."

The stewardesses are supposed to make sure everyone's belted in for takeoff. If they do nothing else, this is the one thing they're supposed to make sure of. Now Mary Lou knows what this is about.

When Jill finishes crying, she stares at her suitcases with red and sore-looking eyes. She looks pure ugly. She doesn't take a shower. Maybe she's in shock. She never does remember why Mary Lou is home at this time of day, and Mary Lou never tells her, even after Angie calls to see how Mary Lou is doing. There's the expectation of drama in Angie's voice as she asks about the abortion, less like concern than curiosity. So Mary Lou tells her about the plane crash instead. She puts Jill on the phone and the two of them talk for half an hour. The next day, on a morning flight, Jill's gone.

• • •

One of Mary Lou's fiances, Darryl, used to get after her for not making more specific plans. "But what do you want to do with your life?" he'd ask after he picked her up from work at the Hecht Company and she complained about her job. "I mean eventually?" She supposed at the time what she wanted to do was be Darryl's wife—although, as also happened with her other two engagements, when it actually came time to pick colors for bridesmaid's dresses and patterns for dishes she would use for the next twenty years, she never could. She did not want to plan her life, she wanted to live it. But now, for once, she wishes she had it all mapped out.

After Jill leaves, the rain begins in earnest. Every afternoon there's a downpour, and sometimes it rains all day. The weather is less hot than damp and jungly. Mold grows on the window sills and in the bathroom. Angie scrubs at it every time she's getting ready for a trip. No one swims in the pool—not even Bettina, who's back in school, hardly ever here with her aunt. Lucas resumes taking Mary Lou to dinner, but when he asks her how she's feeling she says sharply, "Listen, I don't want to talk about it, Lucas. I'm fine. That's all. Let's leave it there." Even as the words come out, she knows they're undeserved and unfair. Lucas doesn't say a thing. He never mentions the abortion or his offer of marriage. To Mary Lou, it feels as if they're conspiring to hide a secret.

One night she goes to Big Daddy's alone, which she never does. At the crowded oval bar, in the dim orangish light, she orders a screwdriver and pays for it herself. When guys ask her to dance, she does, but she doesn't stay with any of them. Jill used to feel insulted that Mary Lou invariably got asked to dance first. Mary Lou knew it was only because she used her power better than Jill did—the way, from the age of twelve or thirteen, all a girl had to do was think about guys coming over and they would. She tried to tell Jill this was not about being good-looking; it was about knowing that any time you called you'd be answered. Having power was just a matter of believing in it. But Jill never quite believed.

Mary Lou's pondering this when a man's voice says over her shoulder, "You're a little thing, but you sure do come on strong." She doesn't have to look back to know it's Glenn. The vodka in the screwdriver makes her feel mellow, not dizzy the way she might from gin or bourbon.

"You still mad at me?" he asks.

When she doesn't answer he says, "You are."

Mary Lou doesn't know she's going to say the next thing until it comes out of her mouth. "You got me pregnant, but I took care of it," she tells him.

"Oh yeah?" Glenn works at not smiling. Finally he does. He's too pleased with his manliness to keep a straight face. Mary Lou can't believe she ever mistook him for a pilot. She knows she'll see him everywhere from now on. She feels herself drifting on a wave of orange juice and vodka and knows it's time to go.

Usually the flight to D.C. is smooth, and she can look down through banks of fluffy white clouds to where the sea meets the land, watching the shoreline as they fly north. But today there's nothing but gray outside. They rise through one cloud layer and another, then drop, struggle upward, bump. A stewardess makes her way down the aisle, clutching the backs of seats for support. If it were Jill, the rouge on her cheekbone would be like a red circle of fear. Mary Lou knows Jill won't fly again until she needs to get somewhere far and fast, and even then it will fill her with dread. The plane bumps again. Mary Lou isn't afraid of motion. She's afraid of the lack of it. Her body feels still against the wild currents of air—unnaturally quiet, the way things are after great commotion. She misses the humming in her blood. She misses Bettina practicing her dives, a child in perpetual motion. She misses things she didn't even know she had.

When the plane touches down in Washington, Mary Lou doesn't feel any better. She told her family she was coming for the weekend but intended to stay forever. Now she sees that the Washington sky is dull compared to Miami's, compared even to the wreckage of what has become her life. Last night Lucas took her to Centro Vasco one last time, and as they ate black beans and rice he said, "Even if you can't be a stewardess, you could probably get a job as a ticket agent. You'd get free plane travel—if that's what you want." She'd been distressed, as usual, at the idea of his reading her mind. But now it seems imperative to discuss this with him further—to what end, she's not yet sure. As the plane taxis to the gate and comes to a stop, Mary Lou notes how little she's left behind—how for once, at last, the fact of flying has made no difference at all.

RAYFIELD THE PRESSER

AFTER NATALIE TASTED THE POISONED POTION, she would probably kill Beryl, but Beryl didn't care. For an hour Natalie had been watching the test pattern on Bubby's TV, sulking because they had to come here again after school. Mother and Daddy were out at a meeting, preparing for the Hearings. Bubby and Papa were downstairs working in the tailor shop. There was nothing to do.

"You're freezing me here!" Natalie yelled when Beryl opened the French doors to the porch. Beryl slammed the doors hard, but Natalie didn't get up. "Find something to read," she said.

"Oh sure." Papa's bookcase was full of Daddy's architecture books from college, with tiny words and drawings of houses. On the table was the *Washington Star* and the *Daily Forward.*

"I can't read this stuff," Beryl said. She wouldn't be seven for another month . The newspaper was too hard and the *Daily Forward* was in thick black Yiddish letters.

"Then get me something to drink," Natalie ordered.

At home Beryl would have said, "Make me," and run away from her. Natalie would have chased her until Mother yelled at them to stop. They couldn't do that here at Bubby's. Besides, Natalie hated Beryl too much to play. At that moment the idea of the poisoned potion came to Beryl. She went into the kitchen.

The room smelled of the meat Bubby put on to cook every day while she worked. There were potatoes and carrots in the pot, too, but by suppertime everything tasted the same. Beryl filled a glass with orange juice, salt, and a big handful of Babo cleanser. It frothed prettily as she mixed it, like an orange freeze from the Hot Shoppes.

Natalie sat up in front of the TV looking grumpy. She was mad because of not being able to play with Stephanie Boyd after school. Mother said she appreciated the bonds between ten-year-old girls, but she just couldn't have Natalie and Beryl walking home by themselves right now, or staying with some sitter who wasn't family, not during the Hearings. Aunt Selma couldn't watch them because she was busy with baby Freddy.

Natalie took a swig of the orange juice. Her nostrils flared and the muscles in her face twitched. "You're dead, Beryl," she said.

Beryl bolted through the dining room and down the kitchen stairs into the back of the store. At the bottom she slowed to a walk in case there were customers. Natalie wasn't behind her.

The workroom was full of soft yellow light, with gauzy specks of fabric floating through. Even Papa's bald spot was coated by bits of lint as he sat at his sewing machine, pinning cloth with the straight pins he spit out of his mouth. Beryl had once asked if he ever swallowed those pins, but Papa said no, he'd been doing it for fifty years; he wouldn't advise Beryl to try it herself.

Bubby looked up from her machine. "You're hungry?" she asked. She didn't look at Beryl but rather at the skirt she had just finished sewing. The family never looked at Beryl anymore, or at Natalie, either. Only Rayfield looked. He was the presser. He stood in front of the pressing machine, pulling the top board down onto the bottom one, onto a pair of trousers. Natalie and Beryl were not allowed near the pressing machine because it had steam inside and was very dangerous. Beryl was afraid of it when she was little, but Rayfield winked and made faces so she wouldn't cry. She wasn't afraid now, when he winked and stepped on the foot lever. A great hiss of steam puffed out. No sound came from upstairs in the kitchen. Natalie would kill her later. Beryl was not afraid of Natalie, either. She was already thinking about something else. She was thinking about the mystery of The Fifth.

Last night at home, the adults were having a meeting in the dining room. It was an odd meeting, because no one laughed or even argued. Natalie and Beryl were supposed to stay upstairs, but Beryl couldn't help hearing Mr. Goldstein say in his deepest, lowest voice: "What are you going to do, Leonard?"

"Of course I'll take The Fifth," Daddy said. "As a matter of principle. What'd you think I was going to do?"

Beryl was confused. She didn't like Daddy sounding angry. The fifth what? Or just *the* Fifth? She hadn't heard any more.

The door of the tailor shop jangled. Someone had come in. Papa pulled his vest down and went to the front, fingering the tape measure draped around his neck. Rayfield got a shirt down to press. He hummed in time with the hissing the pressing machine made before its steam was released.

Bubby stood up. She put one hand to the small of her back and the other to the pile of braids on her head. At night when she took the hairpins out, her hair would come down to her waist. "Maybe you'll help Mr. Rosinski close up," she said to Rayfield. "I have to go give everyone eat."

"Yes ma'am."

Bubby went up the steps. In the front of the store Papa was talking to someone in Yiddish. It might be someone from the Workmen's Circle, and they might talk for a long time.

"Rayfield, can I ask you something?"

"Shoot, baby," Rayfield said. You could always count on Rayfield to tell the truth. In some ways, he wasn't like a normal grownup. He was married to Jasmine, whose name was a flower, and Jasmine was going to have a baby. But Rayfield told the truth anyway. He pressed the shirt—collar first, then sleeves and back. When he was finished, he arranged the folds with swift long fingers the color of coffee. But his palms were pink. Beryl waited for him to turn his hands a certain way so she could see the pink part. It was like waiting for someone to tell a secret.

"What's The Fifth?" she asked.

Rayfield turned from the pressing machine to look at her. He looked down from a long way, through black friendly eyes. He laughed. "A fifth is a bottle of whiskey, sugar—nothing you need to know about right now," he said.

"You sure?"

"Course I'm shore." He took the shirt off the machine and hung it on a hanger. "Don't be asking your grandma or grandpa about no fifth. Hear?"

He winked again, and Beryl felt better. Rayfield always made her feel better. But later, after she went out of the store, she got a picture in her mind of Daddy having a glass of *schnapps* with Papa on Rosh Hashonah. They drank to celebrate happy times, Daddy said. She didn't think he would take whiskey to the Hearings.

"You'll wait right in front of the school," Bubby said. "Papa will come for you by machine." *Machine* meant the car or her sewing machine or anything else with a motor. Before the Hearings, Natalie and Beryl had walked home from school by themselves, and Mother was waiting in the house. If someone had to get them, Mother or Aunt Selma came, or even Uncle Nathan once. Now Aunt Selma was busy with baby Freddy. Beryl was not allowed to hold Freddy, although Natalie was. Mother and Daddy were busy with meetings. Natalie got a dark look on her face when Mother said they might have to go to the tailor shop all week. "You'd think we were going to be attacked," Natalie said.

Mother didn't answer.

"Don't be ridiculous," Daddy told her. "Let me tell you something about witch-hunts, sweetie. Most people know that when you go on a witch-hunt, you're bound to come up empty-handed. Most people don't hold the victims liable."

Beryl felt afraid, though Daddy was smiling. It was a false smile. Witches.

Papa was waiting for them after school. His car was full of clean suits and dresses and coats he had picked up from the dry cleaner's. Rayfield would press them later. Beryl put her head against the clothes to smell the cleaning fluid on them, sweet and dizzy. They bumped over the streetcar tracks and she fell asleep.

She woke up on the couch in Bubby's living room after the sky was dark. Mother and Daddy were whispering to Bubby and Papa in Yiddish. Yiddish was a secret, like the Hearings, that the adults wanted to keep to themselves. Natalie and Beryl were not supposed to understand, but they couldn't help knowing a lot of words. They never let on that they knew.

"*Zul zein*," Mother said when Beryl sat up. That meant leave it alone, don't talk anymore.

Daddy smiled at her. "Well. Did you have a nice nap?"

"I guess," Beryl said. Daddy's face was very white.

"Now we eat," Bubby said. She went into the kitchen and everyone but Natalie followed. Beryl heard the whispered sounds of Yiddish. The grownups pretended to be angry about the Hearings and not afraid, but they talked about them in low voices in a secret language.

She started to get up from the couch. Natalie pushed her back. "*Baby*," she hissed. Natalie stuck her face into Beryl's and talked into her eyes. "Baby still taking a *nap*."

One afternoon there was an article about Daddy in the *Washington Star*. Someone at school had told Natalie it was there. Arriving at Bubby's house, Natalie went all through the paper until she found it. The headline said: *Prominent Washington Architect Called Before McCarthy Panel*. Daddy's picture smiled out from beneath the words.

"Can't read it, can you?" Natalie screamed.

"Yes I can! I'm in the top reading group. Give it here."

Beryl knew *architect*; that was what Daddy did. She knew *Washington*, of course; and *McCarthy* ran the Hearings.

"What's p-r-o-m-i-n-e-n-t?" Beryl asked.

"Prominent. Important. Well-known. God, you're dumb."

She wasn't dumb. Daddy had said McCarthy could ask anyone he wanted to come to the Hearings, and they couldn't refuse. "I don't see why not," Beryl said. She couldn't make out any more of the words in the article. Natalie was looking at her, hating her, with her hands on her hips.

"They have to go, but they don't have to answer, you jerk! If they don't answer he thinks they're communists. He thinks they want to share everything. He thinks Daddy's one. And you're not *allowed* to be a columnist—or didn't you know that?—*baby*." Natalie's voice had little sharp points. Beryl blinked back the stinging in her eyes and went down to the store.

Papa was not at his sewing machine but in front, sorting dry cleaning and laundry on the wide counter. A strong gray light came into the window, reflecting off the three-way mirror where Papa measured customers for suits.

"Here, you'll help me do this," Papa said. He almost never let her help. "You'll put the laundry in one pile, the dry cleaning in the other." His bald spot was shiny in the light, not soft the way it looked back in the workroom. The brightness picked out tiny white whiskers on his face. He looked old in the light.

"Natalie says they think Daddy's a columnist," Beryl told him.

Papa was holding a blue suit. He froze for a minute and then moved the suit up and down in his hand as if he were weighing it. "A columnist," he said. He wasn't looking at her. He was smiling a little, not at Beryl but to himself. "Leonard Rosinski is an architect. A columnist is somebody who writes for a newspaper."

Papa was lying. Beryl knew. Daddy *was* a columnist. He had written a newspaper story about a house he had designed, where two or three families could live at once. They could cook together and take care of each other's children. Some of the mothers could work and others could stay at home. They could share everything. It was easier that way. Mother had explained the article to Beryl and hung it on the bulletin board in their kitchen.

Tears were in her eyes and she couldn't see to separate the laundry from the dry cleaning. Papa was lying because of the Hearings, because of the secrets they told in Yiddish. Rayfield came out of the workroom carrying a bunch of hangers. The light from the window went into his skin. It didn't change him or make him look whiskery like Papa. It went right into his skin.

Rayfield put the hangers on the counter. He winked as if he didn't know Beryl was crying. He always did that. One of the first things she could remember was falling from the high counter across from the pressing machine when she was little, and Rayfield picking her up, lifting her high over the counter, over the sewing machine, saying "Bingo!" in a large cheerful voice, and winking. She was above everyone in his arms, looking at the pink, secret palms of his hands. She had not cried. Rayfield had never said: "It don't hurt, does it?" He had never pretended. He had just said "Bingo!" and winked in a way that made her feel there was a secret between them, and the secret was she had a kind of courage she hadn't known was there.

One day Rayfield's wife, Jasmine, called to say she was going to have her baby. Jasmine was so tall and flat in the middle that you couldn't imagine her puffed up with a baby inside, like Aunt Selma before Freddy was born. But Rayfield left the store, half running and half dancing, so Beryl knew it was true. That happened the very same day Daddy went to the Hearings. Mother said they might not be back until late.

After school Natalie slammed her books onto the dining room table and started to do homework, right on top of Bubby's lace tablecloth.

"You have to take the cloth off," Beryl said.

"Get lost."

"Bubby always takes it off if she does work at the table." Bubby sometimes wrote numbers there, in a big black notebook.

"Get out of here, Beryl." Natalie's voice was like snarling. It was like that because she knew part of the secret about the Hearings. Beryl went downstairs to the store.

It was quiet in the workroom with Rayfield off having his baby. Beryl picked up Papa's statue from the counter—a white stone carving of a man's head down to the shoulders. On the bottom was the man's name, along with the year he was born and the year he died: Eugene Debs (1855-1926). Papa kept the statue because Eugene Debs was a great leader who had helped the working people. They still remembered him even though he had been dead more than 25 years. He had run for president five times.

"Did he ever win?"

"No."

Beryl didn't see how he could be such a great leader and not win, but she never said that. She wished Rayfield hadn't left. Bubby was sewing a hem and Papa was ironing a cuff with the hand iron. There was not even the sound of machines.

She had the statue in her hands, the cool white stone. She was thinking about Jasmine in the store one day, in a red dress with her hair hanging straight to her shoulders like a stiff black sheet. She could not imagine Jasmine busy with a baby's bottles, tucking her hair under a scarf or braiding it like Bubby's instead of letting it hang free. She could not imagine Rayfield holding a baby the way Uncle Nathan held Freddy, stiff and awkward in his arms.

Papa took the jacket off the ironing board and nodded toward the statue. "Some people when they work for somebody else," he said, "they have to work even if it's bad conditions. Somebody like Rayfield needs the money to buy what to eat. Let's say his wife is going to have a baby, he wants to go home. But the owner says no, he needs some suits pressed. What can Rayfield do? He can go home and lose his job. Or he can stay."

"You wouldn't make him stay."

"No, not me. But some people. But let's say he works in a big tailor shop, ten pressers work there. All the pressers can get together and say, either you let Rayfield go home or none of us will work here anymore. That's what's called organizing. That's what Eugene Debs taught the workers to do. Then all of a sudden it's easier for the owner to let Rayfield go home than to hire ten new pressers."

"Oh." She put the statue back on the counter.

After today Rayfield would have a baby. After today Daddy would not have to go to the Hearings anymore. Maybe he would have to stop being a columnist. She had liked his story about the house where several families could live. Nothing would be the same.

A long time passed. They were having brunch in Bubby's kitchen. It was supposed to be a party, but the adults were talking in Yiddish. It was not the way Mother had said.

She had said: "No breakfast—not a bite. *Brunch*." Her voice had been airy, a party voice. They went to the deli to buy bagels and cream cheese and lox. "Later maybe we'll ride over to see Rayfield's new baby," she said.

Aunt Selma and Uncle Nathan had come to Bubby's house with Freddy. "Oh, let me have him," Natalie cooed.

"As soon as you're finished eating," Aunt Selma said. Natalie looked at Beryl in a superior way. Now Natalie was feeding Freddy his bottle. The adults were drinking tea. Papa was sipping milk and *vasser* out of a glass. He held a sugar cube in his mouth and let the hot liquid pass over it. He could talk with the sugar in his mouth, just as he could talk with a mouthful of pins.

The conversation was partly in Yiddish and partly in English. There were words like *blacklist* that Beryl didn't know. She thought of a list made with a black pen, but she knew that could not be right. She understood a lot more than she used to. She knew communists wanted to run the country a different way and columnists wrote for newspapers. But she didn't know what a blacklist was, and she wasn't going to ask.

"*Veden?*" Uncle Nathan said. "It happened in California, it could happen in Washington."

Daddy said he didn't think so; he wasn't worried about a blacklist. Steam was on the kitchen windows. Aunt Selma smiled at Beryl and said, "It's Sunday, isn't it? Isn't something on television on Sunday?"

Outside it was cold after the hot house, even in the sun. Papa, Bubby, Mother, Natalie and Beryl got into Papa's car. Daddy left for a meeting. Aunt Selma and Uncle Nathan took Freddy home. Mother gave Beryl a wrapped package to give to Jasmine. It was a sweater for the baby.

Beryl didn't want to go. Everything would be changed with Rayfield, too. Jasmine would be fat. She and Rayfield would hover around the baby like Selma and Nathan around Freddy, protective and closed.

Rayfield lived in an apartment. Jasmine stood behind him when he opened the door. She held a tiny baby smaller than Freddy, with fine, fuzzy bristles of hair like Rayfield's. Jasmine's middle was a little round, but her arms and legs were still thin. She said the baby's name was Luther.

"He doesn't look big enough for that name," Beryl said.

Everyone laughed. Rayfield and Jasmine didn't laugh away from her, they turned their eyes right to her face. Rayfield said, "Well, I guess he ain't, not yet." Beryl gave Jasmine the wrapped package. She said, "Well just for that, you got to be the first one to hold him." She put the baby into Beryl's arms. He opened his eyes and then closed them again. He was small and light. He didn't cry until after Mother gave him to Natalie.

"That's the dinner bell," Jasmine laughed when the baby kept crying. Her hair hung down like it always did, a black sheet touching her shoulders. "Rayfield, you stay in here with Mr. Rosinski while I feed him," she said. "You ladies can come with me."

"I'll just wait out here," Mother said. She held Natalie's arm. Bubby didn't get up, either, but Beryl was out of their reach. She followed Jasmine into the kitchen.

The two of them sat down at a wooden table. Beryl waited for Jasmine to put on a bottle to warm. That was what Aunt Selma always did and what all mothers did as far as Beryl knew—warmed a bottle and tested the milk on their wrists and fed it to the baby. But Jasmine did the most astonishing thing. She lifted up her blouse and put the baby to her breast. She did not wear a brassiere like Mother and Aunt Selma did. She lifted up her blouse and her breast was right there. It was brown, the color of the kitchen table. It was not as private-looking as Mother's white breasts, because of its nice color. Beryl did not turn away.

Jasmine arranged the baby's head so it was close to her. The baby did not seem surprised. He stopped crying and started to suck. He made his hands into little fists as if it were hard work. Beryl could see a tiny line of milk next to the baby's mouth, but he did not choke or turn purple the way

Freddy did when he got too much milk from his bottle.

Jasmine talked to Beryl while the baby nursed. She acted as if feeding him was no effort at all. The baby's eyes closed and his little fists opened. Rayfield came in to pour Cokes for everyone. He stood behind Jasmine's chair and put his hands on her shoulders. "Well, whaddaya think?" he asked. He sounded as if he were talking just about the baby, but Beryl knew he meant the secret, too. Colored babies could get milk right from their mothers. There were no bottles or pots or pans. Jasmine shared her milk. Beryl knew about sharing. It was like Daddy's house. The families could share the work and everything would be easier. "Nice," Beryl said as if they were talking only about the baby. She would never tell Natalie. Rayfield winked. Everything was gray and cramped around her, but the secret had light in it, like the hidden pink of Rayfield's palms.

SHELL ISLAND

EBAN'S WIFE, WHO HAD LEFT HIM, would eat anything but reds. Stayman, Jonathan. . . occasionally a Golden Delicious. Most apple people felt that way. After Alex was born they had moved from Washington to Smithsburg, Maryland, because Lila's brother had died and she wanted to take over his job in her father's orchard. Autumn weekends she stood on the loading docks selling bushels of reds to people who drove up from the city. "They think you can use them for pies and sauce, but you can't. Reds get an ugly taste if you heat them," she'd say. Not Red Delicious, just reds, the way communists were reds in the '50s.

Eban knew nothing of the apple business. He taught some classes in town and drove into D.C. two days a week for his research. Alex had just turned ten when Lila announced she was moving in with her father's foreman, Larry. "I don't know why, Eban, I can't give you a clear explanation," she said when he demanded one. "Maybe it's because he can tell a red from a Macintosh and you can't. Honest to goodness, maybe that's why."

So it was that at the age of forty-seven Eban came to take a job on the coast of southeastern North Carolina, where there were no mountains and no apple trees and—except in the fall, brought to the grocery stores from great distance and at great expense per pound—no reds.

He took Alex with him. "When you're young, it's good to have all the different experiences you can," he explained to the boy. "We've never lived by the sea." Alex shrugged his shoulders. He had fallen into a state of lethargy and could register only indifference. Indifference to Eban, indifference to his mother, indifference to leaving the school he'd attended since kindergarten. They went at the end of August, before the new term, driving the eight-hour stretch south with only two brief stops for gas and lunch.

The land was flat along the coast, and sandy, with squat houses and scrubby trees. A real estate agent greeted them. Alex had always lived in a house and Eban did not wish to make a drastic change. The agent drove them around under a bright sky she described as Tar Heel Blue, blasting her air-conditioning against 93-degree heat. Tall stands of pines lined the roadways, shedding needles onto exhausted Southern grass. She showed them tiny ranch houses on flat lots, dwarfed by the pines. Eban found them depressing. Alex did not react. The humidity was overpowering.

"Or you could rent at the beach until May," the agent finally said. "People let the houses by the week in summer, but they like long-term tenants after that. September and October are really the nicest months."

She drove them across the drawbridge toward Johnnie Mercer's Fishing Pier, where the evening before they had sat on the beach after swimming. She showed them an apartment jammed between graying frame houses, then a claustrophobic condominium overlooking the marsh. Finally she brought them to an oceanfront house at the uncrowded north end of the beach, which looked like a shack on stilts from outside, but inside was spacious, well furnished, and clean.

"Of course out here you'll have all the little problems of living on a barrier island," she said as they stood on the deck looking out at the water. "They'll evacuate you every time there's a hurricane warning." Alex perked up at the mention of hurricanes. The woman had anticipated that. "Don't worry, these places have been here for a while. They've withstood a few storms, they don't blow down that easily." Alex glowed. Eban himself was beginning to like the idea of living on a *barrier island*.

To the north and south were other, similar dwellings, facing the dunes and the sea. In town, the sad little houses had been landscaped with pampas grass and myrtles, but here even grass did not grow on the lots, only weeds and burrs. There was not a single tree. It suited him. Alex was watching the ocean curl toward them in the late-afternoon light.

"We'll take it," Eban said.

The section of beach on which they lived was called Shell Island. The streets were named for shells—Sand Dollar,

Conch, Cowrie, and Scotch Bonnet. Scotch Bonnet? Eban bought shell books at the souvenir store on Johnnie Mercer's pier, and was surprised to find shells he'd never heard of occupying so much space in his illustrated paperbacks—160 species of cowries alone, commoner than he would have thought.

Except for Eban's job at the university, and Alex's school— a private school Eban had chosen because of the small classes and Alex's emotional state—they had nothing to do but explore the island. Each morning they drove over the drawbridge into the town of Wilmington, where Eban arranged his schedule to coincide with Alex's, picking him up at three each afternoon. They bought styrofoam belly boards to float on in the ocean—Alex at ten, Eban at 47—learning to catch the breakers just so. Alex—lighter, braver, more indifferent— repeatedly skinned his belly on the drifts of shells which washed onto the shore with each tide. He didn't complain. The sun remained intense through September, the weather stayed hot; and all around them was water—ocean to the east; to the west, the Sound.

Alex spent hours fashioning sailboats out of cardboard milk cartons, using straws for masts and Kleenex for sails. Holding the boats delicately in his hands, he crossed the narrow road that ran the length of the island and set his creations afloat in the Sound. Eban's passion was not boats but the sea itself. He stood on the deck, putting off housework and laundry, making note of the colors as the ocean changed from green to deep blue in the late afternoon light. He watched the gulls circle and dip in the breakers. He searched for the dolphins that sometimes came leaping by, breaking water with their fins. Peering through the set of good binoculars Lila had given him early in their marriage, he charted the ships that floated against the horizon. Finally weary of staring, he hiked up a new road that had been built to the northern tip of the island, where construction had already begun on rows of condominiums and a hotel, but where for now there was still an unobstructed view of long-legged water birds in the marsh to the west, and pink-and-gold sunsets over the reeds. Many days, after work, Eban spoke to no one but Alex.

In the evenings fishermen lined the shore as the tide came in, casting out in the areas where the gulls were feeding. At first Eban and Alex only watched, peering into buckets filled with ice and bait and the day's catch. Finally Eban, whose fishing experience consisted of a day on a bass boat in Western Maryland, bought surf fishing gear at the marine store across the drawbridge. "All right, I'm going out to catch our dinner," he said—and by luck or stubbornness he did.

It didn't happen again. He tried different baits—shrimp, which slipped off the hook, bloodworms, which bit, and cut mullet. "You could try for spots off the pier," Alex suggested, knowing his father had a weakness for small panfish. But Eban, thinking use of the pier was somehow cheating, refused. He gave up fishing and returned to his study of shore life, identifying birds in the marsh and shells on the beach. He watched the boats. He bought their seafood at the strong-smelling fish market just across the drawbridge, where mako shark and swordfish steaks were placed on ice and the cheaper fish dumped unceremoniously into bushel baskets. At night, glutted by sight of brown pelicans and sand sharks, by talk of spots and whiting and blues—at night he often slept.

Mornings, he woke from dreams of Larry and Lila together, touching, or of his inlaws having the two of them over for dinner. He had liked his inlaws, before. Country people, they had deferred to his better education, his maturity (compared to Lila's), his lack of impulsiveness. He in turn admired their pulling the orchards through four years of recession. Only their speech, dotted with colloquialisms and bad grammar, embarrassed him. When Lila left, they claimed to be bewildered by her behavior, but they never fired Larry. A long-time foreman, they said, the only one familiar with the work. It had never occurred to Eban that he—the scholar—would become the embarrassment. Waking from dreams of that, he looked out to ocean sunrises rather than blue mountains— red sky, white breakers, hungry gulls. The scenery struck him as exotic, and eased his pain.

They were often stopped by the drawbridge on their way into town. The bridge opened every hour on the hour to let the boat traffic through. Bearing down on the Intracoastal Waterway at 45 miles an hour, they became accustomed to seeing red lights flashing in the distance and wooden barriers coming down, telling them without question that they were going to be late.

Neither of them minded much. Stopped in traffic, waiting for the steel girders to rise, Alex got out of the car and ran up for a closer look. Eban was pleased to see him taking an interest in the boats heading south on the Intracoastal for the winter. For himself, the appeal was being locked on the island seven or ten minutes longer, caught in view of the reedy growth from the bright water, fishing rigs unloading at the market, unfamiliar island life. He rather liked the bridge blocking passage so effectively— making the island a barrier from the mainland as well as the sea: impermeable: safe.

Alex often returned to the car disconsolate—for what reason, Eban could not decide. Perhaps the southbound boats unsettled the boy, traveling so freely while he was due at school. Later Eban realized Alex was not watching the boats at all, but rather the shore itself—shelves of sand rising from the shallows, long stretches of marsh grass, clusters of reeds. Alex had been seeking something there and was disappointed not to find it. But as to the object of the search, which disturbed his son so, Eban had no clue. Then one evening as Alex walked toward the Sound with the day's newly completed sailboat, Eban understood with sudden insight that *his boat* was what his son expected to see, morning after morning. Alex thought somehow that the sea would carry it from Banks Channel into the Intracoastal, and give it back to him the following day. Perhaps he believed that the same law would also bring back his mother.

Eban, helpless, began to buy milk in large plastic gallons, unsuitable (he hoped) for fitting out with sails.

They had been there less than a month when a hurricane warning came. For days there were reports of a storm moving northwest from this coordinate to that coordinate, packing winds of 120 miles an hour, but so far away. A momentary bleep of excitement in Alex's eyes, followed by indifference.

Then one day they woke to a metal-gray sea, churning. All the schools had been closed. If the storm continued on its present course, it would make landfall at Wrightsville Beach sometime the following night. Its power, coupled with the evening's high tide, could make for untold damage. The beach communities were to be evacuated. "All *right*," Alex sang, dancing. Eban pulled the porch furniture inside from the deck and tacked boards (left by the landlord) over the sliding glass doors facing the sea. Alex helped him, having abandoned altogether his previous indifference.

Inside, the phone was ringing. *Lila*, Eban thought. She had called once before at an awkward moment, to check on Alex when classes began. Hearing that the boy was in private school, she'd said bitterly, "Trying to get around that bussing order for racial balance, aren't you, Eban? Don't tell me it never entered your mind." (In fact, it hadn't.) "I never thought you had it in you to be a bigot."

Since she'd left, she'd made a point of lacing their conversations with whatever wounding comments she could. Eban wondered if she was trying to insulate herself against the accusations he might make otherwise, or if the insults had been stored up all the time they'd lived together—directed, in those years, against the reds instead of Eban. He believed that now, secure with Larry, she might have managed to be kind.

"Well, I never thought you had it in you to be an adulteress," he'd replied.

A shriek of wind, shearing over the deck. Eban envisioned Lila wrenched from her distant bliss by a momentary pang of conscience at abandoning her son to storms. The phone rang a fifth time, a sixth. He was annoyed that she'd choose just then to call, when Alex seemed to have recovered a measure of normality.

"Eban?" The woman's voice startled him because it wasn't Lila's, surely: but reedier, and more Southern, a Carolina voice.

"Dennie Mattson," she said. It was a moment before he placed her: the middle-aged departmental secretary whose car sometimes occupied the parking spot next to his, adorned with a bumper sticker that read: "If God isn't a Tar Heel, why did He make the sky Carolina blue?"

She was always inquiring about his adjustment, suggesting sightseeing trips, offering to help. She might have annoyed him except that she seemed so sincere. Once, to make conversation, he'd mentioned the salt-spray glaze that stuck to his windows—a housewifely detail—and she'd said: "We had a place out there once with the same problem, and the only thing we could ever get to cut that stuff was Softscrub"— looking almost triumphant at being able to offer a solution. Now she wanted to know how they had taken the news of the evacuation, what he was going to do.

"We're getting ready to go over to the high school, I guess," he said. "They say it's the evacuation center for this area."

"I was calling to invite you here instead," she told him. "Last year the centers were just misery. Babies crying, and you couldn't get into the bathrooms." Hurricane Diana had hit Wilmington the previous fall, sweeping through the center of town, spawning tornadoes which uprooted masses of trees. "I've got some other people coming, too. We'll have a hurricane party."

"We couldn't really," he said.

"Bring some sleeping bags, and flashlights if you have any. Last year the electricity was off a couple days." She gave directions to one of the flat, pine-woods developments where a month before Eban had refused to rent a house. She sounded—in her Southern way—as if she expected them.

To the east, the sky had grown darker, and the wind had begun to rise. The sea, whitecapped, came almost to the dunes. *Hurricane.* Alex was watching with glittering eyes. On the drawbridge, police in slickers stood in the rain, allowing people off the island but not on. Eban felt suddenly displaced, as he had in the days preceeding his move from Maryland. What if the beach house should be ruined? A vision rose before him of the evacuation center some days hence, in the sticky aftermath of storm: a high school gym dim from lack of electricity, filled with the anxious sweat of unbathed families, crowded bathrooms smelling of urine. And Alex, indifferent. Eban headed not to the school, but to the woman's house.

"I'm so pleased you decided to come," Dennie Mattson said, opening the door to a small beige living room full of people. Introductions all around: an elderly aunt and uncle who lived out on the beach; their son; a fat X-ray technician and her daughter from the house next door.

They all behaved as if his joining them were normal. The adults watched the weather reports on TV, drank beer from cans, ate Cheese Nips out of a box. At some point hamburgers and chips were served for dinner. Alex perched himself by the window to chart the storm, which so far wasn't much. No danger, the broadcasters said, until night. The others talked of the eye of the terrible hurricane last year, a perfectly calm and yellow eye. "There were ten people staying with us, and I'll tell you, that's something you don't forget," the X-ray technician said. Eban had nothing to offer on the subject except the fogs that haunted the Maryland mountains. Driving up from town in the rain, he came to know exactly at what altitude the zone would change, above which the clouds would close in, leaving him to cling to the white line at the side of the winding road. He'd been more wary of fog than Lila had—she had grown up with it, after all—and she had held him (he realized now) in contempt. Her own terror had been of lightning on the mountain, which did its damage, he supposed, but was, after all, in contrast to the fog—*light*.

He didn't speak of Lila aloud. He drank yet another beer, waited for them to ask. No one did. He realized that, from their perspective, he was merely a man alone, with a school-aged child. . . he might have been divorced for years.

The announcer said the storm had begun to turn north. Perhaps it would hit Morehead City, or even Cape Hatteras farther up the coast. The Wilmington area would see only heavy gales. In the dark, with rain slashing and wind whipping, the X-ray technician announced that she'd better go home and feed her cats. Her daughter went with her. Eban heard himself saying (he was a little drunk by then), "And all the rest of us can go out for a walk."

Dennie clapped her hands—a blond, middle-aged cheerleader. "Oh, wonderful!" The elderly aunt and uncle declined, but Dennie and the cousin and Alex went, wrapped in slickers, into the night. The wind buffeted them, less (they all noted) than it would have during a typical afternoon thunderstorm. Even so, Alex's color was high. The hurricane might yet hit. Last year it had changed course several times before making landfall. A few blocks from Dennie's house, a man, watching the storm from his porch, asked as they passed: "Do you need shelter?"

"No, we're just walking." But they were pleased.

Back in the house Dennie and Eban and the cousin watched the news and had a final beer after Alex went to bed. The storm was definitely heading north. Loose and slightly dizzy, Eban realized that he had not tasted alcohol since Lila's departure. In the aftershock of her going, he had stopped drinking altogether—had disciplined himself, rather, to prepare regular meals for Alex, to go to bed (though not always to sleep) at normal hours, marshalling his forces, as it were, to survive the hardship. He had no sense that his difficulties were over. But for the moment, sitting in a stranger's living room in a circle of light, talking of innocuous matters like winds and tides, with the buzz of alcohol between his ears, he felt, mind and body, like a tense muscle that had suddenly unclenched—one of those absolutely still moments he had not known for some time, when life breaks and pauses before it goes rushing on.

By morning the wind was calm; the evacuation order on the beach had been lifted. Dennie wanted everyone to stay for pancakes, but Eban was anxious to get back. The newspaper reported that the ocean had overreached the dunes during the night on parts of the beach. The speed limit was an absurd twenty-five miles per hour, but he observed it. Arriving home, he found everything intact. They removed the wooden boards from over the sliding glass doors just as the clouds blew off and the sun came out, giving them a clear blue holiday, because in anticipation of damage, most schools and businesses had been closed. He and Alex wandered the beach in the dry sunny air. Alex gathered the large, conical shells the high stormtides had washed in. Eban looked them up in his book. "Whelks," he said. Normally whelk shells did not reach shore, he supposed, because they were too large for the ordinary tides to propel them in. The specimens Alex had gathered were mostly broken and worn down to gray, but he lined them up on the picnic table on the deck. So: the hurricane had brought whelks, but no damage. Eban walked the house, testing faucets and outlets. All of them worked.

That was Friday. By Monday the heat had returned and Alex was tired of the whelk shells. "Some hurricane. This is what they give two days off of school for. Big whoop. I'd like to show them a big snow on the mountain."

After that Alex's mood stayed grim. "It's too hot for fall," he whined, as they slid into October and it was. He wanted crisp mornings, gold and auburn hills. He made no more sailboats. Eban could not, or did not, try to offer a defense. He had no wife, no dignity, no mountains and no apple harvest. He watched the sea.

Three days a week he had early classes, so he tended to his students and then brought his research materials back to the beach house. Positioning his desk to face the ocean, he worked until it was time to get Alex, his binoculars by his side. He allowed himself a session of bird-watching instead of a coffee break, gazing at brown pelicans flying in straight lines close to the shore, casing the surf for fish. He lunched to the sight of dolphins, noticing that they almost always traveled south. Perhaps they liked the warmer waters. He did not investigate further. The dolphins cheered him, and he preferred they keep their mystery. He was beginning the draft of his first new paper since the move. The heat was no longer stifling, though Alex thought it was. He turned the air-conditioning off and opened the sliders to the breeze.

Dennie, by virtue of their spending the hurricane together, now considered herself his friend. Days he lunched at the university, she wandered into his office with her own brown bag, filled with sensible egg-on-pumpernickel sandwiches and carrot sticks, much like the lunches he packed for Alex and himself. Had she reminded him in any way of Lila, he might have minded, but Lila was only 35, dark and flirtatious, while Dennie was as old as Eban—a pale, straightforward woman with spindly limbs and a cumbersome bust. Eating her nutritious lunches, she seemed not a woman at all—in the sense that Lila, who lunched on Diet Pepsi, had been— but simply a companion, which Eban could accept.

She read his horoscopes from the newspaper and told him about astrology. "Once we got audited by the IRS and ever after that we mailed the tax when the moon was void of course, and we never got audited again," she asserted.

"And what does that mean exactly—void of course?"

"All I know is, it happens every other day. And any project you start then, you'll never hear anything more of it."

Eban raised his eyebrows. "You have that superior look on your face," she said. "But I bet right now you're making a note to yourself to mail your tax next year when the moon is void of course." And, in fact, Eban was.

She told him the departmental gossip and enthused about Wilmington's building boom. Later, she told Eban about herself. Her son was at college in Chapel Hill; her husband, Edward (she pronounced it Ed-wood) had worked for Corning glass when he wasn't fishing, and died of a heart attack at the age of 53. She spoke of him cheerfully enough. He'd had a boat which she'd finally sold, and had entered the King Mackerel contest every year. "Ever taste King Mackerel?" She made an unpleasant face.

"I've seen the steaks in the fish store. Look kind of dark."

"Terrible, if you ask me." He liked her frankness, coupled with her soft North Carolina drawl. Much better, he thought, than the country quality Lila's speech had. With Lila it was: "Don't wear that, it needs washed," always dropping the infinitive, and once, when Alex was small, "It's new, but I wore it on him once," which annoyed him disproportionately.

"I suppose out there at the beach you do some fishing yourself," Dennie said, biting into a pickle.

"I gave it up," he said, looking at the pickle. "I felt too sorry for the fish."

"Fish don't have feelings."

"How do you know?"

"You eat them, don't you?" That seemed to settle it for her. "I even feel a little sorry for the worm," he said.

She broke off a piece of the pickle and handed it to him, having noticed how he was staring it down.

It was the middle of October and the temperature had not gone below seventy degrees for a week, even at night. There were occasional cool spells, but the tendency of the air was always to heat up. "It's not normal," Alex said.

"We have no way of knowing what's normal. We've never been here before in fall." Eban rather liked the idea of a climate without autumn. At any rate, they had nothing by which to judge it; normal didn't exist.

"Well, I hate it," Alex said.

In the increasingly angled light, the sea was blue-green, fading to darker blue in the depths. "It doesn't look like itself," Alex asserted. But the ocean *was* itself, Eban argued; what else could it be? What did they know of North Carolina waters in the seasons? Yet when he looked at the aqua shallows, he was reminded less of the Atlantic than of the Caribbean, where he and Lila had been on the company trip that ended his marriage. His inlaws had hosted an early December vacation—after the harvest—on which most of the employees had come with their wives. Larry had been alone.

It was then that Lila's affair had begun. She had bought three new bathing suits, one of them a bright turquoise which set off the darkness of her skin. He thought three suits was excessive for a five-day trip. He said she would always have the figure of a young boy, regardless. That was a joke, but Lila glared at him. She looked good in clothes and knew it— everyone said so. There was something lyrical about her appearance. She spent hours preparing for the trip in a tanning salon. She didn't want to burn, she said. She never burned.

The group rented a boat and went out to the reefs to snorkel. Under the water, plants waved tendrils at him and colorful angelfish wiggled by. In the distance, just visible from where he swam, a barracuda lurked with all its shadowy menace. Surfacing, he was so absorbed by the experience that he barely noticed Larry staring at Lila's turquoise bathing suit and approving, and Lila looking back. He'd always felt his failure to observe them just then had left him, later, responsible.

"The boy is bored," Dennie said, "Living there on the beach. That and the adjustment." Most of the houses on Shell Island were empty now, not having been rented for the winter. Their little lane housed a group of college students next door and a retired couple across the way, but Alex was the only child. The bathers and surfers and fishermen that had given the beach its festive quality had deserted. Alex's one friend from school lived twenty minutes away in town. "At least shoot a few baskets," Eban urged, pointing to a basketball goal at one of the abandoned houses nearby. "That's something you can do by yourself."

But Alex would not. "I miss grass," he said, looking at the lot below: weeds and sand. He spent hours watching "You Can't Do That on Television." It was a pastiche of one-liners and throwup jokes: Mother, I think you love Tommy better than you love me. — Oh Alistair, I never loved *you*. Sometimes Alex laughed out loud.

"Just the adjustment," Dennie said. On weekends she invented outings for them, inviting herself along. "Remember, he's been through a lot," she admonished, though Eban had not once offered up the details of his broken marriage. They took Alex to a surfing competition and a chowder tasting at Greenfield Park. "Are you going to marry her?" the boy asked. "Of course not. We're just friends. I don't even find her attractive." "Me neither," Alex agreed. But Dennie had adopted them, swept them up, was out of their control.

She insisted they go to the aquarium at Fort Fisher, where there were slide shows, nature walks, and a shark in a huge tank. A sign announced that it was a nurse shark, one of the species known to attack man. Alex stared at the beast swimming around in circles, its huge skin like pinkish sandpaper, its small blue eyes lashless and mean. "So that's it," he said flatly. "Big whoop."

In the newspaper, the fishing columns lamented the lack of autumn fish because of the warm waters. The speckled trout hadn't come in and only a few mullet were being caught at night. The ocean was ten or fifteen degrees warmer than usual. "God, do you believe this?" Alex said. Eban reminded him of the bare bones of trees on winter mountains, the cold, the death. Alex said he'd never minded. The week before Thanksgiving, the paper ran pictures of azalea bushes beginning to show bloom.

Then there was a spell of dark, rainy weather, spawned by a late hurricane in the Gulf. The first day was cool, like the sober end of the apple harvest, and they thought the season would change. It didn't. Trying to write in the rainy, humid heat, Eban felt distracted. He spent hours sitting on the dunes with his binoculars, watching the frothy gray-green sea, the pelicans dive-bombing after fish. When the hard rains came, he slept. He dreamed of the mountains. From their house he and Lila had had a clear view of the valley—neat rectangular fields, other orchards, other houses—and then more mountains on the other side, a perfect oval around the perspective. He woke to a rainy flatland: of the beach, the sea, his soul.

A terrible dank fishy smell sometimes rolled in from the ocean, the odor of decayed seaweed and rotting fish. Eban slept his afternoons away. He stopped dreaming of Lila and dreamed instead of Todd, Lila's dead brother, whom he hadn't thought about for years. In his dreams, Todd walked beside him on the beach. They walked for miles, for hours, and Eban woke exhausted, as if they really had.

Todd was a dark, rangy man who worked in the orchards

but whose first love was flying. He was a student pilot at first, then licensed, and finally instrument-rated. He flew in winter when there was no work to do, and in the growing season when there was. One day when a fog rolled in, Todd flew his rented Cessna into the mountain. He was 27 at the time. Lila, pregnant with Alex, wanted to name the baby after him.

Eban refused. They'd be saddened every time they looked at a son named Todd, he said. But he begrudged Todd his dying and Lila her orgy of mourning; he begrudged the waste of a life for sport. A few months later, when Lila's father suggested she take over Todd's job, she reacted with surprising emotion. She hated the city; orcharding was the only work she knew. Eban could have his career anywhere. Having refused her on the matter of the name, he was reluctant to say no again. They moved from Washington, where Eban had been happy, to Smithsburg, where he was not. In a way, Eban had blamed Todd for that, too.

But now, ten years later, dreaming, he and Todd walked the beach with no resentment between them. Together they looked out at the sea, at fish and plants which seemed to be visible under the water—the same plants he had seen in the Caribbean—and at gulls and pelicans above. "It wasn't just for sport, you see," Todd told him. "I was in search of another element." Eban nodded, understanding. Todd had no more expected to conquer the air than Eban did the ocean; it was too unfathomable—but just, somehow, reaching, to cope.

Dennie had invited them for Thanksgiving dinner. Her son would be home from Chapel Hill. "Billy will love it," she insisted. "The thing he always hated when he was younger was if we didn't have a lot of people for the holidays. It'll be good for Alex, too." Eban tried to refuse but in the end they went, just as they had gone during the hurricane, because the other alternatives were even less attractive.

The day was hot and sunny—eighty-three degrees by noon—abnormal, as Alex pointed out. Billy turned out to be blond and nondescript and just as cordial as his mother. Seeing Alex lose interest in Dennie's shell collection, he brought out an obviously new and complicated camera, which he taught Alex to use. At one o'clock they ate turkey and gravy and potatoes in the stifling dining room, getting up from the table overstuffed and irritable. Alex might have sulked except that Billy suggested they drive out to the beach, to Eban's house, to try the camera .

"We should shoot you swimming in the ocean," Dennie said when they got there. She'd changed into shorts which showed the fine varicose veins in her legs, under the bright sun. "You can take the pictures up north to your friends." She often spoke of people going "up north," whether they came from Virginia or Maine. It was as if all places north of Wilmington were cold and gray and identical, and could not be distinguished from one other.

"It's not really up north," Alex said quickly. "Maryland is south of the Mason-Dixon line. You can see some of the stones that mark the Mason-Dixon line not far from our house."

Our house.

"I'm getting dressed," Alex told them. "I hate this sand."

Inside, the phone was ringing. Eban had no time to reflect that it might be Lila before Alex grabbed it. Eban heard him saying, "Yeah, grandma—turkey and stuffing and the works. Then we went swimming, believe it or not." His mother-in-law. Eban imagined for an instant that she'd called to apologize for not firing Larry; perhaps even to say Lila had left Larry and wanted Eban back. A lightness bloomed in his chest, where before had been a dark weight. Then Alex handed Eban the phone and his mother-in-law said: "Eban, I know how awkward this is, but I'm calling to ask if you'll let Alex come up here for the Christmas holidays. I know it's not in the agreement." She paused. "It isn't for Lila I'm asking," she said. "It's for me."

Dennie and Billy were in the living room, pretending not to listen. "I'll ask Alex." And Alex danced, shaking sand off his bare legs onto the rug, waving a fist in the air: "All *right.*"

The drawbridge schedule had changed. Instead of opening

at hourly intervals, it went up on demand, whenever a boat needed to go through. In the warm, sunny weather, boat traffic was heavy all through early December. Sometimes, running an errand into town and coming back, Eban was stopped by the bridge on both legs of the trip. One afternoon, late on his way to get Alex, he found the bridge closed, with an interminable succession of boats passing underneath. Alex hated him not to be waiting when the bell rang. Lila had left him too long at a birthday party once, and he had feared ever since being the last one to be fetched. Minutes passed, the car was hot. Eban had to pull the collar of his shirt away from his neck and wipe his sweating palms on his trousers. Boat after boat: sailboats, fishing rigs, cabin cruisers. Eban's heart beat rapidly, an uneven rhythm. His breath came short and fast. (Lila had hyperventilated during labor, and swore the labor would be her one and only.) Chest aching. Breathe slowly, he told himself. The bridge began to open. His hands were trembling. Wooden barriers rising. Foot on the accelerator. Moving now. But it was as if he had been cut off forever: from the mainland, the town, his son.

A gray sky, cooler weather, coming back from a shopping trip for Alex's winter clothes. He would need them for his trip up north. "Don't call it *up north*, Dad. It sounds like you're from here." Dusk was falling, night coming earlier. A line of brown pelicans swooped by them, eerie against the darkening sky. "They're creepy," Alex said. "They look like pterodactyls."

Looking at the ocean, Alex said: "I hate the way the land ends right there, and the water closes you in." Eban thought of mountains ringed by other mountains, deceptive, as if at the end of those hills, everything stopped.

The morning Alex left was blinding-bright with sun, but really cold, for once. Alex was tense with excitement, anxious to get on the plane. Eban hugged him goodbye, but the boy pulled away, embarrassed to be embraced in public. Then he had gone, down the little chute that led to the plane. Eban was sure he'd refuse to come back and had said as much to Dennie over the past weeks. But she'd replied: "Maybe not. Maybe the trip north will get it out of his system."

Driving back through town from the airport, Eban saw there'd been a hard freeze. The first? He didn't know. On the beach the landscape was always the same: sand and weeds; no green, no bushes, no trees. In town the grass was crusty from ice and the tender plants had wilted. It looked surprisingly normal. He was visited by a vision of his Smithsburg house against a muted sky: bare orchards, violet and gray winter, masses of birds. Returning to the beach, he noted that the reedy dune grass was now brown and beaten down by salt spray. The sand was interminable. Except for the ocean, he might have been living on a desert. That had been Alex's view of it all along. He imagined his mother-in-law phoning, pleading Alex's case, begging him to leave the boy in Maryland. He'd been imagining such an outcome for three weeks, and now that he was finally alone, after all that high emotion, he couldn't sustain it. He felt drained, empty. If Alex came back, they would move into town.

Dennie insisted he come for dinner, because otherwise he would brood. She cooked an elaborate meal, wore a silky dress. "Lila wanted to name Alex for her brother," he said. "I wouldn't let her." He had not spoken of such things before and now could not make himself stop. Perhaps insisting on Alex's name had been a mistake; perhaps it had something to do, all these years, with Lila's working so hard in the orchard and Eban's raising their son. Dennie nodded, not disagreeing. "I still think after Christmas he'll be ready to come back," she said.

Sitting in the living room after the meal, she smiled at Eban in what he recognized as a come-hither way. He was vaguely surprised. He saw that she expected him to make love to her, and supposed he would. There was no hurry. In the meantime they gazed at the shells that filled her knicknack shelf, gathered during her husband's fishing days. Among the conchs and the olive shells and the cowries was a long strand of flattish beige disks, almost like segments of a sand-colored lei. He could not identify them at first, and then recognized them from a drawing in his shell book. "Whelk egg casings," he said.

"Yes. Though sometimes I have trouble imagining whelks laying eggs."

She raised her eyebrows and he tried to picture whelks mating; he couldn't, of course.

"These things wash up onto the beach in the summer," she said. "Here, let me show you."

He picked up the papery necklace and handed it to her where she sat. With a long fingernail she slit open one of the compartments and emptied it onto the coffee table. Hundreds of tiny, whitish whelk shells fell out, perfectly conical, perfectly detailed miniatures even to the spiky nobs near their tops.

"You can imagine how many eggs there must be altogether," she said. "I mean, rows and rows of these casings washing up onto the beach. And each one has—what? Maybe a hundred of these little compartments?"

He touched his index finger to his tongue and then to the table, so that several of the little whelk shells adhered to it. He raised them to his eyes. They were small and white, each one capable of a new life, and they struck him as distinctly hopeful.

GARDEN PESTS

THE SUMMER DEBBIE DIED was the year we had the tomato hornworms. I was afraid of them so my daughter, Ann, picked them off the plants with tongs and drowned them in paper cups of water. One morning I walked out into the bright sunshine and discovered the leaves of a Better Boy clipped off neatly at the top. On the mulched soil beneath the plant was a trail of green feces. I knew the hornworm must be in plain sight, if only I could distinguish it from the stems. My arms broke out in goosebumps. I lifted each branch, afraid I'd accidentally touch the segments of the creature before I saw it with my eyes. Then there it was, its little hooked feet attached to the bottom of one of the branches, chewing on the young leaves. Except for the tiny whitish horn on its head, it was as green as the plant itself, a devil disguised as Mother Nature. It was a good four inches long and as fat as my thumb. I backed away.

Inside, my sister-in-law, Belle, was on the phone, Debbie's mother, calling with her daily report from the hospital.

"How's she doing?" I asked.

"Better than yesterday. She seems in good spirits."

"Good."

At that time Debbie had just become ill again after a remission. With all the talk of advances and cures, we were hopeful that she'd respond to further treatment.

"Are you going to see Debbie?" Ann asked when I hung up.

"I guess so. I really should."

"I wish I could go with you."

"You know you can't go until you're twelve. There's a hornworn on the plant right there," I pointed. "How about getting rid of it for me?"

"Yeah. Okay," Ann agreed.

My mood was ruined now that I'd said I'd go to the hospital. I was not much attached to Debbie. Even before her illness, she'd been a spiritless child, too obedient and too neat, with limp hair and eyes the color of dishwater. I went to the

91

hospital as a duty I felt I owed to Belle, though she was David's brother's wife, no real kin.

Ann sent Debbie one of her stuffed animals. Beasts of every description cluttered her room. Though she'd outgrown playing with them, she still slept with several and could recite all their names.

At the hospital, Belle was replaiting what was left of Debbie's hair. My niece, seeing the animal I was carrying, puffed air into the area between her top lip and her nose, a gesture of approval. "Aww, the Calico Cat," she said. "That was nice."

"I'll tell Ann you said so."

Belle finished the pigtail and rose to go. While she was gone, I was to read Debbie a mystery Ann had recommended. I wasn't unwilling to help Belle when I could. Debbie sighed.

"Aren't you feeling well?"

"I'm okay. You know what?"

"What?" I asked.

"Everybody smiles at me."

"I think that's nice."

"Why do they smile at me?"

"Because you're cute, probably," I lied. Debbie wasn't cute.

"It's because I'm sick," she said.

"I don't think so."

"It is. The nurses and everybody smile at me, even people who don't know who I am. They think I'm funny."

"No. If they thought that they'd turn their eyes away. It's because you're cute."

"It's because I'm sick."

"Debbie loved your cat," I told Ann later.

"Did she? I wish I could see her. Maybe I should send her Bear."

"Then who would protect you from the monsters of the night?"

"Oh *Mommy*"

"Don't get too involved with Debbie, Ann. Debbie is very sick."

The last two weeks in July Ann went to camp. The tomato hornworms grew worse. I got out the tongs and removed them myself. I couldn't bear to put them in the cup of water like Ann did, to watch them squiggle and drown. I wanted a quick end to it. I cut them with the kitchen knife, chop chop chop, one two three, over with, like a chef dicing vegetables for soup. When they were wounded or in danger, the hornworms made a small sound: click... click... click. They seemed capable of no greater frenzy or volume. That, more than their green ugliness or the slimy jelly that fell from their innards when they were dead, disturbed me. I would have been happier if they shrieked or screamed. But I meant to have my tomato crop.

In August, Debbie deteriorated rapidly. Her face became a watery puff; she stopped eating and whined with discomfort. Belle brought a rocking chair to her hospital room. When I came in the afternoon, Belle would be in the chair with Debbie on her lap, rocking her. "She often dozes," Belle would say, "but she never really sleeps."

"How is she?" Ann would ask then.

"Worse."

"It isn't fair."

"You've got to try to think of other things."

At the very end they put Debbie in an oxygen tent. Belle no longer left during my visits. I sat in the rocker and read Debbie stories while Belle rested. Before her medication, Debbie became uncomfortable and tried to toss from side to side. She was too weak to roll more than a few inches in either direction.

"See how she's looking at us?" Belle asked after the oxygen was installed. "She wants to be held."

"The doctors say no, Belle. She has to stay in the tent."

By then Debbie's face was moon-shaped from cortisone, her eyes swollen to slits that made her look retarded. Her breath began to rattle. After it was over Belle said, "We were stupid. We should have held her."

Soon after the funeral, we canned the last of the tomatoes. Ann dipped them into boiling water with the tongs to loosen their skins, and I took care of the jars and water bath.

"Let's not have tomatoes again next year," I said to her. "I couldn't stand another season of hornworms."

Ann shrugged. "If you don't want to. But the tomatoes taste good. And it's not like we don't have enough."

I didn't say it was really the hornworms' incessant clicking that disturbed me so. Some things a child can't understand. There was so little else they could do to protect themselves, and their sound was so small.

THE EXTRA

My MARRIED SISTER, LACEY, seems all right when she gets off the plane. She seems all right when we pick up her luggage and even when we start off in Mama's car, which Lacey notices I drive very smoothly for someone who's had her license only three months. All this is a big relief. Before I came to the airport, Mama said: "Don't ask what's bringing Lacey all the way down here right after Christmas, you hear, Mary Beth? I will not trust you with this car if I have to worry about you saying something tactless, like is there trouble between Lacey and Brian." If you could see Brian, who married Lacey on the ninth of May, you would know why we don't want them having trouble.

Lacey still seems all right when we pull out of the parking lot where the attendant does a double take when he looks at her. Lacey has dark, thick lashes and enormous eyes, one of which happens to be brown and the other blue. This is because of Mama having German measles when she was pregnant. Brian says he could never decide if he liked brown-eyed girls or blue-eyed ones, "So I figured once I got both in the same woman, I'd better hang on."

Lacey nods at the parking lot attendant as if his staring is perfectly polite. She even has the good manners to comment on the crisp sunny weather, saying "I haven't been this warm in months." So it takes me by surprise when we pass the "Welcome to North Carolina" sign and she says with an unmistakable catch in her voice: "I don't remember that."

"I think it's mainly for the film people," I tell her, being something of an expert on films. By the time you land in Wilmington you have flown over most of North Carolina practically to South Carolina, so you're kind of surprised to see a state welcome sign. But if you think of it as Southern hospitality for the actors and directors coming in from California. . . well, that makes a lot of sense. Mama says don't get started on the film people and especially not the movie I'm in, which was released three weeks ago and which I plan to take Lacey to see. But it's not my fault the welcome sign is there, or that we have to pass the film studio on our way into town.

"We didn't shoot at the studio," I say to make conversation. "We shot on location the whole time, and to this day I have not seen the sound stages inside the studio itself." This is the type of thing you can say to a married sister who lives in West Lafayette, Indiana, where there is no film studio at all.

"Well, maybe next time," Lacey says. She understands that being an extra in one teen film is not going to be the end of it. By the time we reach the mall, where Mama manages The Boutique, I think after all Lacey has come home mainly because she's tired of cold weather (as she's said many times on the phone) and wants to visit while Purdue University, where Brian goes to school and Lacey works, is still on break.

A bunch of seagulls lives in one corner of the mall parking lot. The ocean is just a few miles away, so the only reason I can figure them living here is that eating the leftover food people throw out is easier than catching fish. The birds flap up as we drive past, then settle down.

"Do you know how long it's been since I've seen seagulls?" Lacey sighs.

"Middle of May, I guess." Myself, I can't get too fired up about seagulls.

"Middle of May," Lacey says with that catch in her voice again, as if it were a million years ago.

Inside the mall, every girl between my age and Lacey's seems to be shopping at The Boutique's after-Christmas clearance. Mostly it is only cold enough here for a few heavy sweaters, so it's nice if you can get them on sale. Mama had hoped to take off the rest of the day, but she says to Lacey: "Honey, there's just no way I can get out of here with this crowd. How about if we meet at K&W for dinner? Then tomorrow I'll have the whole day."

Lacey looks a little disappointed, so I say, "After we eat, I'll take her to my movie."

"Now Mary Beth, I told you to let Lacey get settled first."

But Lacey says to Mama: "There's nothing I'd rather do tonight than see Mary Beth on film."

The next thing we do is drive home to let Lacey unpack. Between our house and the one next door is Mr. Williams' camellia hedge, which has pink flowers that give off a sweet, spicy smell Mama says reminds her of winter holidays and the brief dimming of the Southern light. Mama is very poetic about flowers. When we were little, before Daddy died, Lacey and I used to judge how soon Christmas would be by the camellias—sort of like an Advent calendar. They started blooming at Thanksgiving and were almost finished by Christmas—the way they are when we get out of the car— with a few flowers still hanging on the bush but a lot of petals on the ground. Lacey takes one look at the hedge and begins to cry.

"I almost missed the camellias!" she sobs. This strikes me as odd because she and Brian deliberately spent the holidays with Brian's parents in Indiana in hopes of its being a white Christmas, which it was. Myself, I have never seen a white Christmas except on TV.

I go over and put my arm around her shoulder. "You had a fight with Brian, didn't you?"

"You know what grows in Indiana at this time of year?" she cries. "Nothing. Nothing!"

"You can tell me about it," I say. "I mean, everybody has fights."

She looks at me with her brown eye and her blue one, both of which are now bloodshot. Then she recovers herself. She takes a tissue from her pocket, blows her nose, and tries to smile. "I know you won't believe it, but this has nothing to do with Brian." I nod, but she is right that I don't believe her.

Later we are sitting in the K&W Cafeteria right across the street from the mall. Lacey used to make fun of K&W's country cooking but tonight, because Mama has only a few minutes to gulp her food, Lacey doesn't complain. She eats no meat, just four different kinds of vegetables—okra, cabbage,

black-eyed peas and turnip greens—which is odd for someone who never in her life ate a vegetable unless Mama
nagged her. I wonder if she and Brian have become vegetarians, which is a common thing for college students to do. Of
course Lacey herself isn't a student, only married to one. She
tells Mama about the professor she works for in the psychology department. She doesn't say much about Christmas at
Brian's parents' or the snow.

"It's just your typical teen movie," I tell Lacey when we get
in the theater. I've seen it seven times, but I don't want to
make it any big deal. "There're two scenes where you can
see me real good."

What was Troy Wicket like?" she asks, having been a Troy
Wicket fan even before she met Brian.

"Pretty normal. I mean, after you shoot a scene together
twenty times, it's hard to be too puffed up."

I can tell Lacey wants to hear more, so I go on: "The first
day this one extra said to him: 'Mr. Wicket, can I ask you
something?' But he said right away, 'Not Mr. Wicket. Call me
Troy. Don't make me feel like an old man.' After that we all
called him Troy. I mean, he's only twenty-one."

"Is he as good-looking in person?"

The truth is, he isn't. He has pits in his skin you can't see
on the screen. I don't want to admit this to Lacey. "Not as
good-looking as Brian," I say.

Her face loses all expression. I think: uh-oh, Mama is really
going to let me have it now. But right then the lights go
down. I sit back and wait for Lacey's reaction when she hears
me say my line.

Lacey doesn't know I say a line in the movie. Mama and I
agreed to let it be a surprise, because we didn't know until
the movie was released whether the line had ended up on
the screen or the editing room floor. Last spring when we
filmed, Lacey was so caught up in getting married and going
off to Indiana that she didn't pay much attention.

Everybody had said Lacey and Brian would turn out to be

just a summer romance, him coming here to work at the beach two years ago and then going all the way back to Purdue. But he spent all winter calling and coming to see her. He sent her records like "Pretty Blue Eyes" and "Brown-Eyed Girl." When he finally proposed, Mama said jokingly, "I guess that's because he can't afford to keep up this courting anymore."

After that it was all Mama and Lacey could do to prepare for the wedding in May. There wasn't much money, so Mama baked the cake and Lacey sewed the dresses. There were hundreds of errands to run. But since I didn't have my license yet, I mostly got in the way. Finally my friend Marianne said, "Come on, go to the casting call with me, they don't really need you here." So I did. We filled out an application and attached our snapshot. A week later they called us, along with two hundred other high school kids who wanted to be extras.

The opening credits come on, superimposed over Troy Wicket riding his bike through an intersection when a car runs a light and hits him. He's not badly hurt except his leg. The rest of the movie is about Troy coming back to his high school and going out for track to build up his injured muscles. First you see him with a cast on, limping around school. Then the cast comes off, but he still limps. Then he tries running. I am in a classroom scene that was filmed the week before Lacey's wedding and a scene at the track filmed the week after. I don't tell her it took five whole days to make two scenes, or that most of the time was spent waiting around. I only tell her it was fun, which it was.

The director told us it cost twenty thousand dollars to shoot a minute of film. He said that's why "Quiet on the set" really meant it. There were dozens of tech people around. They had blackout screens made of wire and black velvet, that they put anyplace they thought there would be a shadow they didn't like. They shined lights into the windows to look like sun. They moved the booms and held light meters up to Troy's face, and they said things like: "We have sound," and "Rolling." One man even had a camera attached to him by straps and springs, so he could run beside Troy, bouncing up and down, and the camera would stay perfectly level. I have never seen anything like it in my life.

"That's you!" Lacey whispers when the track scene comes on.

"Just wait," I tell her. We are all sitting on the bleachers and Troy is running the four hundred. He is in the lead when suddenly his leg gives way. He limps off the track. The camera focuses on the bleachers again. A boy sitting behind me yells down to the coach: "That's what you get for running a cripple!" We girls look back at the boy. I stand up. My face is set and angry. I don't look ugly, I just look strong. "You better shut up," I tell the boy, "Or *you're* going to be the cripple." Later, of course, Troy will begin to win.

Lacey's mouth drops open. "You didn't tell me you spoke, Mary Beth."

"Didn't tell you I got paid almost four hundred dollars to say it, either!" I say.

"Ssshh," says someone in back of us.

On the way home, I tell her the rest. How the director decided there ought to be a little commotion in the stands. "You," he said, pointing to the boy behind me. "You're mad at the coach for letting Troy run. And you—" he pointed to me, "you're the one who's going to defend him." It wasn't even in the script!

Later the lady from the casting agency said to me: "There must have been something about you to make him notice you over the other girls, Mary Beth." I hadn't thought about it before, but I guessed there was.

All spring I'd been feeling sort of invisible. There was Lacey, with Brian hanging around her. There was Mama so busy with the wedding. And me not even able to drive. Then there was the wedding itself, me dressed up to be maid of honor, but every eye on Lacey in her drifts of white. All spring Lacey was like one of Mr. Williams' camellias, her life opening out and out like layers of petals, pink and perfumey. And me a tight little bud. It wasn't that I was jealous. Nobody loves Lacey more than I do. But I was tired of being invisible.

After the director chose me to say my line, I felt as much a part of the movie as those tech people doing lights and props and sound. I wasn't invisible anymore. The director had picked me. I could work summers as a production assistant. After high school I could study film. Become a film editor. A director. A star.

Instead of my thirty dollars for being an extra that day, I got a contract to be paid Screen Actors' Guild wage—almost four hundred dollars to say one line I'd have been glad to say for nothing. More money than I made all winter babysitting for the Moores across the street.

"Do you believe it, Lacey? I was rich."

Lacey is laughing, hearing all this. "I envy you, Mary Beth," she says.

"Are you kidding? That's when you were on your honeymoon with Brian."

Lacey sighs. "I wouldn't mind a chance to be in a movie."

It occurs to me for the first time that, in spite of being married to a hunk like Brian, Lacey is stuck working in the psychology department all day and here I am, in movies. Pretty as she is, with one blue eye and one brown eye, Lacey is probably too confusing-looking to be an extra.

The next day we all go to the store to buy chicken for supper. It's natural Lacey wants to look around, her being a married woman now, but she lingers at the produce section so long that I wonder again about her and Brian being vegetarians. Finally she picks up a bunch of collard greens and says: "I doubt half the population of Indiana even knows what greens look like—or fresh okra either."

I see then this is not about vegetables, this is about homesickness.

"I remember when I first came to Wilmington, I couldn't believe they didn't grow apples," Mama says to make her feel better. Mama was raised in the mountains where there are apple trees.

"Yes, but at least Wilmington isn't bleak," Lacey says. "I have never lived in such a bleak place in all my life."

"The *only* place you ever lived was here," Mama tells her.

"Yes, and last summer you said West Lafayette was the cutest little college town you ever saw," I add. "You said some parts of it were almost as pretty as Chapel Hill."

"That was before the winter," she says, looking at me fiercely.

By now we are in the checkout line. Lacey has a pouty look that stays even as we carry the groceries to the car. We drive down a street lined with live oaks so thick they blot out the sky. Lacey and I used to ride our bikes here, under the tunnel of branches hung with Spanish moss, and pretend it was the black hole of Calcutta.

Now Lacey says: "You're lucky to live someplace green in winter. In Indiana, everything is brown."

"One live oak is pretty," I say. "Twenty in a row are spooky." It's as if she doesn't remember the way things actually are. "Anyway, out there you have snow."

"Try driving in snow. Try having snow melt down the inside of your boots, Mary Beth."

I figure all this has something to do with Brian. I figure we will get to the real problem in a minute.

"You'll get used to snow," Mama says.

"No. I don't believe I ever will." But still we do not say anything about Brian.

Only two good things happen the rest of the day. First, Brian calls and Lacey talks to him as if they still like each other. Second, Mama makes the fried chicken and Lacey eats it, proving that she is not a vegetarian.

The next day is Lacey's last full day home before she's scheduled to fly back. Up 'til now the weather has been crisp, but in the morning when we wake up, it must be close to seventy degrees. It's the beginning of one of those balmy spells we get all through the winter. Mama is due at the store at eleven, but when Lacey oohs and ahs over the warm weather, Mama says without hesitation: "We'll spend the day at the beach."

Never in all the years she's been working has Mama called

in sick when she wasn't. She says this is something you can-
not do when you are supporting a family. But today she
does. She calls even though the beach is fifteen minutes away
and she could be back in plenty of time. She's acting almost
as strange as Lacey.

The next thing I know we are walking on the sand,
wrapped in sweaters against the wind. In spite of the warmth,
the breeze is cold coming off the ocean. The water is green
and foamy, and the sky is not sure if it wants to be gray or
blue.

Bunches of seagulls gather on the beach and then take
turns flying out over the water, searching for fish. They circle
and dip, their wings broad and white. They look nicer here
than they do in the mall parking lot. Lacey is so serious that I
think she's going to get misty-eyed again. But when she finally speaks, it has nothing to do with birds.

She sits down on the sand and says, "I can't go back."

"Oh?" Mama sits down, too, in such a way that it's clear
why she broke her rule and called in sick.

Right on cue, Lacey bursts into tears. "I just can't!" she
sobs.

Mama scooches over on the sand and hugs her. "Well, let's
have it," she says.

"Do you know what they did at Christmas, Mama?"

"What?"

"Here I was, so excited about a white Christmas and all . . ."
She starts crying so hard that she can't even speak. I figure
something terrible happened. Then she blubbers: "They
opened their presents Christmas *Eve.*"

Of course this doesn't have the first thing to do with snow
or Indiana, much less with Brian, but since Lacey is crying
her eyes out, we have to take it seriously. Finally I see the
problem. All my life I have never opened a present Christmas
Eve, only Christmas morning. And Lacey, either. Daddy used
to read us "The Night Before Christmas" and we used to
imagine Santa coming to our house while we slept, sneaking
through the den inasmuch as we didn't have a chimney. But
how can you tell a kid about Santa coming if you open your

presents Christmas Eve?

Mama is wiping Lacey's tears away like she's still a little girl. "You and Brian won't always spend Christmas with his parents," she says. "You could open presents whenever you want to, when you have a family of your own."

"No, Mama. I mean, it wasn't just that. It was everything. The cold, the brown grass. . . and then on top of that"—she starts to sob again—"the idea of opening presents on Christmas Eve!"

Mama rubs Lacey's shoulder and says in a soft voice: "And then you told him you needed a little time to think. Right?"

At this, Lacey begins to cry even harder. "I *love* Brian!" she sobs.

Right then Mama's attitude changes. She moves away, leaving Lacey by herself on the sand. "When I first came to Wilmington, I hated everything about it except the beach," she says. "I hated the flatness and the sandy soil and the fact that there was no fall. Where I grew up, the trees used to turn such beautiful colors."

Above us, the gulls have spotted something and start to get excited. "Now I've been here twenty five years, wife and widow," Mama says above the calling birds, "and the fall is still too warm and I still wish there were more trees that changed colors."

"Oh sure," Lacey wails. "That's easy to say. No snow all winter. Camellias. Sun."

"I hated the warm winter as much as you hate the cold. It didn't seem normal to me."

"Then why did you stay?"

"Because of your father, of course."

She lets that sink in. Then she waves her hand at the water. "The only thing I liked was coming to the beach. You know why? Because if you look at the ocean long enough, you see that it's more powerful than you are, and more lasting, and just keeps going about its business. Like you ought to be doing."

Mama's face is so stern that I almost think she's play-acting. Then I remember the year Daddy died, and how we came to the beach all the time. I thought it was because Daddy wasn't around and there was nothing else to do. But maybe it was to watch the ocean go about its business. It's surprising the things you don't know about your own mother.

The next day Lacey gets on her plane without even blubbering. I expect Mama to act relieved, but she doesn't. She lets me drive back into town, saying I can drop her off at work and keep the car if I'll pick her up later. She stares out the window.

"It really isn't just homesickness, it's more like culture shock," she tells me. "I don't think she ever thought about wearing heavy old wet boots to work in the snow."

"I guess."

"It's just. . . living there with him. The permanence."

I nod. I am still not sure what could be so terrible about living with Brian.

Mama opens the car window to let the warm breeze in. We pass the film studio and she braces as if she's trying to keep from saying something that will just kill her. A TV miniseries is filming next month, using a lot of extras, and I want to ask about going to the casting call. But of course I keep my mouth shut.

Finally she says: "You know, when I was pregnant, everyone thought there would be something terribly wrong with Lacey, after my German measles. But it turned out there was just the eye color. We were really very lucky."

So why does she sound like she's about to cry? Getting out at the mall, she seems plumb out of ideas. She must expect Lacey to come running back home any day, this time for good, maybe ruining her entire life.

The seagulls in the parking lot are fighting over some stale rolls as I drive away. They look gray from exhaust fumes, permanently stained and nasty. I think maybe they've been here for generations, their ancestors coming because of the easy bread crusts, and now they've lost their way to the sea. It's like every choice you make cuts off another one, so your life gets narrower as you go along. Like Mama working so much she never gets to the beach, and Lacey loving Brian but wanting to live in Wilmington. I know when we passed the film studio Mama wanted to warn me I could be a director or an editor but probably not both at once. And probably not a star. It makes me mad to think about it. The gulls are all over each other, making a racket. "You're supposed to eat fish, not bread, idiots!" I yell out of the car. The ocean is only a few miles away, and if they really wanted to, the fool birds could get there.

It's funny how your body sometimes knows what to do before your mind ever thinks of it. I find myself heading for the grocery store, walking to the produce section. I rummage through the bins until I find a bunch of collard greens about twice as big as the others. I know exactly what I'm doing. All the time my hands are sunk deep in leaves and stalks, my mind is thinking it was no accident the director chose me to tell that guy in the movie he'd be a cripple if he didn't shut up. I am just the type to make it happen. I'm thinking how I'll direct my film and star in it both, maybe even do the editing. Mama will just have to see. Lacey will be all right, too. At home, I pack the collards in a box and take them to the post office. They don't weigh all that much, and the postage is less than I expect when I send them first class mail to Indiana.

FRACTURE

BY THE MIDDLE OF AUGUST Anne is having a recurring dream
about her husband's accident. In the first scene Bradley is
falling off the roof again, in slow motion. The fall goes on
interminably. She does not see him hit. What she does see is
his calf, neatly folded like a piece of paper, the thigh also
slightly out of line. His face is crumpled with pain.

In the second scene Bradley is in his hospital bed, looking
pale and contrite. "Why are you angry?" he asks her. In real
life it is he, not she, who is angry.

"You've been in the roofing business nine years," she says.
"How could you be so stupid as to fall off?"

She wakes, invariably, with her heart racing, shame and
guilt lumping in her throat like cold cooked cereal. She gets
up, walks the hall to the girls' room, checks their breathing.
She switches the air-conditioning off. Their unspoken agreement—hers and the girls'—is that in the interest of economy
they will run the air conditioner only at night, after she
returns from the hospital. By morning heat has mingled with
the trapped cool, and already the house is sticky. Enid is five
and Josie is seven, but they never complain.

Each morning they clean. They are there so little that the
house is never really dirty, but they have their rituals. The
girls do the bedrooms; Anne does everything else. In the
dense heat she sometimes feels as if she's moving through
water. She doesn't mind. This week, especially, she is content
to bob and tread in her usual routine, riding the ebbing wave
of summer as long as it will hold her. Not anxious for the
change of seasons, afraid of the news they are to receive on
Friday, wanting only to maintain her precarious balance a few
days longer. At noon she sets out paper plates and mixes
tuna fish with mayonnaise: another ritual. The air in the
kitchen is like glue.

The phone rings: Josie rushes to answer. Anne hears her
whispering from the other room. It must be Josie's friend,
Sonia. Josie likes to impress her.

"Yeah, he gets four shots of it every day," Josie says. "If it doesn't work by Friday they'll have to cut off his leg." A flourish on those last few words, a note of triumph.

"Sure it'll hurt," she says. "What do you think?"

"No. I have to go to my cousin's. Maybe after supper."

"Come on, Josie," Anne calls. "Aunt Molly's waiting."

The girls grab bathing suits and fling themselves into the car. Molly, Anne's sister, lives two blocks from a neighborhood pool.

"Seat belts," says Anne.

"Oh Mom."

"Listen, this family doesn't need two casualties."

Each afternoon as they set out for Molly's, Anne has difficulty relinquishing her morning fantasy: that time looms ahead of her as it has in other summers, a flow of sameness and sun. Molly's daughter, Rosalie, is six months older than Enid. Molly infuses all of them with normalcy: the eating of popsicles, the smearing of suntan lotion onto bare shoulders. When Anne pulls into the driveway, the girls bound out and Molly approaches: barefoot, in cutoffs, garden gloves in hand. A version of Anne a year ago, which she recognizes with nostalgia.

"No news yet, I guess."

Anne shakes her head.

"Listen, no matter how it turns out, you'll be just fine," Molly says.

"I'm too old to be fed pap," Anne tells her. But she is smiling, she is comforted.

She backs the car up, turns in the direction of the city. At this moment, precisely, her morning self drains like water from a tub. The afternoon self is weaker: clenched jaw, shaking hands. She heads for the hospital, all heartbeat.

There is, in the trunk of the car, a briefcase filled with Bradley's work schedule, two different construction magazines, and a pad of note paper in case he feels up to scribbling some instructions. Since the accident in May, Anne has been the titular head of the company. In fact, Jerry, the foreman, took over the pricing of shingles after the first month, and even before that was routing workers from job to job.

Between infections, Bradley has periods of relative health when he directs the work. The economy is bad enough without two amateurs running the business. All of Anne's training is in education.

Once, at the beginning of the first infection, Anne rushed into Bradley's hospital room completely absorbed in a crisis. The wrong shingles had been delivered and the supplier refused to accept responsibility. Bradley, greenish pale and pierced with tubes, listened to her outpouring coldly, then peered down at his cast.

"Jesus, Anne, I'm wired in here, half drugged, in pain. What the hell do you expect me to do?" Now she consults the foreman, Jerry, for anything pressing. At home, in the evenings, she does the company books.

South of the beltway she drives through the lowlands of the city—shabby apartments, traffic lights every block, almost no trees. Black boys stand on the sidewalk in little groups, hair cut short, radios to their ears, restlessness shivering down their limbs like palsy. Their entrapment in the city is more permanent than hers in the present situation, but the effect is similar—an outcropping of nerves. And she suspects music is as tenuous a hold to the world as love. The boys make her think of an afternoon she spent mopping milk from the kitchen floor the year Enid was two—confined, angry about it—at the moment Bradley was negotiating a bank loan to save his company. At times like these, she always thinks she will put her name on the list for substitute teachers—to help out in her own way—but she never does. The boys gaze at her with hardened eyes, but she is no longer afraid. She feels perfectly suspended: between them, and housework, and whatever will happen two days hence. She doesn't even try to make every green light all the way downtown.

No: fear is Bradley's territory these days, though he refuses to say so—fear of being relegated to his office, forced to sit and think, of being unable to move. He has always been too muscle bound for quiet sulks before—too much a man of action. A swimmer of furious laps at the Y. But a one-legged swimmer? At best, the leg may never be right enough for roofing.

The hospital sits on three landscaped acres, a green oasis in the hot concrete. Still, the parking lot is an ocean of tar, and it depresses her. She has arrived; logic dictates that she go in. Moving slowly, a swimmer under water, she locks the car door, removes the briefcase from the trunk. Away from the parking lot near the building, the air hangs damp and fecund, heavy with the smell of grass. The swinging glass doors are constantly in use, but always flawlessly clean. She pushes hard, hoping to leave a handprint.

Inside, air-conditioning. A steady seventy-two-degree chill, ordered and artificial. The elevator arrives. What if Bradley is dead up there, newly dead, as yet undiscovered by the hospital staff? A recurrent fear. She wedges herself between two candy-stripers and an empty stretcher. If he is alive—she suspects he will be—what will they talk about? Anne is certain he prepares topics in his spare time, after the pain pills but before the lethargy. She prepares a few herself.

"Coming out." A white-coated attendant pushes the stretcher into the hallway. The candy-stripers giggle. Anne is thinking about appendages. Not just those that come attached, but also more recent additions: the car, the children, *Sports Illustrated* every week and the *New York Times* on Sunday. When it gets down to basics—fingers, toes, arms and legs— she is in serious territory indeed. What could she do without? The left leg? The right? Fingers? Arms? Eyes? (No!) The intelligent thing would be to make a list in order of importance, and never expose anything vital.

Can Bradley live without his leg? She has her doubts.

She gets off on four and turns right. Nods at the nurses. Doesn't trust nurses. . . they jabber among themselves. Have they been in the room recently? She hopes so. Her throat is dry, fear mixed with anger. This is no anger at the situation, at her inconvenience, not that at all. It is anger straight from her dream, at Bradley for being so stupid as to fall off the roof.

In his room he is intact. Alive, conscious, and less green in the face than she remembers. There he reclines, his leg in the clumsy cast, his smile a bit forced. They exchange guarded hellos, feel their way through the first opening phrases, careful not to offend. Anne hopes they won't repeat yesterday's discussion. . . what they will do *if.* "Even if I lose it," (it—never the leg—always *it*), "I'll be okay. Of course it may take a while. . . . " A while?

"What about the disability?" Bradley asks at last. "Did you talk to the insurance guy?" Ah, yes, they both relax a little. Practicalities are easy.

"They still aren't convinced you're disabled," she says.

"What do they want, a profit and loss statement?"

"Something like that." Actually a profit and loss statement is what they *do* want. The insurance company says Bradley works with his brain, not his leg. If he is disabled, it ought to show up on the bottom line. Bradley says his physical presence is required at the job site. How can his business *not* suffer? The argument could go on forever. If the worst happens, Bradley will do well to remember he works with his mind.

He shakes his head. "Christ. And we've paid them all that money for. . . how long?"

"Eight years."

"Bastards."

She nods. Bradley scratches his cast; his skin beneath it itches where he can't reach. "Better this than nothing," he says, running his fingers over the plaster. "It gives the illusion." Sometimes her own leg itches at night: violently, unceasingly, until she startles awake to scratch.

She wants to ask him how he feels, but she is afraid he will answer curtly, a clipped word or two. His face looks pale, and usually he is golden in August. She was wrong to think the greenish tint had vanished. She looks away from him, out the window onto a strip of flashing, a glitter of light.

The phone rings. Out of habit, both of them pick it up—Bradley on his extension and Anne on the one that might belong to a roommate. Bradley has not had a roommate since he began getting this new drug.

"Daddy," comes Enid's enthusiastic voice. "Guess what we did!"

"Tell me."

"Oh Daddy, *you* know. We went to the pool." All summer Daddy has receded farther and farther from the flow of every-day activities. He has probably forgotten the pool. Does Enid notice?

"Mommy?"

"Yes, I'm here."

"Aunt Molly wants to know if we can stay for supper. Can we?"

"No, we were there on Monday. We can't stay so much. Maybe another time."

"Okay." No complaints, no argument, even from a five-year old. Everyone is so agreeable. "Daddy?"

"Huh?"

"Daddy, they say they might have to cut off your leg. Is that true?"

Anne draws her breath sharply. *No*, she thinks. *This is against the rules.* But she remains silent. Bradley is on the other line. Her palm begins to sweat against the phone. There is no set punishment for this particular infraction, it is so unthinkable. After a summer of drill, practice. . . after all that, *this*. Her throat begins to close; she wheezes slightly. Bradley sits in his bed like a Buddha.

Then he begins to speak slowly. "We don't know yet, hon," he tells his daughter. "It might happen. You're not frightened, are you?"

"Oh no, Daddy. I was just wondering."

"We won't know until Friday." All very casual, very light.

"Oh. Okay."

While they are saying goodbye Bradley glances in Anne's direction. She reads censure in that look, irritation. In his moment of anguish, the children come to *him*, not her, for comfort; she can handle nothing. Oh, he is wrong; if he were not so devoted to his leg he would see. She is a good mother; the children are upset, they are bound to have their lapses.

Then she meets his eyes and the look holds none of that— not censure, not annoyance, nothing. The eyes are empty— or at least benign.

"It's all right," he says when he puts the phone down. "It doesn't matter." But shame is running in her blood today, and nothing is all right.

"What about Jerry?" he asks after a time. "Nobody yet," she answers. Jerry is trying to hire a man for the rest of the summer. Unemployment is up and they thought it would be easy.

"Most guys would rather draw unemployment than earn an honest day's wage," he says. He warms to this topic; he talks almost with ease. She finds her own voice; they speak as if conversation were natural to them.

"Enid'll be in school pretty soon," she says. "There's no reason I couldn't get on the substitute list."

He only shrugs. "Whatever you think." She remembers: he has never spoken to her of her working: a taboo. For a time she keeps looking at him, wanting something clearer, disapproval or relief. Then her anger chokes her and she swallows the rest: that she has gotten comfortable with the company books, considers the books the one normal link between them now, would not give them up even if she got a chance to teach full time. Two can play Sphinx as well as one.

In the silence she notices that the plastic hospital chair is sticking to her legs. Bradley gets restless in late afternoon: so little movement. Such long minutes, and their posture so strained. Dinner trays clank in the hall: quarter to five. Two more days of this. Can they bear it? She rises to go.

"Anne! I'm glad I've caught you." She is waiting for the elevator when the voice freezes her, draws her in. Bradley has, altogether, five doctors, sometimes six. They are leery of the surgeons, but his doctor, Al Conrad, they trust. As he guides her into the visitor's lounge, she is struck by a familiar thought: that his voice is too rich.

"I just want to talk to you for a second. I promised not to say anything until Friday, but I wanted to get your input. . . . " Sometimes he tries to disguise his meaning, but the voice gives him away. Buoyant, confident today, with none of the gray undertone of worry.

"The drug is working," she says .

"It looks like it, yes. What does Bradley say?"

"He says he always feels better no matter what drug you give him because he wants to feel better, and he's not making any predictions."

"Yes. That's what he tells me also."

"When are you going to let him know?"

"Not 'til Friday. I can't afford to be wrong and saddle him with an amputation."

"No, of course not. But. . . it *is* good news?"

Al Conrad smiles. "Very good news." He puts his hand on her shoulder and walks her back to the elevator. So far she has felt nothing. She is too busy attending to protocol. The doors slide open. She gets in, waves and rides downstairs alone.

Of course even now she must react with a certain control, she tells herself. But the truth is, she still feels nothing. A warm sap surrounds the knot where she keeps herself, but it doesn't penetrate. She tries to imagine herself racing through the lobby, heady with joy, but she walks sedately as ever and leans on the swinging glass door. Outside, she is smacked in the face by damp heat.

Uncivilized stuff, she thinks—it begins to peel her veneer. The knot melts. The news sinks in slowly, water into parched ground. She drives. Ninety-degree car, thickening traffic, the unhandsome slums of the city: a study in relief. She imagines the schedule she and the girls will follow after they leave Molly's—drinking lemonade in the yard, grilling hot dogs on the patio, letting the air-conditioning cool the house. Her mind caresses the time-worn routine, lets it become precious. Bradley will come home intact: will walk, will swim. Climb roofs? They will not have to change. The nastiness that has hung over her summer begins to lift; she feels a clearness inside. The lights are synchronized along this stretch and as the car gathers speed it seems to her that she is weightless, floating.

Then a light turns red and she slams on the brakes, aware only of her beating heart. A grinding stop—and then she is assaulted by sound. A boy on the curb holds his radio to his ear, a gleaming chrome rectangle larger than his head. The music is shot through with static, the melody is indiscernible. Heat shimmers up off the pavement into the boy's eyes, but he is too busy to notice. He is listening to the music, he is not even there, his face is black and beaded with sweat, his expression is intense. How can he stand it? Who is she fooling? She might be looking into a mirror. She has squirmed like a pig through the last four months of her life, and Bradley has, too, and for all she knows they are contorted as the face of this boy feeding music straight to his brain. Changed beyond recognition.

Traffic moves again, but her clearness is gone. Her underarms are wet, her blouse is stained. Much too soon for relief. Tomorrow she must sign up for substituting; bring her own strength to this mess, whether he likes it or not. Tell Bradley she wants to keep on with the company books. So much to do, all this heat. A little breeze blows into the car as she swings out of the city, but it doesn't make her cool. Can she manage? Or are they locked into this summer forever, into clotted skies and jarring music, and is the amputation complete?

ADJUSTING TO ALTITUDE

IT WAS THE MIDDLE OF JULY, ninety degrees in the parking lot of Stapleton airport, and Jake's Daddy, Sam, was smiling as he heaved Jake's suitcase into the back of the van. "Before this day is out, son, we're going to have a snowball fight," he said.

"Sure, Dad. Snowballs."

"Wait and see." Sam's weightlifter's muscles pumped, and his teeth gleamed in the glossy mountain sunshine. He slapped the side of the van companionably. "Borrowed from a friend," he said. A woman friend, Jake feared.

One set of seats was folded down to make room for a tent, sleeping bags, groceries. They were headed to Steamboat Springs where Sam worked in a sporting goods store. On the way they'd camp overnight in the mountains.

Jake's mama, Leslie, had disapproved of this plan on the phone. "Oh, I see, a father/son ritual," she'd said stiffly. So it wasn't until Jake got off the plane that Sam announced that their father/son cookout would be preceded by a hike up above the tree line, "To see what snow feels like in the middle of July."

Though it was only marginally cooler in Denver than in this morning's dripping Carolina heat, Jake noted that the snow-capped peaks of the Rockies did indeed rise impressively in the distance. He was twelve, just off his first solo flight. Two weeks in Colorado lay before him. Snowballs? Why not?

They drove north from Denver to Fort Collins, then west into the mountains, his Daddy talking all the time. "I bet your landing was rough, wasn't it? That's because of the thermal currents coming up from the valley floor. The heat gathers there all morning and then rises up. That's why it's rough if you land in the afternoon."

And then, before Jake could respond: "You'll need a sweat-shirt when we get up beyond the tree line. You have a sweat-shirt, don't you? Well, hell, your mother probably put in your winter coat."

Jake laughed because she nearly did. She said living in a pocket of warm air along the Carolina coast gave you a false sense of weather. Everyplace else was colder.

His mama's boyfriend, Albert, said, "Let him be, Leslie. It isn't that cold in July, even in Colorado." Albert was in a good mood because Jake was leaving.

The road ascended into the mountains, into spectacular scenery Jake had seen before only in postcards. The sky was so blue and the trees so green that they seemed almost unnatural, more like a movie or a dream. Or else last night's lack of sleep was catching up with him—being keyed up, flying west, gaining two hours. He got this hazy, detached sensation a lot when he was tired or bored—in school after lunch, or in summer after a swim workout, after he'd walked home in the heat. The sensation wasn't unpleasant, just weird. And very possibly the first step toward craziness. He couldn't afford to be crazy, not now.

He said to himself: this is actually happening *right this minute*. I am here seeing these mountains.

His Daddy was talking about the jagged peaks, high and uneven because they were so young, geologically speaking. *Concentrate*, Jake thought. Sam pointed to the tree line—an actual line almost straight around the mountain at a certain height. "As if all the trees got together and decided they just wouldn't grow above that point."

Jake laughed because the trees *did* look like they'd agreed not to grow any higher, and the detached feeling suddenly went away.

"Depending on my schedule, I'm hoping we can go on one of those white-water rafting trips while you're here," his Daddy said. Sam was an expert at planning outings. He'd been in Colorado only since spring, and in Florida and Arizona before that—moves that kept him from getting to North Carolina often. But when he did come he took Jake on outings every day, water skiing or deep sea fishing or to the batting cages and the beach. They ate picnic lunches and suppers at Taco Bell. He took Jake home tanned and happy and too tired to talk.

"Your Daddy means well," his mama would say then, "but he's too unsettled and too rough." Her idea of an outing was a movie with Albert.

"They say the rafting trips are for tourists and pretty tame," Sam said. "But it might be fun."

Better than a stroll around the park with Albert, Jake thought. He began to feel excited and a little afraid the way he always did when his Daddy was around. By the time they reached the turnoff for the campground, he was completely awake.

"There." Sam pointed to a mass of snow on a peak above them. "That's where we're hiking to." Jake followed the finger upward, beyond a stand of dense trees to a harsh rock-and-grass incline leading to the snow.

Sam unfolded his topo map. "We're at eighty-six hundred feet," he announced, "and about to go up." Except in an airplane, the highest Jake had ever been before was five thousand feet when he and his mama drove the Blue Ridge Parkway.

They set up the tent first. Jake had never done this, so Sam showed him how to hammer in the tent pegs, tie the knots. His Daddy probably did this all the time. Then they gathered firewood to use when they came back from their hike.

"Ten of three," his Daddy said. "Just time to get up and down the mountain before dinner." Sam slung two canteens of water over his shoulder and instructed Jake to tie his sweatshirt around his waist for later.

The trail began with a footbridge over a stream of water, shallow and fast-moving and so clear that the smooth oval stones beneath it seemed almost magnified. "The Laramie River," his Daddy announced.

"Looks like a creek. Too small for a river."

Sam laughed. "In the West, this *is* a river." And then seriously: "The water all looks clean out here. But never drink from these streams. There's stuff in them that makes you sick." Poisoned water! Adventure! Jake knew his mama would hate the idea of streams that could make you sick.

The trail led through a field of wildflowers, then up the

mountain, on hard-packed dirt and rocks, switching back and forth as it snaked upward between the trees. At first it was wide enough to walk two abreast. "There's a waterslide you'll like in Steamboat. And a big pool," his Daddy said. "There's a boy your age in the condo next door."

When the trail steepened and narrowed, Jake fell behind, watching the canteens bob on Sam's narrow hips, watching his sturdy, muscular arms swing, tanner than Jake's own arms though Jake was in the sun all summer.

Sam's legs were sturdy, too, and covered with dense brown hairs above the running shoes he always wore. Jake knew he'd be just as muscular; he'd start lifting weights soon as he was old enough to use the weight room at the Y.

Sam kept talking, glancing back to make sure Jake heard. Then as if it were a normal question, he asked, "You get along okay with Albert?"

"Yeah, fine," Jake lied. Albert was a photographer, a vegetarian, and a pussy. Jake had moved some of his clothes into his mother's bedroom and his darkroom into the laundry room. The day he set up all his trays and equipment, Jake swiped six bottles of chemicals and buried them in the dumpster outside the apartment. Albert might think they were lost in the move, or he might suspect, but he'd never know.

"Have you been messing around in here?" Albert asked later. "There were some bottles. Right here."

"I didn't see them."

Albert squinted and glared. "How about keeping out of here then? With all this stuff in here."

"What if I'm doing laundry?" Jake never did laundry.

"Seriously, buddy," Albert said. "How about making like a tree and leave?"

"An old joke, Albert."

"Not a joke, Jake." When Jake's mama wasn't around, Albert didn't even bother to be polite.

Jake's plan was to tell his Daddy only the facts about Albert. That Albert liked to eat Chinese, take pictures, spend Sunday mornings in bed with Jake's mama. He'd let his Daddy make up his own mind about whether Jake ought to go back to Virginia or live here in Colorado.

Sam got so quiet that Jake figured either he was thinking about Leslie, which seemed unlikely, or walking had begun to occupy him. At least it had begun to occupy Jake. Despite the switchbacks on the trail, the path was steep. They were in the trees and couldn't see much. Jake was a little winded; thirsty, too. He'd have taken a quick drink, but Sam had the canteens. Why was his Daddy carrying both?

Jake wouldn't ask to stop because they'd been walking only maybe half an hour. The air was already cooler, just as Sam had predicted. Soon he'd need his sweatshirt. It was odd being so thirsty without being hot. Why was his mouth so dry?

"Take it easy the first couple days," his mama had said. "People need time to adjust to altitude. Don't let him take you on one of his Olympic marathons."

Maybe he was adjusting to altitude. He pictured the drinking fountain outside his homeroom at school. Pictured water coursing out in a thick silver arc.

Abruptly, in front of him, as if he'd read Jake's mind, Sam stopped and shrugged the canteens off his shoulder. They'd come around a bend. A far mountain was visible in the distance. The snow seemed not so far above them. A flat-topped rock hunkered above the trail.

"Up here," his Daddy said. They scrambled up and sat on the rock, surveying the trail below them and the mountain in the distance. Jake waited for his Daddy to open the canteen and offer it to Jake. Jake drank for a long time.

"Tired?" his Daddy asked.

"No," Jake lied. He handed the canteen to Sam, who drank and gave it back. Jake slipped the strap over his shoulder. "I'll carry this one," he said.

His Daddy nodded and jumped down from the rock to the trail, a long way, maybe seven feet. Jake felt he had to jump down, too. Leslie had made him wear hiking boots with no spring in them. He shoved off, hit the dirt trail hard. His Daddy watched him. He wished for running shoes like his Daddy's.

"How's swim team coming?" Sam asked, walking off again.

"Okay," Jake said. Another lie.

"What's your best stroke?"

"Freestyle." Actually he was better at breaststroke but got disqualified every time for doing scissors kicks. He never felt himself doing them, so getting d.q.'ed was always like being punched in the stomach.

"You can't expect to win your first summer," Sam said, striding out now, making Jake work to catch him. "The first year you have to race against your own times and against the clock. Second year you start worrying about the competition."

"Yeah, I guess." He didn't say most of the kids had been on swim team for three, maybe four years. Nobody started at twelve. How could he ever catch up? He was swimming because Jake's grandma said, "That boy is raising *himself*, alone in that apartment while Leslie works and then sees that man." *That man.* Besides, Jake liked "raising himself." Making his own peanut butter sandwiches, playing Nintendo.

But Sam and Leslie and his grandma were of one mind: "You need a summer sport, Jake." Next thing he knew he was signed up for swim team. The pool was in walking distance. Practice was at seven in the morning. The chlorine left his vision blurred and his head stopped up. After the first month he could win in practices but never at meets. He lost because of clumsy starting dives, an inefficient stroke, getting disqualified. Going fast had nothing to do with it. He detested swimming.

His Daddy pointed at a break in the trees where they could see mountains in the distance again. Dark clouds had gathered behind the peaks. "Let's hope we get up there before it rains. It almost always rains in the afternoon at this time of year." As if they'd chosen to hike in rain deliberately. "Thunderstorms sometimes." His Daddy winked.

Jake was out of breath again. His boots were weighting him down. His Daddy got farther in front of him. His mama used to complain that when Sam was walking or biking he'd forget anybody was behind him. He'd get so far ahead of her that she wouldn't see him for hours. "Why does it always have to be a race? If I want to go twenty miles, why does it always have to be fifty?" Her voice grew shrill and high then, which Jake didn't like. "Why does it always have to be an endurance contest?"

It hadn't been five minutes since they'd had their drink, but he was thirsty again. He took a swig from the canteen. Drinking and walking at the same time made him more out of breath. Didn't satisfy his thirst, either.

A laughing couple passed, coming down the mountain. Descending toward the shush of the Laramie River. Soon they'd be dipping cupped hands into the clear water, marveling at each oval rock highlighted on the riverbed underneath, as if in one of Albert's faggot photographs. No one would believe anything toxic could grow in such clear water. It would taste cool, delicious. False.

He concentrated on things outside the dryness in his mouth. Rocks embedded in the packed dirt of the trail, the pale leaves of the aspen trees, their white trunks. The sound of his own breathing.

He was getting cold. If he put his sweatshirt on without stopping, the act would take more air from him. His Daddy was walking fast.

Another stream now. Above the water, the air shivered. They balanced on rocks and went across. On the other side, they waved to a scout troop that had pitched tents and built a fire. A corner of red plaid flannel protruded from one of the tents—the inside of a sleeping bag. Jake imagined pulling the cloth around him, catching his breath, being warm.

Jake wasn't just winded now; his head felt foggy, too. Not detached like in the van earlier. No, this was a fog of sickness. His stomach was jumbled. He didn't feel well at all.

Sam moved fast, not looking back. Jake remembered his mama giving up biking, staying home, her anger and restlessness filling the apartment like fever. Sitting motionless except for her teeth against her nails, biting away. Her disposition snappy and mean. Jake knew even then she'd quit biking because she was weak. His Daddy left because of her weakness. Albert was weak, too. When Sam went around a bend and couldn't see, Jake stopped a second to catch his breath.

It didn't help; he was too sick. He couldn't understand why he wasn't in better shape after swimming all summer.

His nose started running. He wiped it with the back of his hand. His hand came away red. Blood. He'd never had a nosebleed in his life. The light dimmed and brightened through the trees with the movement of the clouds. From the distance, far away, came the rumble of thunder.

He wiped the bloody hand on his sweatshirt and went faster, getting his Daddy in sight. Sometimes they came around and saw other mountains jagged against the sky. They had been walking—how long? An hour? Two? Jake squinted at a far peak, trying to assess the angle of the sun. He couldn't judge. He was still on Eastern time, confused by the foreign pattern of clouds and brightness.

His nose was bleeding, his stomach jumbled, and now his hands tingled, too. His hiking shoes weighed more than they had at sea-level.

"Me, I'm an ocean person," his mama had said, claiming some people liked to live near the ocean and others in deserts or mountains. "It's as if in a certain environment, they automatically feel right at home."

Jake didn't care about the ocean now that he had to swim every day at the pool. Where there was ocean, there was Albert. But in the ocean the danger was not from the water but from other things—vicious fish or vicissitudes of weather. Here the mountain itself was treacherous, the cold dry air, the very light.

His Daddy stopped short and whistled through his teeth. Jake caught up. The trail had ended, a huge clearing opened ahead. "Look at that. An avalanche must have come through."

Before them lay a forest of downed trees. Slender whitish trunks—some kind of fir. Every tree for a hundred yards across had been completely uprooted in the avalanche's path.

Above the expanse of trees was bare slope, steep and rocky. The tree line. Patches of snow. Behind the peak, the clouds were dark as the rock. A few raindrops splattered down. Sam sat down on one of the tree trunks. Patted a spot for Jake. Opened his canteen and drank. Jake was too sick to be thirsty. In a minute he was going to throw up.

"You all right?" Sam asked.

"Fine."

Sam eyed the distant trail, across the wreckage of downed trees. Sam studied it so long that Jake began to see what he had in mind. The tree trunks provided hundreds of footholds, even steep as the slope was.

"What do you think?" Sam asked.

"We could go across the trees," Jake said. "Straight up."

His Daddy stood, pleased. Jake did the same. The air made his lungs burn. He swallowed to keep his lunch down. Not weak like his mama and Albert.

Graceful in his running shoes, Sam made his way across the tree trunks. Jake followed. In slow motion, boots heavy, stomach really sour now. Drizzle misted his face and hair. Not a lot of rain, but cold. It might not be really happening except that the rain was so cold.

He had to be careful where he put his feet. The tree trunks were wet and slippery. Sometimes they were so close together that he had to step on top of them. Other places the trunks were farther apart, and he could step over them and put his feet on the ground, torn and furrowed by the violence of the avalanche. His Daddy moved faster, lighter, looking up at the snow.

Then his Daddy stumbled. Pitched forward slightly, then back. He seemed to sit rather than fall. His shoe was wedged under a tree trunk.

"Oh, shit," he said. Sitting on the wet ground, knee bent, he wrapped his arms around the hurt leg, resting his head on the knee. "Shit," he said again.

"You hurt?"

"I twisted it." Sam pulled down his sock. The ankle was already beginning to swell. "I'm all right," he said.

Jake helped his Daddy up. "Can you walk?"

Sam tried to put pressure on the ankle. He grimaced. "Not really, but you can always hop down a mountain." He tried to smile, but his face went gray and rough. It was as if he didn't have a suntan.

Jake remembered something. He was four, and Sam was whirling him above his head, letting him fly on outstretched arms. The hot green twilight blurred into a single splash of color. His Daddy circled faster. Jake closed his eyes. He was dizzy and the world was apart from him.

A single slice of pain brought him back. It was the first pain that made him think he was living solely in the part that hurt—that all his life had knotted and clumped into the few inches between hand and forearm. His wrist was broken in two places. He screamed. His Daddy didn't stop right away. He thought Jake was having fun.

"Are you okay, really?" Jake asked now.

"Sure." Sam sat down again. "Give me a minute."

"You want to wait a while?" Jake asked. He knew what he had to do.

"You don't need to go after help," his Daddy said. "I can get down."

"I don't mean that." Jake pointed up the mountain. Beyond the fallen trunks the trees stopped, and beyond the tree line it was a couple hundred feet to the snow.

His Daddy regarded him—proudly, Jake thought. "I can wait," his Daddy said.

Jake felt air stabbing his lungs as he made his way across the remaining tree trunks—hot metal points of air. His lunch and his heartbeat were in his throat. No matter. If his Daddy wouldn't keep him, who would? Albert?

The trees gave way to bare ground. Across patches of thin grass, outcroppings of rock. The incline almost forty-five degrees. A steady rain now. Slipping over the wet rocks. Not really walking anymore—more like crawling. His Daddy had known it would rain. Why hadn't they gone back? He leaned forward, clutching the grass, clutching for balance at whatever protruded from the ground.

Dizzying movement in his stomach. In his head. Sick.

Up.

Kneeling, crawling.

He clung to a rock. Red drops of blood dripped from his nose.

Chest on fire. Head whirling.

Then a wave of weakness. He couldn't move. His mama said take it easy, but she never said altitude would light candles in his lungs, turn his stomach, force blood from his nose. If she had, would he have believed it?

Maybe he was dreaming. He'd never felt so bad inside a dream. But no, the rock was cool beneath his cheek. Finally he turned his head to the side and threw up.

In front of him, in a circle of dirt, a dandelion bloomed. Dandelions grow above the tree line, he thought.

If you could think of something outside of yourself, you were all right. He imagined the hiss of air on the plane, hissing from the overhead nozzle, thick and luxurious, whole milk after a diet of skim. He breathed that air.

He squiggled along a little on his belly. Above him, snow. Glistening, even in the rain.

Strength trickled back into him. Put him on his feet. Hard shoes digging into the hillside. Holding on as if to the side of a building. A wall. Up. Inch by inch. Foothold to foothold. Up.

Detached now. His Daddy a speck among the fallen trees below.

Belly to rock, wet, raw. At the end he couldn't see his Daddy at all. He didn't know it would be so simple. Reaching up, higher than he had ever been before, he opened his hand to whatever it might grasp, and found he was touching the snow.

A POLITICAL FOOTNOTE

AT ONE O'CLOCK ON THE AFTERNOON of Morton Opak's funeral, Annie Katz and Bernie Levitan were studying cat muscles in their comparative anatomy lab at the George Washington University in downtown D.C. Normally their friend Seth would have been with them—they were all in pre-med together—but it was Seth's father who was being buried.

"I still get the origins and the insertions mixed up," Annie said to Bernie, peering at a tangle of exposed shoulder muscles. She kept wishing her boyfriend, Sandy, could go to the cemetery with her instead of Bernie. Partly she just wanted him there, and partly she kept thinking Sandy would be good at formal occasions because of all the years his father had been a Congressman.

"Yeah. It's hard to remember every muscle. In every cat." During the exam they would go from one lab bench to another, identifying muscles the instructor had indicated by a straight pin. It was easy enough to get them right in your own cat, that you had been working with all semester, but the other cats were larger or smaller, put together slightly differently.

"We're gonna be late getting to the cemetery," Bernie said. They were studying an extra hour because they'd skipped so many classes the past two weeks, in order to be with Seth while divers were searching for his father's body. Morton Opak was one of nineteen Navy bandsmen who had been killed three thousand miles away, when his plane collided with a Brazilian airliner over Rio de Janiero harbor. The band was on a South American tour, being flown to Rio to play at President Eisenhower's reception for the Brazilian president.

"The ironic thing is, Morton didn't even want to go," Seth's mother, Pearl, said day after day. "None of them wanted to go." For two weeks they sat in Seth's living room while the bodies were being recovered, listening to Pearl Opak cry even while she was talking. Annie and Bernie tried to distract Seth—usually that was easy—but mostly he sat around listening to his friends but not really hearing them, looking like his face had been shot full of novocaine. The rumor was that when they finally found the bodies, they recovered only *parts.*

"God, I don't even like to think about that," Seth said. "I wish nobody'd told my mother that."

All the bandsmen were to be buried at Arlington National Cemetery after individual funeral services earlier. Bernie and Annie decided to skip Danzansky's funeral home to study for the lab exam, and then drive directly to the cemetery. They both needed to maintain B averages if they expected to get into medical school.

Dave Weinberger, the lab instructor, came over. "You about done?" Weinberger was good-looking, but too short. He was going to the University of Virginia medical school in Charlottesville next year.

"Yeah, I'm afraid done might be the word," Annie said. She knew Weinberger had let them stay late so he could look at her. Her sweater was tighter than normal, the only black sweater she had. She liked flirting with Weinberger even though she was in love with Sandy. Sandy was a law student and would never know.

"Yeah, we're done," Bernie said. "We have to go to the funeral." Weinberger got a serious look on his face.

"I was sorry about that," he said.

"Come on," Bernie said. Annie gathered up her books and Bernie more or less shoved her out the door. Sometimes he told her she acted like a bubblehead around Weinberger, though that didn't stop him from using the lab time Weinberger allowed her. Bernie said Annie was the smartest girl he knew, but he doubted if either Weinberger or Sandy knew she had a brain in her head.

It was cold and sunny outside—the pretty, deceptive cold of Washington in March. Annie's dark skirt and sweater were too thin, her good coat was flimsy, and she had on high heels instead of loafers, which let the wind wash over her feet. They had walked west on G Street past G.W.'s parking lot, then down two blocks toward the river, to the construction site where Bernie liked to park. Annie was shivering.

"I've never been to a funeral at Arlington National Cemetery," she said. "We usually just take company there to see the Tomb of the Unknown Soldier."

"Yeah, we do, too." Bernie had on his winter jacket and gloves. It had snowed the week before, and little patches of ice still clung to the grass by the river.

"Sandy's not coming to the cemetery," Annie said. "He's meeting us at Seth's house after."

Bernie grunted something. Sandy wasn't Jewish, and he was older than they were, both of which Bernie held against him. Annie might never have met Sandy if his father hadn't come to lecture to her history class. Denzell Williams was one of the Congressmen who were always asked to speak at the university because their children were students. Sandy had come to hear the lecture, too. Afterwards Annie went up to ask a question, not so much because she was interested in politics as because Sandy was standing by the window with a bar of sunlight illuminating his blond hair—the same color hair as Annie's—and he looked so handsome that Annie was drawn forward. Right away Sandy said, "Is it anything I can answer?" and moved her away from the clutch of students around his father.

Normally Annie dated boys from the undergraduate Jewish fraternities. She'd gone out with a few other law students, but they were Jewish, too. She'd expected her parents to object to Sandy, but they hadn't. Bernie said that was only because they admired Congressman Williams' politics. Sandy was going to spend the summer helping his father campaign in Connecticut for re-election. Annie thought he might ask her to marry him before then, so she could go with him, and she found the idea of campaigning exciting. She didn't tell Bernie that. Bernie said the minute Sandy opened his mouth people would know he'd started boarding school when he was five, and that would lose his father all kinds of votes, just wait and see.

Annie blew into her hands to warm them. They smelled slightly of formaldehyde. Bernie moved closer and for a minute she thought he would put his arm around her, to make her stop shivering, but he didn't. He hadn't touched her since freshman year—the afternoon he'd talked her into leaving chemistry lab early so he could show her the porn films from his stag party.

He'd brought the films to Annie's house because both her parents worked. He'd used her father's projector to show them on her living room wall. They were the first porn films Annie'd ever seen, and she got excited. Bernie must have expected that. He took her blouse off while the woman in the black garter belt was still undressing, and he started working on her bra.

"Hey Bernie, don't," Annie kept saying, but she couldn't bring herself to stop him. He got her bra all the way off and stood her up. He raised her arms so he could look at her breasts in the mirror across the room. Then Elmira Birnbaum, her mother's friend from next door, came knocking on the front door. The houses in Riggs Park were attached on one side, and maybe Elmira heard something through the wall.

"Annie, are you all right?" she was calling through the door. "I saw all the shades were drawn. Are you all right?"

"Yes, I'm fine. Wait a minute." She motioned Bernie to hide in the kitchen while she put herself together. Bernie turned off the film and Annie started rewinding it. She let Elmira in.

"I borrowed this chemistry film from the instructor," Annie told her. "I was just finished with it."

"I thought I heard someone talking." Elmira was looking all around the living room.

"Maybe the voices on the film."

"Well, I just wanted to make sure. You know, I told your mother I'd keep an eye on the house in case anything ever looked funny." Annie's mother worked as a typist for the Department of Labor and her father had a dry cleaning store down near Gallaudet College, the school for the deaf. Elmira Birnbaum was a widow in her fifties who didn't work. Some people said she'd never actually been married. She was too ugly—six feet tall with a hook nose and kinky hair that ballooned around her head like a Brillo pad. She had a way of

130

always saying anything that came into her mind.

"Did you call your mother?" Elmira asked. Annie was supposed to call her mother every afternoon when she got in, but she never did. She never started the dinners her mother told her to start, and she kept her room looking like a pigsty. When she was twelve she'd quit Hebrew school two months before her Bas Mitzvah, and hadn't been back to temple since. These were her main crimes in life according to Elmira Birnbaum.

Elmira obviously didn't believe her about the film. She started walking through the dining room, toward the kitchen. Annie had to keep from smiling, thinking what would happen if Elmira found Bernie. He was crouched under the kitchen table, which was to the side and against the wall. If Elmira looked down he'd probably jump out and say, "Boo!" What the hell? But Elmira didn't see him; she just glanced around the center of the room and left. Bernie stayed under the table until Annie came to find him. She sat on the floor with him and started to laugh. Bernie's legs were crunched under the table, but he started laughing, too. Annie put one hand over her own mouth and one over his, so Elmira Birnbaum wouldn't hear them through the wall.

They were late getting to the cemetery. Cars were parked all along the roadway. They could see the huge crowd around the burial site—families of all the men, friends, the other hundred odd members of the Navy band who hadn't been on the South American tour. Bernie wound up a hill and down again before he found a parking space.

"We'll never get there if we go by the road," he said after he got out. He started walking cross-country, between gravesites, up the slope.

In town, most of the snow was melted, but at the cemetery there was still about an inch on the ground. Annie's high heels sank into it, and into the wet ground underneath. She couldn't keep her balance. Bernie took her wrist in his gloved hand and pulled her up the hill. The sun was shining, melting what was left of the snow. Chunks of snow were melting down Annie's ankles, underneath her hose. Bernie kept pulling her, she couldn't have gotten anywhere without him, and finally they were at the top.

The Navy band widows were sitting in chairs by the caskets. So many caskets. The families stood behind the widows. It took Annie a while to see which widow was Pearl, in her black coat and a hat with a veil. Someone must have given Pearl a sedative. She held a tissue in her hand, but her eyes were dull and dry. Seth was standing behind her, his hand on her shoulder, his face slack as if he'd taken sedatives, too. A hard brittle sunshine glittered off the snow. Annie's mother was in the crowd, but her father couldn't get away from the store. Cold water was seeping into Annie's shoes. She started to sway a little, because her feet were getting numb.

The caskets were draped with flags. Probably only part of Morton Opak was in there, and parts of other men in the other caskets. She didn't want to think about that. For two weeks they'd sat in Seth's living room not knowing when divers would bring up his father's body, or if they would. The funeral was kind of an aftermath. Every day they'd brought Seth his homework and pretended he was going to do it, to take his mind off things. He never did homework even when there was no crisis; he always wanted to let life slide around him too much, but it was hard not being able to make him study just then. Everyone sat around Seth's living room, on furniture that had been brought together into a circle for the guests, the dining room chairs as well as the upholstered pieces. It was as if they were sitting *shivah* already.

Seth's friends cracked jokes and talked about Coolidge High School, where everyone from Riggs Park had gone. It was awkward because they were all at different colleges now, with different friends. Sharon Greene, Bobby Goldbaum and Paul Siegel went to the University of Maryland, and Mel Epstein was at American University. They kept trying to remember things they had in common. Once they were laughing over the time Bobby Goldbaum traded his Passover matzoh for a baloney sandwich in the Coolidge High School cafeteria, but when they turned to Seth his face was completely blank, and in the background Pearl was crying.

One night Seth said, "I'll probably drop out of school. It's been almost two weeks already."

"You don't have to drop out," Bernie told him. "We'll help you make everything up." They were used to tutoring Seth; it was their normal way of life. Sophomore year Seth had taken weeks to catch on to solution problems in qualitative analysis. Annie and Bernie had stayed up late with him every night until he could do them, but they had never minded.

"I'm not sure I want to make everything up," Seth had said.

A man began to walk along the line of widows, shaking hands with them. At first Annie could see only the back of his dark overcoat. She couldn't tell who he was. Then the man reached Pearl, who shook hands with him in a dull, mechanical way. When the man turned away from Pearl, Annie could make out the jowls and the ridiculous slope of nose. She noticed that her mother was crying in the tight, glittery way she did when she was angry.

"Oh no. . . not Nixon," Annie said. She leaned on Bernie, because her feet were entirely numb. Bernie put his arm around her and held her against the cold.

Annie's mother had always hated Nixon. The morning after Dwight D. Eisenhower defeated Adlai Stevenson in 1956, Annie came downstairs to find her sitting with Elmira Birnbaum in the kitchen. They were listening to the radio, sipping tea and crying.

"Stevenson's too smart to be president," Annie's mother sobbed. "They don't like an intellectual."

"It frightens them—that somebody would know better than they do." Elmira was smoking a cigarette. She only smoked when she was upset.

"They'd rather have a dolt. A war hero."

"And *Nixon*." Annie's mother shuddered.

Annie took a bagel from the table next to the teapot. "I can't see that it's anything to cry over," she said.

"Just hope you marry rich," Elmira said. "Just hope you don't have to depend on making a living working for someone else, or with a little store somewhere." Elmira believed Annie's father would be old before his time, trying to run a dry cleaning business two blocks from Gallaudet, getting robbed every couple of years. "Your mother will never be more than a GS-3," Elmira said bitterly. "Whose fault is that?" Everyone in Riggs Park had wanted Stevenson to be president, but in Washington you had no choice.

Eisenhower should have had the decency to come to the funeral himself, Annie thought. He'd gotten Morton Opak killed, but he hadn't showed up at the cemetery, only sent Nixon; the Navy bandsmen weren't important enough for the president himself. She remembered a play from her Shakespeare class where a lovesick Duke was listening to music. When he got tired of the song he clapped his hands and the musicians went away. He never thought about them again, because musicians weren't really part of the play, just the servants. But if a Senator had been on that plane, Eisenhower would have been here.

Nixon had finished shaking hands. He was moving away, with his contingent of Secret Service men around him. He had a mean, mournful look on his face, like a parody of someone being serious, someone who couldn't care less.

Annie leaned into Bernie's jacket. Her earlobes began to ache from the cold—or rather not from the cold but from the warmth of his coat, which brought feeling back into them. Her ears had been colder than her feet. She had a funny thought—that she could crawl right inside Bernie's jacket and be perfectly happy.

She pretended Bernie's arm was Sandy's. Sandy would make her feel better here. Denzell Williams had been in Congress so long that Sandy had learned all the right things to do at times like these. It wasn't just manners. Sandy had picked her up at Seth's house every night during the past two weeks. He knew without her telling him that she was too upset to go home. Every night he'd driven her all the way downtown to his apartment near G.W., to talk and make out until he decided her color was good. He didn't try to get her into bed those nights; he only held her and tried to cheer her up, telling her about campaigning for his father, teasing her about wanting to be a doctor.

"I didn't want to be a doctor until Elmira Birnbaum said I should go to nursing school," Annie told him. "Elmira said it was cheaper than medical school."

Sandy laughed. "I see you more in peach chiffon," he said. That struck her as odd, but sometimes in those weeks he really did make her forget Seth, and she thought she loved him all the more for that. She was sure Sandy was going to ask her to marry him, once this was over.

They had folded the flags and given them to the widows. The twenty-one-gun salute began. The crack of shots into the cold air made Annie jump. Bernie let go of her. The guns were shooting and they were lowering the caskets into the graves. Seth was clenching his teeth. Annie thought how Morton Opak's body would be in that casket, under the ground, covered with dirt. Pearl was crying and Annie was crying, too.

Afterwards Paul Siegel asked Bernie for a ride back to Seth's house. Annie couldn't find her mother in the crowd. On the wet road going down the hill to Bernie's car, Annie's shoes were soaked through and she kept slipping. She could hardly feel her feet. Paul Siegel was watching with half a smile on his face, because he'd love to see her go down on her can.

"Here, let me sit in the back," Annie said when she got to the car. "My feet are all frostbitten, I need a little room. I can't even feel them."

Paul gave her a disgusted look and slid into the front seat next to Bernie. He had bushy black eyebrows that almost met in the middle, like a Russian spy.

"Even at a time like this, all you can think about is yourself," he said.

"Leave her be," Bernie said.

She pulled her shoes off and started rubbing her feet. It was as if she were rubbing somebody else's feet, as if her feet were far away.

"So where's the lawyer?" Paul asked. It was always the lawyer this, the lawyer that, like she was dating some octogenarian. When they were in high school Paul had once said to her, "You really think you're a good-looking girl, don't you?" Just like that. "Well, you're not," he said, without giving her time to answer. "I'll tell you who's good-looking." He named a just-average girl in Annie's home room. The truth was, Annie did think she was good-looking. Everyone did. But afterwards she felt she could never get the better of Paul.

"Sandy won't be a lawyer for another year," she said in a cold, distant way. Under her stockings, her feet were more white than usual, an unnatural white.

"He'll never practice law. He'll go right into politics," Paul said. He made *politics* sound like an obscenity. Even Elmira Birnbaum said, "People like Sandy have nothing to do with people like us. We work for the government and they come down here to *be* the government."

Bernie was looking in the rear view mirror, at Annie rubbing her feet. "You okay?" he asked.

"Yeah, I guess." A little sensation was coming back into her toes, the feeling of pins and needles.

"You should've worn boots," Bernie said. "A heavier coat, too."

"I can just see you as a political wife," Paul said.

"Oh shut up, Paul," Annie said.

At Seth's house people from the cemetery were beginning to arrive. Paul Siegel got out of the car but didn't push his seat release to let Annie out of the back. She leaned forward to do it herself, but Bernie said, "Here, get out my side," and offered her his hand.

Annie started to put her foot onto the street. When it touched the ground, she couldn't feel it. She might have been trying to stand on a pile of marshmallows. Her knee buckled and Bernie caught her.

"I don't think I can stand up," she said.

"Boy, you really do have frostbite." He motioned her to sit down again, and he got back into the car. Paul Siegel yelled from Seth's sidewalk: "Hey, what's going on?"

"She forgot something," Bernie said, driving off.

Annie's heart had started to pound so fast she couldn't count the beats, though she had her finger on the pulse in her neck. Her foot was really dead and she couldn't stand up. She had a picture in her mind of white hospitals, white ice, her white toes.

"Give me your house key," Bernie said. Annie's father was at work and her mother would be going to Seth's. He parked at her curb and got out. "Here, hang on to me." Still wearing his gloves, he pulled her from the car, onto her feet. Before her legs could give he caught her under the knees and was carrying her—into her house, through the living room, and up the stairs to the bathroom, where he sat her on the edge of the tub.

"Hey, what's going on?" He took her shoes off and yanked on her stockings. She'd always thought he'd do something like that, but never that he'd take advantage. While he was pulling her stockings down he was running water into the bathtub. The pulse in her neck was uneven, fast; Bernie was undressing her, but she didn't really care; maybe she wasn't fully conscious. She was thinking of the white hospital, waking up to white sheets with a flat place under the covers where her feet had been. She couldn't go to medical school with no feet; she couldn't bear to think such a thing. She wanted to close her eyes and sleep.

The next thing she knew she was sweating. Bernie hadn't taken her skirt off; he'd stopped after the stockings and stuck her bare feet into the water in the bathtub.

"You all right?" he said. The "you" and the "all" came at her from a long way off, but by the time he got to the "right" he sounded normal.

"Yeah, I guess. What're you doing?"

"I'm thawing out your feet."

"I thought you were undressing me."

"No, not now. Maybe some other time." He kneeled on the bathroom floor next to her. "I think we're supposed to rub them until the feeling comes back," he said. "You rub one and I'll rub the other."

They bent over, their heads together, the smell of water coming up at them from the tub, massaging her feet. Any other time she would have felt foolish, but just then she didn't.

"You feel anything?" he asked.

"I can feel that the water is warm."

They kept rubbing, as if they were doing something absorbing and important. She imagined they would bend over a patient like that, or over surgery, with their faces not quite touching, concentrating. She stopped thinking of herself under white sheets with white bandages on her stumps. The unnatural pallor of her feet began to give way to a pinkish color under the water. Then the pink turned bright red. Her feet itched something terrible.

"God. This might be worse than the numbness."

"Here, don't scratch." Bernie handed her a towel. "The itching is normal. Dry off and I'll wait for you downstairs." He went out of the bathroom.

"How do you know the itching is normal?" she said when she got to the living room. She had put on dark stockings and closed pumps, because her feet looked like she'd stuck them under a sun lamp. She kept rubbing her toes together to control the itch.

"I don't know, I must have read it somewhere." He sounded tired, or maybe embarrassed. "Come on, let's get back there before they miss us," he said.

Everyone from the cemetery had arrived, leaving no parking spaces anywhere near the house. "Here, you get out," he told her, pulling up in front. "We're not doing that collapsing number again." So Annie got out and Bernie went to park. She was waiting for him when Sandy came toward her from around the corner where he must have left his little Triumph. He took her arm as if he'd expected to find her there, and led her into the flow of people near the door.

Inside, the mirror by the entryway was covered by a black cloth. The night of their first date, Sandy and Annie had caught sight of themselves in a mirror together. Their hair was the same color, a white-blond. Annie's was loose on her shoulders and Sandy's was combed back. In the mirror Annie had thought they looked almost like angels, and she wondered if Sandy was remembering that now.

But what he did was pull himself up like someone at attention, and lead her through to a place against the dining room wall. "How was it?" he asked.

"It was all right." She wanted to tell him about her feet, but people were standing on both sides of them and it seemed too private.

"I've been to funerals like this before," he said. "They're always a mob scene. Very weepy. Did they send reporters?"

She didn't know why he would care about reporters. They were crushed against the wall by a woman who pushed past them with a platter of whitefish and sable and lox. There was deli and rye bread on the dining room table, and people were bringing cakes and strudel .

"Anything sensational, you usually get the press," he said.

"Nixon was there," she told him. "I think Eisenhower should have come." The woman was trying to set the platter on the table without dumping it on her dress.

"Traditionally the vice president represents the president at funerals," Sandy said.

"Eisenhower was the one who ordered them to play at the reception."

"It's protocol for the vice president to go," Sandy said. "They always do it that way."

People were jammed into the whole downstairs. Pearl was on the living room couch, receiving whoever came in.

"Let's get something to eat," Sandy said.

"I'm not hungry. You go ahead." She realized she couldn't campaign with no feet, either, but she hadn't thought of that back in the bathroom; maybe she didn't care.

Sandy went over to the table. Annie's mother was coming toward her, holding an old lady's hand. "This is my daughter Annie," she was saying. "Annie, you remember Mrs. Ginsburg—Steve and Lois's grandmother."

"Oh, of course." Annie didn't.

"All grown up," Mrs. Ginsburg said. "I remember when you were this high."

"She's a junior in college. She's in pre-med. She's going to be a doctor. Would you believe?"

For just a minute Annie's line of vision cleared and she could see Pearl on the couch, talking animatedly because so many people were around her, wishing her well. Seth was with her, but nobody was talking to him just then. His face was vacant and Annie knew he really was going to quit school.

Her mother and the old woman moved away. She remembered it was during those nights teaching Seth solution problems that she really decided to be a doctor. It wasn't just something she was proving to Elmira Birnbaum. She thought about having her feet cut off, and not being able to be a doctor because of that, and Seth not being able to be a doctor because his father had died. After the cold outside, it was too warm in the house. The young men were filling their plates at the table; Paul Siegel was cutting lox with a plastic knife. She was looking for Bernie. She wanted to tell him she was worried about Seth quitting school. They would cheer Seth up. They would tell him her feet had frozen at Arlington National Cemetery, and Bernie had thawed them out in a tub of water, though he'd never thought to stoop so low as to rub Annie's feet. "Other parts maybe, but never her feet." Seth would laugh, and they would make him study so they could go to medical school together. It was what they had always planned. One of the young men at the table caught her eye. It took her a minute to realize it was Sandy, standing among all her dark-haired friends eating bagels and lox. Finally she smiled at him, though he had nothing to do with her, never had, not now or in the brief moment before she knew who he was.

A TROPICAL CLIMATE

COMING FROM VIRGINIA, raised by gentle-voiced Southern women, Jess was distressed to realize that her daughter's heritage would include no brisk winters or springs of tulip and azalea. Amy would have to weave her dreams of bougainvilea and hibiscus—raw tropical magentas, sharp reds—and of leathery evergreen trees. South Florida was not a gentle place to raise a child.

They'd settled there because Bates loved it. Jess never did. "The town's growing, baby—they want teachers," he'd said when they came there as newlyweds. "I'll try anything for a year." During their courtship, there'd been no hint of the pioneer in him, and Jess was surprised to find him so entranced. The second year he quit teaching, stifled by dress codes and rules, and went into the insurance business.

"This is a boom town, baby," he told her then. "People coming in all the time. This is the place to make money."

She, pregnant, changed the subject. "Don't call me *baby*, hear? It makes me feel like some little helpless thing." But he kissed her and ignored that, holding *baby* as a measure of his power over her.

Amy was two when the insurance broker Bates worked for decided to retire, giving Bates first refusal on the business. "A stroke of luck," friends said, "him being able to buy in so easily." But other men had always chosen Bates first for clubs and teams, so Jess wasn't surprised. It was only that she resented having to stay in Florida, when she'd wanted Amy's childhood to be a mirror of her own in Virginia. She recalled cool mountains and oak trees, lilacs under a spring sky. And what would Amy have? Squat one-story houses plopped into the sand, a St. Augustine lawn that looked like weedy crab grass. Heat so dense it seemed to shimmer with evil.

Most of the people in their subdivision were from farther north. They'd come because they were restless, searching. A few were distinctly unstable. One man, a big muscular fellow, walked by each evening with a large black umbrella tucked under his arm, apparently for protection. He headed briskly

141

for the Everglades just east of their development, greeting no one. At dusk he hurried back, unwilling to be caught by darkness where sidewalks gave way to palm trees and swamp, or the nightly onslaught of insects from the bush. Tending to Amy on the lawn, Jess grew edgy with the sense of his madness.

Bates was unphased by all that. Whatever the cool rolling hills of Virginia hadn't provided him, the cheap insect-life of South Florida did—acres of sawgrass, dark waters, spiny palmettoes—echoing some raw edge of his spirit she'd never seen. He bought a small boat and took it into the swamp, seeking out turtles and lizards and fish. Once he brought home the slimy corpse of a water snake, dangling it at Amy, crying, "Look. Look!" until the child screamed with terror and delight.

On weekends, as a concession to Jess's more civilized needs, they headed west to the Gulf, letting Amy gather sand dollars along the shore. Bates always seemed glad to return from these tame forays. He preferred his weekday activities, working in shirt sleeves, drinking beer with the maverick developers he sold insurance to, who'd come to the Florida boom towns to make a quick profit.

As for Jess, her dissatisfaction wasn't constant. It ran in her veins like sap, ebbing and flowing with the heat. In Virginia they'd taught her that if you had a daughter to raise, you shared the task with a man. She endured but didn't adjust. Amy was three, then four. The town was overbuilt. The good economy gave way to recession. Bate's construction clients left or went bankrupt, leaving him with a narrow base of life insurance policies and local merchants.

"I don't need that building trade aggravation, baby," he said then, never suggesting they move back to Virginia. But Jess knew he'd enjoyed working with men who wore suits in the morning to negotiate bank loans, then stripped down to drive backhoes barechested in the afternoon. He began coming home early, loading the jeep with fishing gear, spending his time in the swamp.

"You be careful out there," Jess warned, afraid he'd come

to harm in the wild. He looked at her irritably, annoyed at being too much mothered. "You trust me to take care of myself, baby," he said. "Hear?"

She began to imagine him falling off the boat, into the swamp, struggling with the muddy waters, leaving her alone. When her fear spilled onto Amy, she enrolled the child in a swimming class. As a toddler, Amy had paddled happily in the Gulf, almost swimming, until the September rains cooled the waters. By the next March Amy had lost interest, refusing ever since to venture deeper than her knees. She was strong-willed even at four. "I don't care what you do to me!" she screamed. "I won't go to swimming lessons. I won't go!"

At night Jess began to dream of drownings. Gulf drownings, swamp drownings, fallings into the drainage canals that crisscrossed the town. She began to long for Virginia, where no preschool child needed to swim for survival's sake. She dreamed the night away and woke with terror caught in her throat. In the morning she spoke to Amy of the sweet reflected light that could glisten up from the canal at the end of their block, beckoning little girls closer and closer to the drowning edge.

In early spring, before the rains came, smoke rose from the winter-dry Everglades, from cypress and sawgrass and palm. Scattered fires took their toll of the bush, leaving the air heavy with ash. Bates shot a water bird, a graceful thing with long legs, shredded by the bullet, reduced to gray garbage.

"Disgusting," Jess said.

"Tasty, though." In Virginia, Bates's mother cooked the deer his father hunted, soaking them in milk to get the game taste out. But that was the yield of the cool autumn mountains—normal, tasty food—and not this abundance of slimy green life.

"You kill that pretty bird with not enough meat on it for the three of us—and you want *me* to cook it? Cook the blasted thing yourself."

After that he put his kills in the freezer. Jess wouldn't cook even the fish. They spoke somewhat less, though they maintained a cool show of manners. Bates was absorbed in the swamplife and Jess in the death-dealing waters that threatened her daughter. One day she found a photograph album from the year they were married. She marveled at the blond, clean-cut Bates she'd fallen in love with—a man with a wardrobe of pale blue shirts and the matching level gaze of an orderly mind. She wondered if she'd been stupid or just naive.

He was fishing and Amy napping when a developer named Drew came to the door. He built retirement houses on the edge of the swamp—one of the few still hanging on through the recession. He needed an insurance policy and hadn't found Bates in his office. Jess thought it only right to invite him in. They drank bourbon and 7-Up until Amy awakened. Jess introduced Drew as "one of your father's clients," but never mentioned him to her husband.

Drew came back the next week and sat with Jess and Amy on the lawn. His own child lived with her mother. Jess said Amy was afraid of water, wouldn't learn to swim. "I remember," Drew said. "Mine didn't learn till she was six." Jess felt reassured.

She finally let him take her to bed, in the guest room where Amy wouldn't look if she woke from her nap. Afterward Jess said it wasn't safe, she couldn't very well hide from her daughter.

"Then come out to my development," he said. "I've got a house that isn't sold, we can use that."

Jess thought he was joking, but he wasn't. She didn't think she'd really go, but she did. It was June, and the rainy season had come, quenching the fires to the east. Dark clouds filled the sky each day by noon, and by one there was a downpour. Knowing Amy wouldn't go out into the rain to drown, Jess left her with friends and went to meet Drew. They had a quick drink in the empty living room of his unsold house and then made love on the plush gold carpet, over which he spread a clean white sheet. They met several times a week. By July when the rains ended, she felt as quenched of desire as the Everglades were of drought.

"I'm not coming here anymore," she said. "It makes me feel cheap." He took her instead to his furnished apartment near the beach. A longer drive, an extra hour away from home. Shades drawn against the white sun, blotting out the glut of high summer. Jess thought of Amy while she submitted to his embrace. Of Amy running barefoot on the stubby St. Augustine grass. Of the long flat plane of the neighbor's yard, unshaded because the development was so new, because Florida trees were so squat. Of Amy drenched in sunlight and heat, drawn like a magnet to the cool, killing waters of the canal.

"Don't be silly. If the kid's afraid of water, it's for sure she isn't going to jump into a canal," Drew said. Jess heard impatience where before there'd been gentleness. She made excuses and fled.

He pestered her to meet him. Threatened to tell Bates otherwise. Sometimes she went. Amy tiptoed barefoot along the canal banks with a giddy new terror. August, then the start of preschool. By the time the rains resumed in September, Jess felt as wild-eyed as the man with the umbrella.

She enrolled Amy in another swimming class. "I don't care how much you scream and yell, you're going," she said. She dropped her at the indoor pool and walked out into the ferocity of the rain. She called Drew to say she couldn't see him. Ten minutes later he was on her doorstep. She had no choice but to invite him in.

His skin, damp from the rain, seemed too oily, too slick for love. She took him to the guest room, reasoning that he'd finish quickly and leave her alone. She undressed mechanically, listening to rain beat against the side of the house. She felt so detached she might have been dreaming.

She didn't hear Bates come in until he'd flung open the spare room door. He looked at her with a strange stillness in his eyes, as if he'd come, finally, to the place he'd been seeking. Then he began to yell. He pulled Drew away from her, yelling in a low primal voice she'd never known from him, garbled as if from under water. He punched Drew and kept screaming. Drew's defense was feeble, uncoordinated, heavy from love. Bates kept punching, pounding Drew's head against the wall. Jess curled up under the covers and watched.

There was no blood. Just the battering and then the snapping of the neck. The way it took so long before either of them realized what had happened. Panic might have risen in her if she'd been in the same woman who came south from Virginia, but even as her stomach churned and weakness spread through her hands, her mind was entirely clear.

"He's dead," she said.

Bates stood in the corner of the room, his breath coming ragged. "Amy'll be finished swimming," she told him. "We'll have to close this door."

Bates didn't move.

Jess said, a little louder, "We'll have to close this door."

She picked Amy up from the pool. Her fingers shook only a little as she drove, her voice not at all. "How was swimming?"

"I hated it. They make you put your head under."

"Is it really so bad?"

"I hated it," Amy said.

She ordered pizza and served it on the patio. The afternoon shower was over, the sun was bright. Bates couldn't eat and neither could she, but Amy didn't notice. Jess did the dishes, gave Amy her bath. Her stomach kept contracting. If Bates went to jail, Amy would be labeled the child of a criminal. She had no mind to buy disgrace for her daughter.

"We have to get rid of him now," she said when Amy was asleep. Bates didn't argue. Together they dragged Drew's body out to the garage and the jeep, leaving the lights off so the neighbors wouldn't see what they were about. She felt sick but kept working. When Bates drove off toward the swamp, Jess cleaned the spare room—washed the walls, vacuumed, changed the sheets. Bates returned and showered. He made love to her slowly, ceremoniously, as if to reaffirm who was married to whom. She understood that now he had extracted his price from himself and could live at peace with the swamp. You dealt with the man or you dealt with the woman, not both. And Amy would learn to swim.

There lodged within her a double coiling knot: of guilt, of pleasure. She wondered if she'd ever be able to leave this place of heat and water now: maybe not. No matter. She could stand it if she had to.

Bates was almost asleep, but she didn't want to lose her advantage. "You know what I think?" she said.

"What, baby?"

"I think before it's too late we'd better take Amy home."

SORORITY

IN HIGH SCHOOOL IN THE LATE '50S, Lois Ginsburg was friends with two bad girls, which was something she could do even with the standards that prevailed in those days, because she was so good. She was neat and well-mannered. She kept her room straight and observed her curfews. She was careful to maintain a B average in school to please her parents, who lamented that her brother Steve was lucky to come home with C's and D's. Lois had large dark eyes and a nice figure, which no boy had ever explored because she was too good to let them.

So it was safe for Lois to choose Sharon Greene and Roo Weinberg as her best friends, even though both had doubtful reputations. She liked having someone to worry about. Her parents wouldn't need her concern until years later, when Steve quit college to go off with his band. Steve was a year older but still in the same grade after being kept back as a child. His one talent was the ability to play any musical instrument he could get his hands on—a calling he nurtured by ignoring his studies and pretending Lois didn't exist if she walked into the living room while he was picking out tunes on the piano. By contrast, Sharon and Roo appreciated her. She would help them, if necessary, even in the middle of the night.

"Talk to me. It's black as death in here," Sharon would whisper on the phone after her parents had gone to bed. Sharon was so afraid of the dark that she imagined herself trapped in her room, waiting for some knobby hand to grab her from outside in the hall. To hear her tell it, she almost never got a wink of sleep.

"Where were you before?" Lois would ask groggily. "I tried to call you."

"I was out with Sam (or Frank or Joey)," Sharon would say. "I had to help him with math (or English or science)." Sharon was an honor student allowed to go out on weeknights as long as it didn't affect her grades.

"You slept with him, didn't you?" Lois would accuse.

They'd known these boys since grade school—old friends and neighbors with whom Sharon's behavior seemed incestuous.

"Well, why not?" Sharon would say. "He wanted to so badly."

"Oh sure. . . why not? You could get pregnant or you could get a disease."

"I'm careful."

"Besides, you don't even like him."

"I like him well enough."

"Sharon, you know what I'm saying."

This never got very far because both of them knew Sharon had sex with boys out of a sense of decency and kindness (as well as fear of the dark)—reasons difficult to debate. Afterwards Sharon talked to the boys about algebra, sports, their girlfriends, as if they'd never touched her. To Sharon, sex was no more noteworthy than thirst, the act itself akin to offering a glass of water. The boys weren't ungrateful. Every one of them worked on Sharon's campaign when she ran for class treasurer, sending her to victory two years in a row.

It was different with Roo. Roo didn't have a soft heart like Sharon, and wasn't afraid of the dark. She was so beautiful that boys would have wanted her even if she hadn't let them so much as hold her hand. Her red hair fell in natural waves around her face. Her cheekbones were high, her nose perfectly aquiline. Her eyes were a wide-set blue topped with double rows of golden-red lashes. Roo tried to cover the lashes with dark mascara, but Lois could always see where the golden color met the eye, which was somehow endearing. Roo hated her pale and freckled skin. But her figure was perfect—small-boned and long-limbed (though she wasn't very tall), with plenty of bust.

"You forget what I looked like in seventh grade," Roo would say when people complimented her. It was as if she wanted them to remember her in a state of incompletion—hair short, teeth encased in braces, eyes invisible behind glasses. But by high school the apparatus was gone and she was stunning. Lois couldn't understand Roo's lack of confidence, though publicly she ascribed it to the insults her friend had suffered in grade school because of her hair.

Roo's real name was Davidina, but in elementary school the boys never called her that. It was always, "Hey Red!" or "Whatcha doing, Red?" while they grabbed at her pony tail. Roo's mother tried to point out that these jibes were actually a sign of affection, but Roo wasn't convinced. She responded to the name-calling scarlet-faced, yelling, "It isn't Red, it's Davidina!" The boys pretended not to understand. They brought frogs to put in her desk, they asked her if it was possible to count so many freckles on a single human face. One day in fifth grade, Roo ran sobbing from the playground to the girls' bathroom and refused to come out until her mother was summoned to take her home. All the boys got detention.

Then a grandmotherly neighbor intervened, saying to some of the boys: "Look, you want to call Davidina by the color of her hair? Then call her Rouge, which is French for Red—it has the exact same meaning—but maybe it won't give her a temper tantrum and you won't have to stay after school."

To Davidina she said, "Rouge is a very exotic name. They may think they're calling you Red, but using French makes it entirely different, believe me."

Roo suddenly smiled. "It does make it different, doesn't it?" Nor did she seem upset as the years passed and Rouge got shortened to Roo. But in high school, when Roo's hair gleamed like a beacon in the cold hallways, when people stopped to stare at her because of her great beauty and reputed looseness, Roo always pretended not to notice, just as the boys had once pretended not to hear her cries for mercy. And it was then that Lois wondered if in the genesis of Roo's nickname there hadn't been a deeper wound than anyone imagined.

There was a junior sorority at the high school—Alpha Delta. Two Greek letters to distinguish it from the college sororities, the real sororities, which had three. Lois's mother said, "Well, it might be nice to see what a sorority is like before you make a big commitment like living in a sorority house when you go to college." It had always been a given of Lois's future that she would go to college and do well, and in the process live all that life her parents had missed, growing up during the Depression. She wouldn't have let them down on the matter of the sorority even if their interests had not coincided. Steve was so unreliable—leaving his homework unfinished to work on his songs, humming his tunes at all hours of the night—that getting a rounded education (socially as well as scholastically) was the least Lois felt she could do.

At first Sharon said she wasn't going to pledge with Lois, what did she need with a sorority? It was like Sharon to assert her independence. Frankly, Lois worried that her friend was only trying to protect herself in case she didn't get a bid because of her reputation. But two girls offered to "bring her up"—which indicated to Lois that a bad reputation wasn't going to hurt Sharon as long as the boys she slept with worked on her political campaigns.

As for Roo—she was noncommittal. "I don't know—I don't really know any Alpha Delts that well," was all she would say. But the truth was, Roo liked people's approval. Why else would she cater to boys? And if a whole sorority gave her its blessing, Lois reasoned, surely she'd feel less need to bed down with half the school. That fall, Roo was going with Joel Gordon, the quarterback on the football team. Lois's brother Steve pointed out that this was an important plus. "Your ritzy Alpha Delt buddies couldn't care less what she does with Joel Gordon as long as she shows him off at their social functions," he said.

"Very nice, Steve. Very delicate."

"Watch. Somebody'll offer to bring her up. Wait and see." Steve was so infatuated with Roo that he felt the need to disguise his affection with crude comments. Though most of what he said about her could be discounted, in this case he turned out to be right.

"You owe it to yourself to pledge," Lois maintained when Roo still hesitated. While Sharon was sensible and focused, Roo was often too dreamy to be swayed by practical concerns. "Think about me, if not yourself. How will I feel if my best friend won't pledge with me?" When Roo finally agreed, Lois was proud to have been the one to convince her.

At first, pledging was even more agreeable than they had anticipated. So much to do! While the members planned the big Chrismas Night Dance at the Sheraton Park Hotel, the pledges worked for various charities. Lois and Roo and Sharon manned bake sales, visited an old age home, helped handicapped children don their coats after class and wheeled them down ramps to waiting buses. They smiled and felt useful. On Wednesdays after school, they discussed these charitable efforts at their pledge meetings. Elaine Marshall, the pledge mistress, was as sweet as she was cute. It was a pleasant, easy time. Lois was elected vice-president of the pledge class, and Sharon became treasurer. Even Roo seemed content.

On Sunday afternoons, the pledges had to attend regular sorority meetings at various members' houses. Here they sat in a separate room waiting to be "brought down" and questioned. Though the waiting was tense, Lois believed it was part of the closeness. Members and pledges alike arrived at the meetings dressed up in skirt-and-sweater sets and heels. They emerged from cars in groups of three and four, smoothing skirts, touching freshly painted nails to just-washed hair. Inside, the scents of their perfumes mingled—a fresh and interesting effect, never sour. Lois was profoundly touched by that. Standing among the well-dressed sweet-smelling girls who would soon be her sisters, she felt part of something large, secret, different from anything she had known. It tickled her nostrils, floated on her tongue. She loved the sound of it: *sorority.*

"Marilyn, Gayle asked you for mints in school last week and you didn't have any," the members would say when the pledges were brought down. Pledges were required to carry gum and mints for members, to follow a list of rules. A record was kept of their demerits. Or it could go the other way. Once, the president complimented Lois for selling three dozen sub sandwiches at a single fund-raiser. A pledge's whole life was on the line. Members could discuss anything about her that seemed either outstanding or unbecoming. She had to be a lady. A lady! Of course! Members even had the power to blackball a pledge they didn't think would be an asset, though no one had heard of that happening. Lois knew she felt as all the other pledges did, in her desire never to do anything to make the members think she was unworthy.

All through the fall, there were more social events than Lois had ever attended in a single semester. Mixers, teas, parties. Lacking a regular boyfriend, a pledge had to find a series of boys to escort her. Given the prestige of the sorority, this was never a problem. The social season culminated in the formal Christmas Night Dance, with a live band and a memory book that listed everyone and their dates. Sharon was the only one Lois had ever heard say a word against it. "We can get the ballroom Christmas Night because no one else wants it," she asserted. "But imagine if you were part of the help. No one wants to work Christmas Night, either."

"Oh Sharon. In a big hotel, someone always has to be on duty," Lois argued. To her, Sharon's comments sounded sour and unfair, a slur against the sorority. And Lois noted that Sharon's sympathy for the help didn't stop her from inviting Bernie Levitan to the dance—a boy even better in math than Sharon was, and good-looking as well. Roo came with Joel Gordon the quarterback. And Lois got up the nerve to ask Marty West, whose eyes were darker than Lois's own, and whose skin was so warm there might have been a fire beneath it.

That night, Roo and Joel danced close even when the music didn't call for it. Lois was surprised she'd do such a thing in front of so many Alpha Delts, in a big formal place like the Sheraton Park ballroom. She noticed that Sharon and Bernie, wisely, didn't dance close at all. After the dance everyone changed clothes and went to a party at the house of the sorority's president. A few of the senior Alpha Delts started making out with their boyfriends who were college students. These girls were pinned or even engaged. The basement was dim and cool. Marty West and Lois danced to the slow songs on the record player. He held Lois close. The music was soft, and Lois's stomach was turning over in a pleasant way. She let Marty hold her as tight as he wanted.

Then she saw Roo sitting on Joel Gordon's lap, kissing him and stroking his neck. Not a single other pledge was making out. Roo looked small and slender in her skirt and sweater, but her hair was disheveled and her face smudged with a serious, desperate look that Lois knew was the look people got when they were ready to have sex. Roo was pressing herself into Joel Gordon's chest as if she could crawl into his rib cage and melt. Joel was rubbing her back. People were watching. There was something wrong with Roo—with the desperation on her face, with what she was doing, what she would do later. This—*this*—was why they called girls *bad*. Lois disengaged herself from Marty, tucking her blouse in so no one would think it had come loose because of something he had done. Her stomach stopped its churning.

Joel Gordon broke up with Roo a few weeks later. This seemed somehow inevitable. But Roo showed no emotion. She began going out with one boy after another. Lois felt uncomfortable, watching Roo socialize so much. She kept picturing Roo on Joel Gordon's lap at Christmas. It seemed wrong to behave so seriously and desperately about a person if you were not going to set aside even a single weekend to mourn him. "I think you're making a mistake," she told her friend. "I think you ought to find just one or two boys you really like."

"You think so? Well I'm looking." Roo's tone was so flip that Lois knew she was hurt and bitter. But she kept going out with anyone who asked her.

"She better watch it," Lois's brother Steve said. "She's only safe with someone who'll protect her." He was not criticizing, only rushing to Roo's defense. His concern was pathetic. If he were Roo's date, he said, he'd never tell what went on between them. "But most guys don't think like that." He was picking out a new song on the piano, hitting the same three notes over and over again. Lois knew he was writing the song for Roo, who was on his mind all the time. There seemed something tentative and unworthy about his talents.

But there was a kernel of truth in what he said. Roo seemed to let those boys touch her in some important way that Sharon never did. The boys always knew Sharon was doing them a favor. With Roo it seemed the other way around.

Steve was intent on his melody. Their mother called into the room, "Lois, Marty's on the phone." When she picked up the receiver, the sound of his voice made her chest feel as if it were being squeezed. She was afraid of the warmth of his skin, the heat of his black eyes, the way her stomach churned when he held her. Her heart was pounding and blood was rushing through her ears. What was she afraid of? It was only his voice. She sensed this was the way Sharon felt when nobody was around late at night, when she was alone and stranded in the dark.

During Easter week, just before the pledges were usually let into the sorority, Roo went out three nights in a row with a boy named Allan. He had been dating Marlene Zimmer, an Alpha Delt who was spending Easter in Florida with her parents. No one liked the idea of Roo moving in on another Alpha Delt's boyfriend. That was mostly because they were jealous of Roo and not because they liked Marlene, a brusque, authoritative girl who was the sorority's parliamentarian.

The pledges never knew what Marlene actually said to the members, because they were sitting upstairs during the Sunday afternoon meeting. But the story got around that when Marlene got home from Florida, Allan told her he'd taken Roo out just to see what he could get, which turned out to be quite a lot. "He's asked me to take him back," Marlene supposedly said, "But I'm not sure I can after that." Tears reportedly came to Marlene's eyes, which no one would have believed because of her toughness. She could not bear the thought of belonging to a sorority with a girl who would do something like that, she had sobbed; she could not bear the thought of the entire group being tainted by Roo's reputation. She invoked social rules the way she invoked Robert's Rules, but with considerably more emotion.

Something had to be done.

Outside the sun was bright, the tulips were blooming. The den where the pledges sat was warm and stuffy. All twenty-two of them thought, secretly, that perhaps this was the day they were going to be made members. The initiation ceremony was secret, but very beautiful, they had been told. Usually the girls were brought down in pairs. That day Roo was called first. She was called alone. She was down there for perhaps ten minutes, but to the pledges the time seemed interminable.

When Roo came up, the pledge mistress was with her. They were both silent, with hard grim expressions on their faces. Roo did not come back into the den. She walked through the hallway and out the door. She held herself stiffly, as if she wanted to cry but would not give them the satisfaction. Lois knew she ought to follow her. She knew Roo was waiting for her mother to pick her up. She remembered Roo waiting just like this in fifth grade, after the boys called her Red. For a moment it was as if nothing had changed in all the years in between, and the least Lois could do was go out there. She felt an aching in her chest at the sight of Roo, standing so stiffly in the sun. But Lois's legs would not move to carry her out of the den. She kept smelling the perfume the other pledges were wearing, seeing their long, stockinged legs under springtime skirts, and it was as if going out that door would be the end of the large, secret thing she was part of, and she could not bear it.

It was all she could do to whisper to the pledge mistress: "What happened?"

"You'll find out in a minute." Outside, Roo's mother pulled up in front of the house in her car, and Roo got in. Then all the pledges were called downstairs at once and lined up against the wall.

"A very serious thing has happened," the president said. She spoke in a low dramatic voice and paused at the end of her sentence. "We've had to ask one of you—one of our Alpha Delt pledges—to depledge."

A murmur went through the pledges, though all of them

expected this.

"This is something we don't do lightly, girls," the president said. It was something that was only done in a case of utmost seriousness, when a girl turned out not to have the qualities—the ethical and moral qualities—that Alpha Delta expected of its members. She hoped this would serve as an example to the other pledges of how serious Alpha Delta's commitment was to admitting girls of good character only. The basement was cool, lit with recessed lights. The members stared at the pledges without blinking. Marlene's mouth was drawn into a tight line. Everyone knew what Allan must have told her about his dates with Roo. Boys like Allan had to say such things. Lois tried to catch Sharon's eye, but Sharon was looking at the floor.

Afterwards, Sharon came back to Lois's house because neither of them wanted to be alone. They didn't know quite what to do. Seeing them come in together, Steve demanded to hear the story. He said, "You have no choice but to depledge." His words fell on Lois's ears like stinging shards of glass. Of course he was right. They had to stand up for Roo. As officers of the pledge class and Roo's good friends, it was their duty.

For the rest of the afternoon, the two of them made their plans. Lois felt as if she were being sucked into a whirlpool. There was no way to get out. They would ask to be brought down together at next Sunday's meeting. They would make a little speech about fairness and, at the end, depledge. Sharon, who knew something about politics, said that was the most dramatic, the most effective way. All week Roo stayed home from school with "flu," and wouldn't come to the phone. Lois called every day anyway; it was only right. When she and Sharon went to Roo's house one afternoon, Roo's mother said she was sleeping. There was nothing else they could do. Marty West came over twice. "You've got to get your mind off this," he said. He pulled Lois close, but she couldn't bring herself to respond. "Wait a while," she told him. She was filled with an image of Roo—not of the girl who'd stood stiffly outside the sorority meeting waiting for her mother, but of the desperate, evil one kissing Joel Gordon Christmas Night.

On Sunday, Lois was sick with nerves and shame. Once they depledged, no Alpha Delt would ever speak to them. They'd been careful not to let anyone know what they were up to—not even Roo herself. They asked to be brought down together, and the pledge mistress said, smiling, "All right," as if nothing were wrong. The pledges started being taken down five at a time. When it was their turn, Lois and Sharon were blindfolded at the top of the stairs. A pleasant melody reached them as they descended in the dark. They could make out the words of a song, the voices of a choir. At the bottom, their blindfolds were removed. They stood in cool half-darkness, illuminated by halos of yellow flame. The smiling members stood before them, each with a lit candle in her hand. They were singing the initiation song. So before Sharon and Lois could depledge, they were members.

Lois smelled the perfume of the other girls and watched the candles flickering in the dark. She didn't think of Roo, or of Sharon standing beside her, or even of the happiness she knew her mother would feel knowing Lois had been installed after all. She didn't think of any one person or one thing, because she was part of something larger. She was warm and complete. She whispered to herself: "Sisters."

Marty West took her home. He kissed her before she got out of the car. She felt a little sick. When she walked into the house, Roo was sitting on the piano bench with her brother Steve. Steve was playing a song he'd written for her. Roo looked beautiful and desperate. The music was sweet, but Lois was part of a sorority now—she couldn't help it—and knew the two of them could only cause her shame.

ACTS OF CHARITY

KATIE'S SECRET PLAN TO LEAVE TOWN for college and forever was in jeopardy because she couldn't find a full-time summer job. It was 1980, and the town was in recession. Half the workers from Mack Truck were laid off; nobody else was hiring. People told Katie she was lucky to be restacking books half a day in the library. She didn't think so. On top of everything she had a summer virus which left her feeling as if her blood were being extracted drop by drop. Nineteen years old and crumbling.

She couldn't tell her mother, Ruth, about either the virus or her secret plan. Ruth had been oversensitive to illness ever since Katie's father died, and now she had financial worries as well. All Katie could do was save up for tuition. Every afternoon she napped so she'd feel well enough to feign health when her mother got home from work. One day she'd just fallen asleep on the couch when the refugees came down from their apartment in the other half of Ruth's double house, talking and laughing and rustling things. The refugees never knocked anymore. Why didn't they knock?

Katie had trouble opening her eyes, making them focus. Maybe she was dreaming. Then Sue Ann's long hair dangled onto her chin. Irritably, Katie swiped it away. This was no dream.

"You tired?" Sue Ann asked, looking down with such seriousness that Katie had to smile. Sue Ann's real name was Xuan, and she was six years old. People from the church had given her the American name the week she'd arrived a year ago. In her red shorts and T-top, she looked like she'd been here forever.

"I'm okay," Katie said.

Lin, Sue Ann's mother, and Tu, her father, paraded past, carrying food into the kitchen—a container of rice from the big sack they kept upstairs in their apartment, raw chicken and shrimp in a pot, a bunch of scallions. Tu was also carrying the baby, Billy—an American citizen by virtue of being born here.

"We come to cook," Sue Ann said. The refugees made dinner sometimes to thank Ruth for helping them. Sue Ann was their spokesman because even after a year she was the only one who spoke much English. Tu worked at a bakery. Lin was home all day with the baby, talking on the phone to her Vietnamese friends. At dinner everyone would gesture and laugh to make up for their lack of a common language, and Katie would be annoyed.

Sue Ann followed her family into the kitchen, and Katie reluctantly got up. Her neck hurt, her glands felt swollen. "I'll help you," she felt obligated to say.

Tu sat at the kitchen table, clapping Billy's hands together, pat-a-cake. Katie gathered that Vietnamese men avoided kitchen duties but were willing to help with babies. Lin had been pregnant when they left Vietnam, pregnant on the boat trip, pregnant in the resettlement camp in Malaysia.

"What can I do?" Katie asked, watching Lin chop pieces of chicken on the cutting board and Sue Ann scrape carrots. Lin barked something in rapid Vietnamese.

"Nothing. . . she say there's nothing to do," Sue Ann translated.

Could such a gruff outburst mean something so ordinary? Katie doubted it. Her mother would say of course it could, Vietnamese was a tonal language, you were supposed to raise your voice.

Not surprisingly, the thought of her mother made Ruth materialize at once. The screen door opened, Ruth lumbered in, cotton skirt wrinkled from sitting typing all day, overdone perm frizzed from humidity. Tu jumped up to give her his chair, but Ruth waved him down. "No. Sit. Sit." She tickled Billy under the chin and took another chair. Sitting, she kicked her shoes off, rubbed her feet.

"The heat always gets me," Ruth said to the refugees. She believed they understood more English than they spoke, which led her to carry on long, one-sided conversations. Heat's been hard on me ever since I gained this weight."

"Ever since you started getting up at the crack of dawn," Katie said.

Her mother scowled at her. Ruth rose at 5 a.m. to drive Tu to the bakery because no buses ran at that hour. She'd been doing this for months, ever since the bakery owners tired of picking him up. "In this economy, who knows if he could get another job?" Ruth always countered when Katie objected.

Lin took a handful of shrimp chips from a package and dropped them into a pot of boiling oil on the stove. Seconds later, they exploded into pink puffs the consistency of Cheetos.

"My favorite," Ruth said, pushing a strand of fuzzy brown hair back from her face. The perm was nearly a month old and still hideous, but when Katie suggested her mother complain to the hairdresser, Ruth refused.

Lin spoke to Tu in Vietnamese, and he laughed.

"She say how nice to cook in a big kitchen like this," Sue Ann explained. Upstairs, Lin and Tu had the smallest apartment in the other half of Ruth's double house, the only one that was vacant last year when the church decided to sponsor the refugees.

"We have four people," Tu said. "You—only two."

When I leave home, Katie thought, they'll talk her into moving into the apartment so they can have this house. She rolled her eyes at Ruth, who stood up and said, "We better set the table." Katie rose to help. Her head and hands felt heavy, as if someone had attached weights to them.

The next day, the library decided to let Katie work part-time in the fall while taking a few courses at the community college. This spoke well for her secret plan to go away as soon as she had enough money, and in celebration she spent the afternoon teaching Sue Ann to play jacks. By four o'clock she was achy and feverish, wondering why, instead of napping, she was sitting on the porch demonstrating how to swipe two jacks away from a third.

"Now you try."

Sue Ann laughed. "I don't know if I can."

"After a year in America you can do anything." Katie winked.

Ruth was planning a party to celebrate the anniversary of the family's arrival, and Sue Ann was already excited about it.

A year ago, Katie and Ruth and Pastor Melnik from the church had picked up Lin and Tu at the airport late at night. Normally Katie avoided church-related activities, but since the refugees were going to live with them, she went. Lin and Tu got off the plane bedraggled from three days of traveling, Tu with sweat stains on the armpits of his shirt, Lin tugging on an ill-fitting sundress pulled tight over her pregnant stomach. Both wore flip-flops on their feet instead of shoes. Tu carried a single shopping bag containing what was left of their belongings after their boat was attacked by Thai pirates.

"It's lucky the woman and her daughter weren't raped during the pirate attack," Pastor Melnik had said. "That's what happens to most of them." It was like Pastor Melnik to explore the dismal possibilities.

Sue Ann, dazed after the long plane ride from San Francisco, shivered from the airport's air-conditioning. In the car on the way home, she fell asleep against Lin's belly. Katie thought: maybe they *were* raped and didn't tell us. The idea made her sick to her stomach.

The next day Ruth described the arrival to everyone who came over, saying, "They were such a mess after all that traveling, they even smelled like they hadn't taken a bath through it all, poor things." It was then Katie realized her nausea must have been caused not by the thought of rape but by the odor.

The congregation was organized into committees. One was to take the refugees to the health department for check-ups, another to find Tu a job, a third to see about English lessons. Hearing about the scene at the airport, people began bringing more dishes and silverware for the apartment than anyone could use. Each day, Lin and Tu looked a little less bedraggled, and each church member felt personally responsible for the improvement. Finally someone gave them a black and white TV.

"Lin like it okay," reported another Vietnamese woman who'd been in the country two years and spoke some English. "But she like color TV more—like you have."

Ruth just laughed. "Tell her even a black and white TV will help her learn English."

But Katie was annoyed. "How can you laugh when they keep asking for stuff? What a lot of nerve."

"Oh, honey, they think color TV is just another throwaway people will give them. They don't realize how expensive it is."

But Katie wasn't sure. Though Tu soon went to work at Laird's Bakery, the family kept telling the volunteers about the items they still needed, and allowed them to run the family's many errands. By winter when the committees were tired, Lin and Tu seemed no more independent than before. People began wondering when they'd move away to one of the cities where the refugees had congregated. Donations stopped; the supply of volunteers dwindled. One day when Mary Laird drove Tu home from work, Lin came outside and said to her, "We so happy you help us. Maybe you get us color TV?" After that, the Lairds stopped driving Tu to work, leaving Ruth to get up at 5 a.m.

Sue Ann tried to sweep up all ten jacks at once, but they trickled out between her fingers. Lin emerged from her side of the double house, carrying Billy.

"Katie, you take me?" she said. "I need. . . " She licked her index finger and pressed it to the opposite palm. Katie didn't understand.

"Stamps," Sue Ann said. "She want you to take her to the post office."

"I can't right now." Katie really did feel woozy; she'd be asleep if she hadn't gotten the idea of teaching Sue Ann jacks. "You could walk to the post office. You could put Billy in his stroller and walk." But Lin shook her head no and laughed a nervous laugh.

That night, Ruth sat on the couch with her swollen feet on the coffee table and nibbled Lin's leftover Vietnamese eggrolls —delicate, finger-sized rolls filled with pork and vegetables.

"I don't see how you can eat them cold," Katie said. "They taste like cold grease."

"I don't think so," said Ruth. "You ate your share."

"Sure, yesterday when they were *hot.*" Katie did like Lin's cooking—rice with little shreds of chicken and carrot and mint. Healthier than Ruth's meaty dinners, which Katie believed were responsible for her weight as much as sitting typing all day.

Katie rose and turned on the TV. "Tu could afford a used car," she told her mother. "You're not helping him, being the martyr, getting up before it's light. What if you're sick one day? *I'm* not doing it."

"A car is expensive. . . gas and insurance and all."

"It wouldn't kill him." Katie left the sound low while she switched through the channels.

"It's a small thing—driving him to work," Ruth said. "He needs to save up for later."

"Later. When's later? It's a year now. It's later." In the beginning, the church paid Tu's rent, but once he started working he was supposed to pay it himself. Ruth charged him only half on the condition that he do a few of the chores Katie's father used to take care of—painting the second-floor apartment, shoring up the banister. But Tu was no handyman. When he wasn't working, he was visiting Vietnamese friends. "You should at least make him mow the grass," Katie admonished. "You're turning him into a baby."

"I enjoy doing the grass. It relaxes me." Ruth leaned over and poked at her swollen foot.

"Yeah. You look so relaxed you're falling apart."

"You don't look so chipper yourself," Ruth said.

Katie made one more run through the channels, then snapped the TV off. The same old reruns. She believed her mother performed her acts of charity to thank God for the good fortune she didn't in fact possess. Katie wouldn't burden her further with tales of a summer virus. "I'm extremely chipper," she said. "Extremely."

Ruth lowered her legs to the floor and picked up the dish with the remaining eggrolls. "You know why Billy and Sue Ann are almost six years apart? It's because Tu spent all that time in jail for siding with the Americans. Think about it. Compared to that. . . . "

"Yeah, I know. Taking him everywhere is a small thing. Taking him to work. To the grocery store. To the doctor. Lin wanted me to take her to the post office this afternoon. You'd think in a year she'd learn her way."

"She's in a strange country. She doesn't speak the language. Have a little sympathy."

"I guarantee you if I'd been in Vietnam for a year, I'd be able to make my way to the post office."

"You don't have two little children. You never had to escape from someplace on a thirty-foot boat with over a hundred people in it." Ruth held the eggroll plate in one hand and put the other to her temple to rub away the tension.

"She makes great eggrolls," Katie said. "But she's still a leech."

By Sunday Katie had developed another symptom, a sore throat. She lay in bed listening to Ruth get ready for church. Katie herself hadn't gone since her father died, after Pastor Melnik told her church was especially helpful in a time of bereavement.

"I'm not going to worship any God who knocks people off at age forty-three after three months of torture," she'd said.

Pastor Melnik had put on such a calm, reason-in-the-face-of-lunacy expression that Katie wanted to slap him. "You're not really angry with God. You're angry at your father for abandoning you. It's perfectly normal for a sixteen-year-old to view the death of a loved one as abandonment."

"Just screw that," she'd said. "Just screw it!"

Instead of reacting with the fury Katie expected, Ruth told Pastor Melnik Katie wasn't coming to church "while she feels so strongly about her father's death." That was three years ago.

"Roo?" Lin had come into the house without knocking, and was calling up the stairs to Ruth. "You go to church, Roo?"

Of course Ruth was going! She'd driven Lin and Tu in every Sunday for a year, even when her face was red from poison ivy. The church was sponsoring Tu's family and expected them to show up .

Ruth knocked on Katie's door, then stepped in. "We're going now. You sleeping in?"

"If it doesn't get too hot." Katie's voice came out a little hoarse from the sore throat. She was beginning to think she had a strep infection and ought to have a throat culture before Ruth got suspicious.

Ruth smoothed the skirt of her summer dress—a pale yellow with slimming vertical stripes. Her hair, newly washed, seemed less frizzy than before. If she looked like that more often, Katie mused, she might even find a second husband.

Katie engaged in this fantasy often—of her mother remarried or at least with an active social life outside the church. She envisioned a companion who'd take Ruth to the city on weekends, to shop and visit the zoo. Who'd paint the second-floor apartment. Who'd allow Katie to enjoy her own vision of going away to the university while Ruth was stuck here typing.

"The dress looks nice," Katie said.

"You think so?" Ruth pivoted on her toes to model.

"If you weren't so busy driving Lin and Tu around, you'd probably be out with some man."

"Oh, Katie," Ruth said, but she sounded pleased.

Lin called up the stairs again in her small beggar's voice. Today Ruth would drive them to church and tomorrow she'd get up before daylight to take Tu to the bakery. Tuesday Lin would want to go to the Oriental grocery store. Ruth wouldn't have time for a social life even if she were thinner.

The entire congregation had been invited to celebrate the anniversary of the refugees' arrival. Not many of them came. The Lairds sent a cake from the bakery along with their regrets. Half of the congregation was away for vacation. The others found it hard to talk to people who didn't speak English. Their embarrassment showed each time Lin and Tu said they were poor, because each one had given a piece of furniture last year, or a bag of groceries or a winter coat. Ruth said American charity was enthusiastic but short-lived. She made finger sandwiches and iced tea, and invited Tu's

English instructor and some of the other refugees to make sure the house wouldn't be empty.

For a time, Lin and Tu smiled and nodded and tried their best to talk to everyone, but the mood was strained. Finally they drifted toward their Vietnamese friends. The party split into Vietnamese and American. The only ones who seemed to be having a good time were the children.

At the end, one of Tu's Vietnamese friends came up to thank Ruth for inviting him. "God will bless you for helping Tu so much," he said. Pleased, Ruth smiled and blushed before being drawn away by another guest.

The man turned to Katie. "God will bless you, too."

"Well, yes, I hope so," Katie said. "We could use a few blessings around here—especially my mother, who'd be working her ass off even if she didn't have Lin and Tu to drag around."

Whether the man understood she didn't know. He nodded and smiled as if he'd heard no insult.

After everyone left, Lin and Tu scurried to clear the dirty plates and glasses. They sent Sue Ann upstairs to listen for Billy while he took his nap. Katie's head throbbed. She was certain now she had strep. It always gave her this peculiarly unreal feeling, as if she were floating off the edge of herself. By contrast, Ruth seemed clear-headed and focused.

"You know Taylor Wilan?" she asked Lin as she filled the sink with water. "The big dark-haired man who works at the hospital?"

"Yes," said Lin—her standard response to Ruth's questions.

"He says they're looking for housekeepers there—you know, mopping and dusting and all." Ruth made mopping and dusting motions. To Katie she said, "They're looking for minorities to fill the affirmative action quotas." There were very few minorities in town—a handful of blacks, a dozen Vietnamese.

"Billy's old enough to stay with a sitter now," Ruth went on, warming to the topic. "It'd be good for you to work." She sloshed iced tea glasses in the sink, then handed them to Lin to dry so Katie could put them away. Her face was bright, flushed.

"The problem is, I don't think they pay more than minimum wage. After you pay a sitter, you might not make very much." She frowned. "I wonder if Bess Fletcher would sit for free."

The dreamy feeling floated around Katie like suds around the glasses. "Why would Bess sit for free?" she heard herself asking. "She charges for the other kids she keeps. What about Lin's Vietnamese friends, if you're looking for a freebie?"

"Most of them work. Besides, I think it'd be good for Billy, hearing English all day."

To Lin she added, "Of course you'd have to be at the hospital by seven. I could take Tu to work, and then Katie, you could drive me to work and then take the kids to Bess's before you go to the library. And you could pick up all of us later."

Katie stared at her mother dumbfounded. Lin and Tu nodded as if it were all settled. "What's wrong with them taking the kids themselves, like everybody else?" she asked. "Tu could get a car. They could be independent. The whole idea of sponsors is to help them get independent."

Ruth looked up from the dishes, pale with shock. Lin and Tu gazed from mother to daughter. Katie wasn't sorry. Clearly Lin and Tu did understand more English than they spoke.

"You shouldn't expect sponsors to keep taking care of you," she said to Tu directly. "It was okay last year. But not now."

Tu held Katie's stare, unblinking. "You could do everything for yourself," Katie told him. "All you have to do is learn to drive. My mother can't do it forever. My mother is tired. Look."

They looked at Ruth and Ruth said, "Katie, that's enough."

"You never said a single word to them about not asking people for a color TV," Katie told her mother. "You let them think it was perfectly all right, like people were going to give them stuff forever." Ruth's eyes were wide and her mouth was open. Katie inhaled deeply.

"If you want a color TV," she said to Tu, "you have to save

and buy it yourself. You can't ask other people to give you one. People will give you what they don't need, but not a color TV."

"Color TV... too much money," Tu said weakly.

"Not if you save up," she told him. And then to Ruth: "See? He does know what things cost."

"You should save up for a car, too," Katie told Tu. "A used car doesn't cost so much. You should learn to drive."

"Please," Ruth said to Tu. "Katie is upset. Maybe if I had a chance to talk to her..." Not wishing to offend, Lin and Tu made nodding motions, rushed out of the house.

Ruth turned from the sink, hands coated with suds. "To talk like that... in front of *them*." She seemed to be holding her breath. "You know what your trouble is? You're empty, Katie. Ever since Daddy died. If somebody wants a full life, you can't stand it. If they want a color TV, they might be stabbing a knife in your back. It makes you that miserable."

"Spare me, mother."

"I've tried to be understanding. I've tried to leave you alone. When you didn't want to go to church . . . ."

"*Church.*"

"I've never seen a girl your age want nothing." She snatched a towel from the drawer and furiously began drying her hands.

"You're the one who'd coddle them forever so you'd never have to make a life for yourself—not me," Katie said.

"Better than sleeping all the time," Ruth snapped.

"Me, all I want is to make enough money to get out of this town and go to a four-year college!" Katie screamed. "That's all I want. You think I only want to sleep? Think again."

"Oh, right." Ruth slammed the towel down on the table. "No doubt this has been brewing in your head for years. You just forgot to mention it."

"I didn't mention it because you've been such a mess since Daddy died," Katie said haughtily.

"*Me* a mess!"

"And I'll tell you another thing. The reason I've been sleeping is because I'm sick. *Sick.*" She clutched her throat. "Maybe even strep. Big deal. Mention a sore throat around here and we go through the whole death scene again."

"You're sick?" Ruth's anger left her face, a kind of serenity filled it.

"See? That's just what I mean. You'd rather worry about my throat than get on with it. You'd rather drive Lin and Tu around forever. Anything to keep from finding a boyfriend."

"A *boyfriend!*"

A tapping at the screen stopped them. Turning, they saw Tu beginning to back away.

"It's all right," Ruth said quickly. "Come in." She opened the screen and beckoned with her arm. "What is it?"

"I think," he said, ". . . maybe we buy a car."

Ruth looked at Katie darkly, as if to say: Look what you've done. "You don't have to decide about a car tonight," Ruth told him. "I think you should think about it."

"We think about it already," Tu said.

Katie liked the firmness in his voice. She had a vision of their mutual freedom: hers, Tu's, Ruth's.

"Neither one of you knows how to drive," Ruth objected.

"Me. . . I know a little," Tu said. "My friend Fon, he teach me."

"See?" Katie said.

Ruth looked a little sick. "Fon taught you?"

"Yes. Fon. My friend."

"I see."

"Maybe you help us find car," Tu said. "Then. . . I drive to work."

"It isn't really necessary," Ruth protested faintly.

"My family. . . we never forget you help us," Tu told her. He bowed a little and let himself out the door.

For a moment Ruth stared blankly at the empty doorway. Then she lowered herself into a kitchen chair. "There's no way Tu can afford a car," she said. "I never minded driving him."

"Yes, but now if Lin goes to work. . . . "

"Passing that driver's test . . . all those questions in English." Ruth's face went completely white.

"He can do it! I know he can."

"I had no idea," Ruth said. She sat so still Katie thought she might faint. As if Tu's asking someone else for help were a betrayal. Katie feared a life for her mother of church projects and visits to the laid-off families from Mack Truck. She'd type all day until she retired. She would never meet a man.

But abruptly, Ruth stood and cocked her head as if she'd remembered something momentous. "Let me see your throat."

"It's no big deal. I'll go to the doctor if it doesn't clear up."

"I want to see it," Ruth said.

"You're paranoid, mother. That's just what I mean."

"Katie, open your mouth." Ruth's voice was firm, her face set. As she moved toward Katie, Katie turned and headed down the hall. Ruth followed. Katie quickened her pace. Her mother did, too. Both of them began running. Down the length of the hallway, into the living room, back toward the kitchen. Ridiculous. Ruth reached out to grab Katie's arm. She missed, then connected. They struggled. Two grown women wrestling! Ruth slung her shoulder into Katie's chest, pinning her daughter against the wall. "I always knew this extra weight would do me some good," she gasped.

Trapped, sweating, Katie made one last effort to lunge away. She hardly budged. Suddenly she started to laugh. She couldn't help it. Ruth took advantage and pried open Katie's mouth. "Classic strep," she said, peering in. "Red with yellow splotches." She rolled her eyes heavenward and flared her nostrils. She let Katie go. She went to the cabinet and took out the aspirin.

"I'd get out of here myself if I were you," Ruth said, relaxing visibly, filling a glass with water to hand Katie with the aspirin.

"Oh sure."

"I would. I think getting out of this town is the best thing you can do."

Katie was so startled that she swallowed the pills without thinking. She could hardly sustain her anger. She cleared her throat to confirm its rawness, to draw ill-will from it, but yelling had dulled the pain.

"You really thought I'd be insulted if you told me you wanted to get out of here, didn't you?" Ruth asked. "What kind of mother do you think I am?"

Ruth smiled gently. Some barrier had been crossed. Tu was to be let go, and Katie as well. Ruth was going to relinquish them all. Katie was momentarily as confused by her freedom as the refugees were. She would have stood paralyzed longer if her mother hadn't sent her forward in a final act of charity.

"At least get a throat culture before you go off to tackle the world," Ruth commanded.

"I intended to," Katie replied coldly.

"And Katie… don't plan me any boyfriends."

ELLENVILLE, 1959

OF THE THREE COUSINS, Fleur was the only one who lived below the Mason-Dixon line, and the other two teased her about it the minute she set foot off the bus in Ellenville.

"How's things down theah in the Say-owth?" Isobel would ask, pushing too-short hair back from her forehead and dancing around.

"About the same as here in upstate New *Yawk*," Fleur would laugh. "You know Washington isn't really in the South." The cousins would look at each other incredulously, and Zoe's atrophied left leg would drag a little, as it always did when she was excited.

Fleur took in the haze-free sky, crisp green mountains, almost-autumnal sun. "Ah, New *Yawk*, New *Yawk*," she said. But Zoe and Isobel didn't hear when she dropped her R's and broadened her words to mimic them. Zoe lived in a Sheepshead Bay tenement in Brooklyn and Isobel had spent all her life on a chicken farm in Ellenville. Each summer they met her at the bus stop thinking it was Fleur—not they—who spoke strangely. Her New York cousins were crazy, and she loved them better than all her Washington kin.

Crazy? In every way crazy—the way they lived, the way they thought. Zoe's project in Brooklyn was twenty-odd stories tall, like a mountain filled with cave-dwellers. Zoe felt no need to leave it for social life or excitement or even food. And Isobel's farm was large and open and messy, nothing like Fleur's own neat house in Washington, where her mother was such a careful custodian of *things*. The farm sat two miles out of town, off a winding road, facing a green hump of mountain. Parking by the candling shack, they forded broken equipment and animals along the path to the house, dodged chickens pecking for seed in the scratched-bare circle of yard, watched kittens dozing on the seat of a broken tractor that had been rusting in the same pool of sunshine for years. Dogs barked at them, ratty-looking things with hair longer than Isobel's—roused from the shade where they'd been cooling their bellies on the dirt.

Fleur loved it. In Washington her mother said pets made the house smell in the humidity, and had never allowed her more than a small blue parakeet when she was eleven. Six months later she tried to grab it in a dark closet to put it back in its cage, but the bird flapped its wings into her father's suit jackets and went crashing to the floor, convulsing for several minutes from a broken neck before fading away. After that, her mother outlawed pets entirely—so it was some comfort that on Isobel's farm animals were tolerated but not indulged. Isobel's mother, Hannah, met them with a dish of scraps in hand, feeding the dogs with the same disinterest with which she hung out laundry, kicking at a cat that tried to get into the house.

That evening, sitting on the porch of the house with the family, they watched the sky change colors above the mountain and listened to Isobel's father, Ezra, give his annual description of the area's two main points of interest—the Neville Hotel, a resort known to every New Yorker with an income above a certain figure, and the prison, which housed maniacs and murderers and thieves. Fleur admired Ezra for telling them about the prison, because it was a fearsome landmark her own father certainly would have kept secret. Ezra did not seem capable of hiding things the way her parents did. One year he even confided to the girls that he thoroughly disliked his chickens, thought he'd been mad to get into the chicken business in the first place, and had determined—at the very least—never to eat chicken under any circumstances anymore.

"Why if a chicken lays an egg and there's any blood left on her hindside, then all the other hens will come and start pecking at her—peck her to death from the inside out," he said. "Chickens are disgusting. Cannibals."

Ezra sighed. Fleur's own father never revealed anything about his life as a legislative aide—and his silence made her apprehensive. Had he been a chicken farmer, he might have sued the man who sold him the chickens in the first place, or written a letter to the *Washington Post*, condemning chickens in a clever way. Fleur could not imagine him staring at the mountain, which in the darkness looked like a large black head of broccoli against a purple sky. And yet Ezra's offhandedness made Fleur feel she would never, after that, be afraid of chickens in any way.

At bedtime the girls picked their way in the darkness to a one-room bungalow adjacent to the main house, which had been built before the rest of the farm and never plumbed or wired. At first Fleur was rather frightened of the absolute blackness there. Such a dimension of darkness did not exist in Washington. If there were no street lights on a certain block, still there was always the glow of them in the distance, a blue-red tinge, a fact of the city: relentless light. She could not envision what might happen in this black and utter void. Then one night she tripped over a big gray cat that sometimes wandered into the bungalow, flew head first over the warm furry hump—falling, shrieking, laughing—and landed on the cot where she slept. After that the fear diminished some—if that were all the dark could do to her. She and Zoe and Isobel talked until they could stay awake no longer, and sometimes she lay on her cot trying to detect any thread of light seeping out from the main house or from cars on the road in the distance. The blackness made her shiver slightly, thrilled—as if she had suddenly gone blind.

The year they were fourteen, on their first morning together, they slept as late as they could, because they had talked until very late and the town swimming pool did not open 'til one. They slept until the sun climbed clear of the mountain and would have slept later had Isobel's mother not come knocking on the door and yelled, "You girls better candle those eggs before the truck gets here." Candling the eggs was their one chore (Fleur liked the word *chore*), after which they could do as they liked. They forced themselves out of bed, into heavy jeans and sweaters. They were squinting into the brightness of the sunny yard, hot and itchy in so many clothes and still half-drugged with sleep, trudging across to the refrigerated candling shack, when Isobel did something strange. She turned directly to Fleur and said, "Doug's brother

Danny will be at the pool with him today. If you like him, tell me and I'll get him to ask you out to the last night of the carnival." Doug had been Isobel's steady boyfriend since March, and Danny was his identical twin brother. They had discussed them at length the night before. Fleur knew with absolute certainty that Isobel ought to have offered the other twin to Zoe.

Had they not opened the door of the shack just then, and plunged into the winter-cold of the candling room, into the dimness after the bright heat of the yard. . . had that not happened at just that moment, Fleur might simply have blurted out, "Why not let Zoe go out with him?" because Zoe, after all, lived closer by and visited Isobel several times a year.

Then the chill brought her to her senses. People often said that Fleur was cute. "You're a cute girl, Fleur, and you're going to be an attractive woman." They never said that to Zoe. For all Zoe's auburn hair and black eyelashes, for all the high swell of her breasts and the white luminescence of her skin, still Zoe was lame. Her atrophied leg hung from her knee thin and misshapen, two inches shorter than the other. Zoe seemed oblivious of it, walking well enough in ugly, special shoes, and even cheerleading back at her school in Brooklyn. But here in Ellenville, where she had to take off the special shoes at the town pool and let the bad leg dangle for all the world to see. . . here in Ellenville she was crippled. And unfit, therefore, for this possible boyfriend, this male—this *twin.*

In the cold, dim candling shack Zoe had already started loading the new-laid eggs onto the conveyor belt that brought them toward a little electric light. Isobel positioned herself by the light so she could examine the eggs for blood spots as they went by, and pass those that met her approval on to Fleur, who packed them in cardboard cartons for market. In her hands the eggs felt brittle and frozen as her heart.

"See, the light makes it so you can see the inside of the egg," Isobel explained. "If there's blood inside the egg, it shows up black. Come. Look." Minutes later a whole bloody yolk passed the light and Isobel called them over again, to see and be amazed. They worked until their hands grew numb, the hunger in their stomachs sharp—for it was past eleven now, perhaps going on toward noon. The eggs with the smallest blood spots Isobel put into a basket for the house; the worst ones she set aside for the dogs. Fleur watched to see if Zoe were suffering at not being offered one of the twins—but Zoe's expression was contained as always, perhaps from cave-dwelling in that Brooklyn tenement, where life was so familiar and safe. When finally Isobel said, "Done," the prospect of sunlight and food and Zoe's continued peacefulness made Fleur want to forgive Isobel everything. So it was with the northern cousins: they were crazy.

They scrambled eggs in the big white kitchen, Isobel breaking them into a bowl, picking out the little blood spots with a spoon. "I don't know why you can't sell these," she said. "The blood's easy enough to get rid of, it doesn't do any harm." Once Isobel had brought a completely bloody egg back to the house, broke it into a bowl for Zoe and Fleur to see. "Oh barf, Isobel, how do you expect us to look at this and then eat breakfast?" Zoe had asked, and Isobel had not done it again. Each day Fleur set clunky white dishes onto the table while Zoe tore lettuce into a bowl for salad. They always had eggs and salad for brunch, because it was all they could think of to fix.

Hannah did not seem to mind. She was usually gone from the house by this time, off to town; or else doing laundry down in the basement—unconcerned with what they ate or did. She offered them a ride if she happened to pass them walking on the road, and she smiled whenever they met, but mostly she ignored them politely, as if they were boarders instead of kin. Even the night they ordered a garlic pizza after a movie, Hannah turned up her nose but let them have it: slabs of runny cheese and tomato garnished with shreds of barely cooked garlic. Later, in the bungalow, Fleur woke with as bad a stomach ache as she'd ever had, too sick to crawl out of bed to the big house for the bathroom and Bisodol.

"I'm dying," she said to Isobel, who slept on her right.

"Go to sleep, you'll still be alive in the morning," Isobel

advised, turning away and snoring. At length Fleur did sleep, and in the morning it was just as Isobel had said. Her nausea was gone, her stomach growled with hunger, and only her breath was sharp as knives.

The way to the pool was through a field. They changed into bathing suits in the bungalow, wore Ezra's shirts over the suits, and tramped through a mile of waist-high weeds. At the far edge of the field was a creek lined with rocks, which they balanced on, and beyond the creek was the pool. There was another route on the road and through the town, but Isobel didn't like wasting an extra fifteen minutes. "Just hold your towel down in front of you in case there's snakes or something," she always said.

Fleur never intended to be afraid. She intended to wade into the field each day unconcerned as Isobel, except that the only live snakes she'd ever seen were in the reptile house at the National Zoo. Besides, she'd been trained to be cautious. At home she checked the doors twice before she went out, to make sure they were locked; she was on the lookout for muggers in Rock Creek Park; she had nightmares about the man who had followed her home from the 16th Street bus stop one night until she'd broken into a run. City fears. In the city you were afraid for good reason, and so you learned some sense. But not Isobel. Isobel would risk snake poison, picker bushes, spider bites, anything for fifteen minutes of sun. She was fearless. Crazy. And with a capacity Fleur simply did not have, for danger, for pain, for tackling things straight on: for offering her boyfriend's twin not to Zoe but to Fleur.

Every summer she suffered. Each rustling of tall grass in the wind might have been a snake approaching; each stinging weed that snapped against her calf might have been the strike. The trek was interminable; she looked toward Zoe, a fellow city dweller, for support. But Zoe never seemed concerned until they reached the creek, where she balanced carefully on the rocks so as not to get water on her ugly built-up shoes, the only pair she had. When it came to snakes, Zoe was crazy, too. Or maybe a crippled leg was already worse than snakebite and once that happened there was no sense worrying about anything less. Fleur's heart slammed against her chest all through the field, and she emerged momentarily overcome with exhaustion, as if she'd run the entire two miles from the farm.

At the pool Isobel threw off Ezra's shirt, raced to the diving board and belly-flopped in, an awkward, thin-limbed swimmer, as oblivious of form as of water temperature. Zoe hid her shoes under the bench by the chain-link fence, so they would not be splashed. She walked flat-footed on the right foot and tiptoed on the left, slightly unbalanced, toward the deep end of the pool. She dived—and was more graceful in the water because swimming lessons had been part of her therapy after the polio, paid for by the state of New York.

"Oh come *on*, Fleur." The two New York cousins pushed wet hair back from their eyes, smiled and beckoned. Crazy. Fleur walked down the shallow-end steps and tested the water with a tentative toe. Compared to Washington, upstate New York had a climate of perpetual fall; the pool was always icy. At home on such a day, her friends would sun on the side, keep their hair dry. The cousins pulled her down. Her toes curled, waves of cramp ran the length of her leg, no doubt her breath congealed into steam when she spoke into the chilly air. "Treat me for frostbite!" she yelled. And yet she swam.

Later, lying on the deck, shivering under the northern sun, she said to Zoe and Isobel: "Let me tell you about heat. In Washington in Summer the temperature is a hundred. The pool is like bath water. The sky is yellow."

The cousins yawned dramatically, wanting no part of eighty percent humidity, of mid-Atlantic haze, of rooms where air conditioning alone gave richness to human life. "The deep Sayowth," Zoe said. Then the twins walked toward them, and with a gesture so small Fleur might have missed it if she hadn't been watching just then, Zoe pulled her extra towel up over the bad left leg. Fleur decided she would dislike Danny Gregory whatever he looked like, Isobel or no.

"So you're from Washington," the twins said, both of them in unison, tall and tan as pancakes, with tan eyes, too. . . and so alike. Alike even to the fine blue veins pushed up from the muscles of their upper arms, as if they had lifted identical weights.

"Can you walk from your house to the White House?" As if every city except New York must be the size of Ellenville.

"Oh *no.*" They were so naive that they would walk past Cardoza High School in the dark if you let them. Undemeath, these twins were crazy, too. Tan-eyed stares focused on her. . . smiling. And so alike.

"How do people tell you apart?"

"I weigh six pounds more than Doug."

"Yeah, and he's twice as ugly," said a boy named Mel who had walked over with the twins. They spoke five minutes, perhaps, and then the boys went into the pool—sailor-dived in, held noses and jumped in, swan-dived in, splashed in—and out again—roaring, shoving, falling.

"Practicing for the swim meet tomorrow," they yelled. Fleur could not tell which one had spoken.

Isobel laughed. "What'd you think?"

"Oh. . . he's nice. They're all nice." But they had not, in five minutes, asked Zoe a single question, though the one named Mel—with tiny brown slits for eyes—had spoken to her for a time.

Night—and their sleep split by the sound of a horn—brash, jarring, louder than an ambulance. They sat up in bed all at the same moment, unable to see, arms flailing out for each other, and when Fleur's voice came she shouted over the blaring of the horn: "What's *that?*"

"The prison," Isobel said. "Somebody probably broke out." On the word *broke* the horn stopped, and the phrase BROKE OUT roared all through the bungalow. The gray cat leaped onto Fleur's cot and Fleur jumped a foot.

"It's no big deal," Isobel said. "They usually catch them right away. Go back to sleep."

Sleep? Fleur stared at the dark for a long time, imagining

the prisoner creeping in on them (there was no lock, hardly any latch, on the bungalow door), snatching her away. When she dozed at last she dreamed not of the prisoner but of Zoe, leading a cheer at school. Her copper hair bounced down her back as she jumped, but her heavy black shoes made her land with a clunk while the other cheerleaders rebounded on the spring of clean white sneakers.

They woke to rain—cold, autumnal—rain that made them think summer was blowing out already, in July. They candled the eggs and made brunch with their sweaters still on, all the while a restlessness crawling inside them, because they had expected to go to the pool again and (though Fleur would not like the boys, no matter what), see them, swim in the meet, live their lives.

"Four of them," Hannah said, wandering in, waving the newspaper story about the prisoners. They'd sawed through the bars of a bathroom, climbed two sets of fences, fled.

"Hey, look, this one's in for murder." Isobel examined mug shots, looked pleased. "They always catch them before this."

Fleur thought: Isobel likes this because there is so little here to *do*. It was barely noon and cold damp daylight stretched before them forever.

It rained all that day and the next. Hannah took pity on them and drove them into town for a movie, but it was not enough, not like wandering through Garfinkle's in Washington, eating in Woodie's tea room, looking at shoes in Hahn's. They grew tired of their aimlessness, tired of each other. At dinner Hannah dished out mashed potatoes—soft dull food for the soft dull day. They spoke of the prisoners— where would they go?—worried the problem about as if the convicts might relieve their boredom by showing up any moment on the damp front steps.

"I'll tell you where they'll go," Hannah said, waving her fork. "They'll go home like they always do. They'll catch a ride down to New York, take the subway to wherever they live, and get caught ten minutes later."

Sure enough, two convicts were captured before the next day, one in the Bronx and the other on the Westside.

In the night they stayed up later and told wilder stories, so as not to die of boredom. Doug had touched Isobel's breast—and other parts, too. Zoe had passed out at cheerleading practice when she had the flu, but the other girls covered up for her so she wouldn't have to tell her mother.

And Fleur?

"Did I ever tell you about the man who followed me home from the bus stop?"

"No. *Really?*" Isobel's voice was high and light: expectant.

She told: how it had been dark; how she'd gotten off the bus where she always did—this was after her piano lesson— and how the man had followed. She knew all the people who lived on her street or were likely to, and this man definitely wasn't the sort. . . .

"Oh *Fleur*, I bet he was awful."

"He didn't even have on a real coat, just a raincoat. Even in the dark you could see his hair sticking out like a bush." Actually she hadn't seen him at all, except for the briefest shadow.

"I kept walking faster but he was keeping up with me. I'll tell you I was scared to death. . . . "

"I bet you were!"

"Shut up, Isobel," Zoe said.

"Anyway, I finally decided if I didn't do something he was going to grab me any minute. So I took a deep breath, I turned around. . . and I kicked him in the shins!"

"Oh, you didn't!"

"Yes, I did. Honestly. Then I ran. Let me tell you, I really ran!"

"That's great, Fleur. That's really great."

"Oh Fleur, think," Zoe said, laughing. "What if he was really going to visit somebody on Holly Street, if he was some poor relative?"

Great whoops all around. "But he wasn't, Zoe. I could guarantee it. You know, you ride the subway. You can tell when they're weird."

"Not me," Zoe said. "I never even noticed. Nothing ever happened to *me*." Her voice was calm, the cave-dwellers voice.

And Fleur was shamed—for lying, for wishing she'd really kicked the man instead of just running—oh yes! and kicked him not in the shins but in the balls. Shamed for making Zoe say nothing ever happened to her, when they all knew the reason it didn't happen—the reason Zoe could afford to be so calm—was not because the big apartment building kept her safe but because she was lame.

The third day brought sun at last, a cloudless sky. Otherwise they would have died for sure. They raced through the snake-ridden field, Fleur in tempo with her pounding heart, ready to swim in the long-delayed meet. At the pool the water was so cold from the rain that the officials were thinking of canceling. Fleur examined the surface of the pool expecting to see the small beginnings of ice. But there was no ice, and everyone complained so much that the meet went on as scheduled.

"I'm signing you up, Fleur, never mind the water. What do you want? Freestyle? Breast stroke? Backstroke?"

"Not me, I'm not freezing my you-know-what."

"Backstroke then," Isobel told her.

"No."

"*Yes.* It's not as cold as you think."

"Freestyle for me," Zoe said.

The boys didn't speak to the girls before the competition. This seemed proper to Fleur: that they wouldn't want the girls' beauty to distract them. When the races began neither Isobel nor Fleur placed, but Zoe came in first in the girls' freestyle. Their teeth chattered for half an hour afterwards . . . and stopped when the boys wandered over, to sit not right next to them, but near.

"How ya doing?" Danny said. Fleur, meaning to be cool to him (for he had not said a word to Zoe) smiled instead. "All right. And you?" As if her manners had come from the Sayowth after all.

When the younger children swam, underwater the length of the pool, they came up blue. Blue fingers, purple lips, goosebumps from head to toe. And one boy—it took so long to notice this—did not come up at all. His frog-motions grew slower, slower, and very nearly stopped. When the lifeguards realized and pulled him out, he was long unconscious, though he had been moving—Fleur was sure of it—moving just a little, until the very last.

They did mouth-to-mouth first and then an ambulance came, screaming through the quiet town, bringing the neighbors to see—mothers with aprons over their slacks, men in hardhats.

"It happened because the water was so cold," Fleur whispered.

"Don't be ridiculous, Teddy was always a lousy swimmer," Isobel said.

But Fleur knew: If Teddy had been a sane city boy his mother would have warned him, and he would have come up when his limbs started aching, preferring to live than win. City people knew enough to run when a man followed them off the bus, not turn around, not try to fight, only survive. They were crazy, these country people. Bored. Wild for action. And Zoe was lame—protective coloration—and lived in a hundred-story mountain, where life was safe. At that moment Danny brought the towel she'd left over by the chain link fence and threw it at her chest, so she had no choice but to catch it.

"You're shivering," he said. She could not understand why her stomach contracted, way down low, when he walked away.

The boy revived, but not for hours, and he might never be the same. At the pool in the sunlight they spoke of the usual things, but of course nothing was usual. The carnival would be here soon, and one of the prisoners was still at large. He was probably camping out in these mountains, now that the weather was nice; he must've had the sense not to run back to the city. And the drowned boy, not drowned but maybe changed forever.

In the gentle northern light, even Zoe's fair skin tanned, though it seemed to Fleur the bad leg tanned not quite as well as the other. . . perhaps a trick of proportions. Isobel splashed in the pool unruly as ever but Fleur held the image of the drowning boy in her mind all the time and stopped going in. The voice in her head was clear as air: cold could kill. She could no more have gone into that water than Zoe could have walked when she was sick. The cousins teased. Cajoled. And finally, sensing it would do no good, left her alone.

Danny sat with her sometimes. She did not mean him to. "He's being nice, he thinks you can't go in the water because you have your period," Isobel said.

"Oh God," Fleur replied. But even that did not make her swim .

Each day Danny spoke to her and Doug spoke to Isobel and some other boy came over to speak to Zoe, usually small-eyed Mel and sometimes a thin almost-albino boy named Phil. Always some *lesser* boy. When Fleur asked Zoe what she thought of Mel, Zoe squinted and made a face, imitating the tiny slits Mel had for eyes. Then she laughed and said, "No, he's all right—really. He's really pretty nice." Afterwards Fleur thought: Zoe should not be making fun of boys who're a little funny-looking. And was shocked that such a thought would enter her mind.

One day the twins walked up to them and Fleur knew that Danny was on the left, Doug on the right. It was not so much that Danny was six pounds heavier as that he seemed larger, dominant, in every way: thickness of hair, deepness of voice. She had thought she was fascinated because the twins were so alike. She did not think she would forgive herself for telling them apart.

The carnival came, with skin-and-bones barkers and only three rides. It was so drab that Fleur could not understand why Isobel wanted to go every night, except to see the boys, who talked to them but would not pay their way until the last night. At home when she was younger, Fleur sometimes went to the Lions Club carnival with her parents, where her mother won at Bingo while her father took her to play the games. Afterwards the three of them circled the Bingo table examining the prizes they could get for her mother's win tickets, until her mother said, finally, "But Howard, there's really nothing here I want in the *house*," before choosing a blanket or a glassware set.

But Isobel did not like the carnival just for the boys; she liked it for the rides. She liked the whip and the Ferris wheel and particularly the Rocket, a long pole with red cages on each end, that lifted them thirty feet above the ground and made them hold themselves in their seats by the sheer power of their outstretched arms. Fleur hated the Rocket. By the third night her arms ached so from holding herself against the metal bar that she imagined losing strength, imagined her stomach pressed against the bar after her arms gave out, steel poking into the softness of her and the macaroni-and-cheese Hannah had fixed for dinner being pushed up and out. This while Isobel squealed, Isobel whooped; Isobel delighted at being whirled upside down and low. Fleur thought: Isobel is so afraid nothing is ever going to happen that she likes *this*. But it wasn't until Zoe said, "It's a good thing I've got a bad leg and not bad arms" that Fleur knew something terrible would happen if she set foot on that ride again.

Now Fleur stood at the bottom of the Rocket watching Isobel spin above them, and Zoe stayed with her out of loyalty. Danny came over to talk. Fleur wanted to say, "Why don't you talk to Zoe?" because he never did. She never said it. She imagined Danny asking her to the carnival on the last night, and imagined herself saying, "Why didn't you ask Zoe? It's because of her leg, isn't it?" She imagined Danny saying, "That has nothing to do with it. Anyway, there's nothing either of us can do about Zoe's leg." She imagined Danny kissing her, imagined his tongue in her mouth. Once she imagined someone saying, "Oh, that's Fleur Gregory, she married one of the Gregory twins." She said, "Come on, Zoe, let's not stand here all night, let's go on the Ferris wheel." But later, in the bungalow, her stomach ached sweetly from the things she imagined about Danny, all the same.

They were too excited to sleep. Isobel sat with her legs crossed on her cot, bouncing—they could not see her, only hear—and said, "If they're going to ask you out, it'll be tomorrow. You never know if they will—how much money they've got."

She bounced higher and the cot creaked as if it would collapse. "What if Mel asks you, Zoe? Will you go?"

"What—and stare all night into his big brown eyes?" Zoe sounded bitter.

"I thought you liked him, "Isobel said.

"Not *that* much.

Isobel stopped bouncing. "He's really pretty nice."

"Then *you* go out with him." Zoe threw her pillow at Isobel in the dark, but it missed and hit the floor.

"I'm going to bed," Zoe said, her voice rough and gravelly. Fleur could hear her foot dragging as she went to get the pillow.

Lying on her cot in the silence afterwards, Fleur thought: Zoe's leg would not be this way if the the polio vaccine had been invented in time. The idea exhausted her.

But Zoe bitter?

The next day the sun was hot for Ellenville, and at the pool they spoke of everything except the carnival. Doug said he thought they got that last prisoner and Danny said no, someone was stealing vegetables from people's gardens; it was the prisoner for sure. Isobel said as soon as she was old enough she was going to get a job bussing tables at the Neville. *Then* see if she wouldn't be rich. Small-eyed Mel and albino Phil sat together not far from Zoe: outcasts all. Fleur thought: there is nothing—really there is nothing—I can do about Zoe's leg, except be kind. Which was not enough.

When Danny came close to her she knew if he asked her to the carnival she would have no power to refuse, even if Zoe had to go alone. She had never had any power in this world. So she said to him, "This morning an egg came through so full of blood it looked *gray* on the outside even without the light." Danny said, "Ummn," and kept coming toward her. She moved toward the pool and jumped in. It wasn't until the cold gnawed right through her that she remembered she, too, could be drowning. Though she did not.

In the dark she woke to the sound of a chicken being strangled. A high thin screech and then silence. The prisoner killing his dinner. Or maybe she dreamed it. Isobel was snoring and Zoe was breathing deeply; she could tell exactly how they lay, so crazy they didn't hear a thing. Wouldn't. A sound came again, of movement, and then a silence as if of caution. The creaking of a door. Her mouth was dry and her heartbeat noisy; probably he could hear it. She fumbled on the floor for the flashlight, a book, anything hard. But the flashlight must have rolled beneath the cots; all she came up with were Zoe's shoes. The movement came again, stealthy. She would wake the others. But no. There was a weight in the bottom of the built-up shoe, heavier than she expected. Let them sleep a little longer. Tiptoeing across the floor she thought: really there is no prisoner, there is no one, only the old gray cat, nothing to be afraid of. But just in case, she moved toward the door—the prisoner, the rapist, the thief—clinging to the shoe with all her might, and ready to take him on.

THE VALUE OF KINDNESS

LATE THE NIGHT OF HER FIFTY-THIRD BIRTHDAY, Cora Russ put on a dark shirt and trousers and stealthily began raking pine straw from her neighbor's yard. Earlier she'd eaten tempura shrimp at a restaurant with her husband, Seth, and her son Jason, a senior in high school, who'd presented her with cologne and earrings and birthday cake. Back at home, Seth watched the updates on Operation Desert Shield until he fell asleep on the couch, and Jason did homework while talking on the phone to his girlfriend. Around midnight, Jason finally went to bed.

The Rutherfords, whose yard Cora was raking, had small children and no time for gardening. Their tall pines had been shedding yellowed needles for a month. Now the pine straw was solid, smothering the grass.

Under her dark clothes, Cora broke a sweat which let her work with feverish energy. It was an almost-balmy Southern night in late fall, moonless and soft. The Rutherford house was dark. Even if they weren't sleeping, they probably wouldn't notice her. If they did, would they have her arrested? Did she care?

Once, Cora had believed anyone of a certain age deserved to die and probably wanted to. She couldn't imagine the passion to live persisting in a soft, wrinkled body. Anyone so ugly would be too embarrassed to want to carry on. But now—if she intended to live out her fifty-third year, she might as well be useful. Besides, what could she be arrested for? Trespassing?

She raked the pine straw neatly into corner of the yard, feeling like Robin Hood. Then she walked home and woke Seth to tell him it was time to go to bed.

"Where've you been?" he yawned.

"Out walking. I was restless."

"Looks more like you were running."

"A little."

He grinned sleepily. "Worried about getting old? Trying to keep in shape?" As owner of a successful employment agency, Seth had time to work out at a health club and run three miles a day. When Cora had first met him, he'd been in the Army training troops for Vietnam. His body had been hard and tan, lighter on the belly, far more beautiful than her own. Now, even with activity, his muscles had lost tone and his skin grown mottled with tiny dark spots—not moles or freckles but the ravages of time—which reminded Cora, especially now, of her age.

The hour of raking hit her all at once, leaving her bone-weary under a hot shower. Because of her birthday, Seth would make love to her tonight. Unnecessary, she wanted to say. And wanted to discuss, too, other concerns of being belatedly menopausal. *If it's not wet, don't touch it. Make it wet first. Then.* Had there been some other man, some other life, she might have managed this, but divulging such privacies to Seth after twenty-three years of marriage was as unthinkable as strutting naked through the house. In any case, there was no discussing the crux of it—that though she loved him, though he was the only man she could have lived with this long and want to continue, even so, for the moment she would just as soon not make love.

"You still have nice legs for an old lady," he whispered as she got into bed. This made her feel doubly evil for the clinical and unflattering ideas she knew would occupy her as they touched: *He's pumping my breast as if it were a cow's udder. He's latching onto the nipple like a baby nursing.* As if "he" had no name. As if she were writing journal entries or a book.

The next day her arms were sore from raking, stippled deep inside with little points of fire. Were the neighbors up yet? Were they puzzled, or did they know perfectly well who'd done the raking, and why?

She dressed for work carefully. Too big-boned for elegance, she opted for formidability—severe, expensive suits and good jewelry. She reasoned that these helped stave off the irate husbands who sometimes came looking for their spouses at the domestic violence center she administered. The truth was, the living quarters of the shelter were on the other side of a deliberate maze of hallways, and the security system was so elaborate that the women were safe even without Cora's intervention. She spent most of her time on the phone or at meetings except when she deemed it wise to give a tour of the shelter to generous patrons.

She was greeted by Shirley Coleman, the shelter's manager, herself once a battered wife who'd taken her two children and left. Shirley was a large vivacious "woman of color," as she described herself. She never used the term *black.* Her office was in the shelter's living quarters, where she greeted each newcomer with such open arms that briefly, even if they came with broken limbs, she comforted them, convinced them there were possibilities.

"Somebody wanting to give us a couch," Shirley said, hanging up the phone as Cora entered, rolling her eyes. They calculated that half their contributions were offered not as charity but in hopes that someone would cart away useless junk.

"I'll have Pauline check it out later," Cora said.

"We have that lunch, don't forget."

"The medical auxiliary?" Or was it Women Aglow? Their talks to such groups almost always elicited a donation. "I should have remembered when I saw you wearing shoes," Cora said.

"Miserable uncomfortable shoes, too."

In honor of the occasion, Shirley had stuffed her feet into black leather heels instead of the canvas flats she normally claimed were all her wide arch could endure. She made no other effort to dress up. Elastic-waist skirt. Cheap sweater. Not, this morning, in her accustomed hot pink or fluorescent lime ("to look a little cheerful, you know?"), but in fire-engine red, and a string of pearls that might have come from the dollar store.

The medical auxiliary, by contrast, turned out in muted silks, which daunted Shirley not at all. Cora made introductions and let Shirley give the speech. As Shirley said in private, "White ladies always like to hear a real, ex-battered wife."

Looking at the well-dressed audience, some of them familiar from the neighborhood, Cora was struck by an urge to
confess: "Last night I dressed in dark clothes like a robber
and went out to rake the ratty pine straw off the Rutherford's
lawn." It was all she could do to pretend interest in the pro-
gram.

Shirley gave her usual zingy talk. Earnest, ebullient, sincere. "What you got to realize is, she's most at risk right now
with the holidays coming up. Or if it would be her birthday.
He don't want her to have no good memories."

The increasingly sloppy grammar made Cora smile. Shirley
knew which audiences responded better to standard diction,
which to the more exotic, ethnic mode of speech.

"What sort of women come to the shelter?" someone
asked. By which she meant: white women or just black?

"Most middle class white women, if they have some
money, they don't come to the shelter. They get on a plane
and take a three-week vacation," Shirley said. Laughter. "Not
that the trip solves the problem. But for women of color—
they don't have the choice. We get mostly women of color."

One by one, Shirley slipped off her heels and stood behind
the podium with her wide feet naked on the tiled floor. The
audience was rapt. "What he does first is, he isolates her. If
she wants to go out with friends, he says, 'You rather be with
them than with me.' He makes her feel so bad she stays
home. Then he criticizes her family. A lot of times, he won't
lay a hand on her until he's got her cut off from everybody.
Until he's all she's got to depend on."

Then Shirley told her own story in a detached, pleasant
tone. So mild, such a sweet pulp. How had she escaped bit-
terness when her ex-husband had broken her nose, shattered
her jaw? Cora tried to imagine rising from unspeakable hor-
ror, going back to show others the way. She'd never known
unspeakable horrors; indeed, horrors of any kind. Having
not, how could she be sure she'd have the strength to escape
them?

"Your yard looks terrific," Cora said to Peggy Rutherford,

her heart thrumming in her throat, blood rushing through her ears. "When did you rake it?"

"You won't believe it, but we didn't. We woke up one morning and—*voila!*" She removed the hand pushing her toddler on the swing and made a quick sweep around the lawn, toward the pile of pine straw. "Overnight. It was bizarre." The swing glided back; Peggy propelled it forward. "We don't have the faintest idea who did it. Some Good Samaritan. The phantom gardener."

"Well, I wish he'd come prune my roses." A double lie. Pruning was one of the pleasures of Cora's warm winter days.

"It's scary, in a way. Suppose he'd had—I don't know. . . less benign motives?"

Had her motives been benign? Perhaps not. Cora considered. "A little scary, yes."

Seth had taught one of his all-day job-hunting seminars and now was sprawled across the couch in the family room, beer in hand, not drinking. The TV beamed out interviews with troops assigned to the Saudi desert since August. They'd eaten Thanksgiving dinner and sounded homesick and bored. "They ought to get in there and be done with it," he said. "You'd think they'd have learned something from Vietnam."

"What's this, War 101?" asked Jason, coming into the room.

"The voice of experience, son," Seth replied.

"Right. The aging but venerable veteran." Jason folded himself into a heap on the floor.

"With the emphasis on venerable," Seth told him.

Seth had been sent to Vietnam when he and Cora were married less than a year, to supervise a mine sweep along a road where dozens of people had been killed. She never knew, until Jason asked his father if he'd ever seen anyone die, that a trooper once had his legs blown off by a mine they missed, and that Seth had held him while they waited for the Medevac helicopter. "All you can guard against is bleeding and shock," Seth explained. To the injured soldier he had crooned, over and over, "Everything is well under control here. Everything is well under control." And when the trooper lost consciousness and his breath rattled, Seth held him closer, did not let go until the breathing stopped.

"Did it make you sick?" Jason had asked.

"You think it will before it happens," Seth replied. "But when it does, you aren't. You just do what you have to."

After that Seth's unit cut fatalities on that road eighty percent. Later, his first months back home, he startled at every car backfire, every sudden noise. A quick tensing of muscles, so subtle that Cora wouldn't have known unless she was touching him (which she often was those days) and felt his fright resonate inside his skin.

A year later Seth resigned his commission. After a stint with an employment agency, he'd started his own, specializing in placing other ex-military. Cora sometimes thought he still missed the intensity of Vietnam. It seemed he'd had some personal thing to prove there, and that he had—for which she rather envied him.

What persisted was his anger at the way Vietnam was perceived. "From watching TV, you'd think every third guy who went over there ended up homeless," he complained. To Jason he preached otherwise. "We'd have won, no question, if we'd gone in with proper force." And Jason, when he was younger, had been infected with Seth's enthusiasm, had spent days running around the yard shooting toy M-16s at the enemy. Now Seth hoped for a quick war of mastery in the Persian Gulf to atone for the shame of the other. For handsome statues instead of the Vietnam Memorial, which he called "nothing but a wailing wall." He stayed glued to the nightly updates on television, irritably waiting for action.

"Here. Sit," he said, patting the couch next to him. Cora did. He slung an arm around her and set his untouched beer on the end table. Years ago he'd prided himself on being able to drink all night and still work the next day. Now a single beer could give him a headache.

"You look beat, Dad," Jason observed, studying him.

"Warding off women wears you out," Seth said. "You know

how those seminars are. Those employment agency groupies."

"Babes, huh?" Jason asked

"There *are* no employment agency groupies, son," Cora said, slipping out from Seth's arm, feigning annoyance. Then the phone rang and Jason bounded out to get it, ungainly as a large dog.

"Sure, go ahead and talk about other women," Cora said with exaggerated petulance, noting the exhausted slash of white along Seth's cheekbones, across the bridge of his nose. "But keep in mind that I'm likely to get up some night while you're sound asleep, and get a giant carving knife, and cut off your wang."

He leaned against her, reviving a little, whispering in her ear: "It'd *take* a giant carving knife, too."

At her desk, explaining to two volunteers how to do a bulk mailing, she was burning up, turning crimson. The hot flashes had been brief at first, pulses of heat beamed from her neck into her face, lasting only a few seconds. So *this* is it, she'd thought, wondering what all the uproar was about. Now she babbled on in front of two earnest thirty-year-olds while heated coils glowed inside her chest, up her earlobes, casting off some horrid inner fire. Thirty seconds, a minute. Any instant she might ignite, making the volunteers party to the crisis they so desired.

"So you sort them according to zip code, and then depending on how many of each category there are?" one of them repeated.

"Yes." Sweat broke out along her upper lip, down her neck. Visible, surely. "Use the conference table if you want to. Put them in separate piles. There's plenty of room."

In a minute she'd be cold. Ridiculous. And unnecessary, her doctor insisted. "What you need is hormones. Not only will they stop the hot flashes, they'll also protect you from heart attack and osteoporosis."

"Yes, and cause uterine cancer instead. I've read about it."

"Where? In some women's magazine?" Oh, snide now, disapproving. "Even if you do get cancer, it's the easiest kind to cure."

"What! Am I hearing right? Advocating getting cancer!"

Not even a grin. "Usually all that's required is surgery."

"*All?*"

"We're finding the benefits far outweigh the risks. You really have no choice."

No choice! She didn't mention two grandmothers who'd survived into their eighties without hormones. She said she'd think about it.

"Think about it soon, Cora." His voice was grave and dramatic, condescending, as if she were too stupid to understand what was being offered.

Whenever Seth went to an evening meeting, Jason camped out on the family room floor. Tonight he held the TV remote in his hand, switching channels every few seconds in hopes of finding a certain video on MTV or VH-1. He had a violent hunger for one song and one song only, almost an anger. Cora did the dishes, straightened up. At nine o'clock Jason muted the sound and called Leah, his girlfriend. A nightly ritual. Before his senior year he'd hardly dated, and now he seemed consumed.

Wandering upstairs to give him privacy, she restlessly stripped the sheets from her bed, fetched new ones. Jason's laugh drifted up the stairs, a short, clipped guffaw. What did he and Leah talk about? In school they exchanged lengthy notes which covered most everything—or rather, Jason received notes which Leah wrote. Instead of discarding them or tucking them away, Jason left them on his desk or bathroom counter, the most public places, as if to be sure Cora read them, which she did.

They were oddly sweet, which made Cora like the girl, who in person seemed unextraordinary. *I really respect your dedication to running* (during cross country season). *It's nice to see someone who really cares about studying* (which was news to Cora). Leah's kindnesses made Jason kind in turn. But now. Lately. *What do you want to do Friday night? I know what you really want to do, but what we actually will do is another story.*

She wasn't sure she wanted to be party to this. She smoothed her bed sheets, rearranged the comforter, then took clean linens into Jason's room. There were no notes in sight tonight, just scattered shoes and laundry. As Cora pulled off the soiled linens, the sound on the TV switched on suddenly, blaring. Rich guitar music, a gravelly male voice singing indecipherable lyrics. In her own wanting days there'd been no videos, only records she'd played so often that the grooves wore down and the sound grew foggy. By then Cora was sated, bloated, as if she'd eaten too much sugar. She could tell Jason there'd be many things he'd hunger for, many things he'd get. She could say it wasn't altogether pleasant, having all you wanted of a thing, wearing out your need.

She shoved his bed out from the wall to fit the corners. On the floor was a J.C. Penney catalog turned to a page of slender models in underpants and bras. An old towel beside it had been crumpled into a sticky ball—what in her own youth her brother had crudely termed a come cloth. She carried it to the laundry room, vaguely disgusted.

The week before Christmas, the shelter was packed. "It's like I told you—she don't leave until her children are out of school," Shirley explained to the busy volunteers. "She always thinks of everybody else first."

The latest arrival was Kenya Washington, eighteen years old, with a two-year-old, an infant, and a badly bruised chin. Her husband showed up outside Cora's office an hour after she arrived. Cora said no, his wife wasn't anywhere nearby, she couldn't say where she'd been sent, it was useless to ask.

"I know you got her here," Howard Washington replied, patient, almost respectful, standing close to the intercom on the porch. "If unknown person comes on premises," a sign on the shelter wall read, "please call 911 or push panic button"—an alarm connected directly to the police station. It hadn't come to that yet. "I'm gonna find her," Howard Washington said, brushing a hand across the top of his tall box haircut, perching himself on the porch railing. "I got time."

Cora called the police. Seeing the cruiser turn onto the block, Howard Washington disappeared. Whenever a husband seemed dangerous, the wife was whisked to a safe house in the community until her man cooled off. Cora instructed the volunteers to begin making calls.

They had no luck. Most of the people who provided safe houses were busy with the holidays. "I'll take her for a day or two if I have to," Cora whispered to Shirley, not anxious for it but aware that a woman and two children might make Jason think twice about bringing Leah home for sex while Cora was at work.

Kenya sat on the couch in Shirley's office, a thin, angular girl with Oriental features and African-black skin, huddled next to the armrest, eyeing Cora's seasonal green suit with distrust. Unnecessarily, she bounced her sleeping baby on her shoulder. Her little girl pulled ornaments from the Christmas tree.

"How long I got to stay in somebody's house?" she asked Shirley.

"Just till we feel like it's safe for you here," Shirley said. "It'll be all right."

"How do I know he don't get the address and track me there?" Her heat filled the room, but she spoke with more fear than anger, and her voice held no conviction.

"He won't follow you. He wouldn't get in even if he did," Cora said. "We train people to make sure that doesn't happen."

Kenya looked down, unbelieving but submissive. Sometimes the women came in filled with healthy fury, but mostly they ran off in sudden bursts of self-preservation, and when the adrenaline wore off, they were more abject than vengeful. Kenya's chin was so puffed out from her pretty, angular face that her jaw actually looked misshapen.

The baby suddenly squalled. Abstractedly, Kenya leaned over and pulled an empty bottle from a shabby purse.

"Come in the kitchen, I'll show you the formula and where

to warm it," Cora said. The shelter would provide food if necessary, but the women had to prepare it. Be independent.
Heal their wounds and give them strength. Ordinarily Shirley
introduced newcomers to the kitchen, but Cora judged that if
she were taking Kenya home, she might as well take charge.

Pale light from a bank of windows fell onto counters of
cheerful tile and wood. Cora showed Kenya around. The girl
surveyed the room not for coziness or function but for safety:
the double locks on the door, the fence around the parking
lot in back (its gate never closed, however, because of fire
regulations). Kenya sat on a kitchen chair, her daughter wide-
eyed at her feet, the baby's head lolling off the edge of her
arm, neck unsupported. *Keep hold of his head*, Cora thought
but didn't say. The baby slurped his bottle, fell into a brief
gluttonous sleep, woke with a start and shrieked.

Cora had taken a woman home once before. Jason had
sulked, his space invaded. Seth had tried to make small talk.
The woman had muttered back in a thick ghetto accent.
She'd stayed two nights, but it seemed like weeks.

Burp him now, Cora thought. The girl didn't. Cora reached
out, gave Kenya no choice but to let Cora lift him up and
away, his body against her shoulder, his hair a soft black fuzz
against her chin. "What's his name?" she asked.

"Robere."

Or it might have been Andre or Jacques. Did every woman
at the shelter give her child a French-sounding name?

Cora had no crib. No formula. No infant seat. She handed
the baby back and weighed her reluctance against the girl's
wound. If she were Shirley, she wouldn't hesitate. Shirley had
taken them home until her landlord threatened eviction.
Otherwise she'd be doing it still. She made Cora feel diminished for balancing the trouble of tending this frightened,
hostile, battered girl against the comfort of having someone
in the house to chaperone her libidinous son.

In the end she needn't have worried. Within the hour a
volunteer turned up and took Kenya off. In her office, away
from the rising pandemonium of waking children and
women ready to fix supper, Cora finally buzzed Shirley. "I

don't think that girl has the faintest idea about tending that baby," she said. "Even though it's her second."

"Wouldn't be surprised. Her people are all out of state."

"What happened, exactly?" Cora asked.

"He got drunk. Beat the shit out of her."

"The usual," Cora said.

Seth was in ecstasy. Oh, Mr. Ecstasy himself. He'd just won his age group in the holiday road race, a 5K, with the best time he'd run in a year. He was still flushed as he stood under one of the leafless willow oaks that lined the road, holding forth to friends from the local running club about the yellow ribbons encircling the trees.

"Yellow's coward's color," he said with disgust. "It means you want to get the hostages out and then get out yourself. No! When you're up against a bully, you have to go in and get him."

This was less a military position than a personal one. When Jason was six and plagued by larger boys, Seth hated seeing him intimidated. He watched Jason stalk the yard, shooting imaginary adversaries with a toy pistols and rifles, afraid to go to school. "What do you expect to accomplish by this? The guns don't even look real," Seth told him. "You have to fight back with your fists." He even showed Jason how. Cora protested that it was wrong to teach violence, better to talk it out.

"And what's he going to do when the kid's punching him in the face?" Seth roared. "Reason with him?"

In the end, Jason faced his nemesis and came home only marginally worse for wear. He wasn't bothered again. Now Seth vented the same driving hatred of bullies against Saddam Hussein, and against the weather-beaten yellow ribbons everyone displayed. For himself, he'd tied a patriotic red-white-and-blue ribbon to the antenna of his car.

"If I were running the show, I wouldn't wait for any January deadline, either," he intoned to the runners. "I'd go to war right now. The sooner the better."

The crowd, mostly runners, nodded and collectively

zipped up their sweatshirts against a sudden wintry wind. Cora scanned the scene for Jason, who'd placed third in the fifteen-to-nineteen division, behind a couple of college boys. But the young people had drifted off, beyond the line of trees.

"We could be in and out of there in a weekend if we put our minds to it," Seth concluded.

"Despite the predictions of some experts?" asked a fortyish woman named Trish, sarcastic but smiling, tugging at the black tights she wore under her running shorts.

"Despite the predictions of some experts," Seth countered, returning the smile. At the recent holiday parties they'd attended, people had mostly agreed with Seth, when for twenty years, on the matter of Vietnam, they hadn't. He challenged Trish's gaze until she looked away, self-conscious, pushing a strand of dark hair from her forehead.

Jason surprised Cora, coming up from behind, laying a hand on her shoulder. In the startled second when she first turned, he might have been a stranger, no longer the target of bullies but larger than the two friends who stood beside him, the bulk of his chest and arms handsome on his slender frame. His running coach had advised him to take up weight training, and the results were recent and startling.

"We're going to take off, okay?" Jason said.

"Sure, go on. We'll probably be leaving soon ourselves." Cora looked toward Seth, but he was talking again to Trish. Cora had met the woman before but not paid attention. She was handsome even with her makeup sweated off, high wide cheekbones, a full lush mouth a bit like Cora's. Was the twinge that went through her jealousy? Or just embarrassment that Jason was witnessing his father's flirtation?

Once, Cora would have been seized by possessiveness. She'd always worked full-time partly because she abhorred the thought of falling into the dependent, narrow lives of women protected and supported by men. She'd seen them play tennis and shop, only to discover one day with shock and outrage that they'd been abandoned. Cora meant to have her own money even if she couldn't lay full claim to her emotions. But now, even when Jason turned hurriedly away, even when Seth and Trish started laughing together over a shared comment, Cora could not have said she was exactly devastated.

She planted Rose Kincaid's Christmas tree in full daylight, in view of anyone who might see her go into the yard; it was not meant to be a secret. Rose's brother-in-law had died Christmas Eve. Rose and Joe were still in New England with the family. Their balled-and-burlapped Christmas tree had never even been taken into the house. It sat propped against the front porch, drying out, looking hapless.

Cora had meant only to go for a walk. The air was cold and restless, reflecting her mood. Rose was a friend; Cora might plant the tree and call the act a Christmas gift. She would tell Rose later. The toolshed in the Kincaid's yard was unlocked. Cora retrieved a spade, dug a hole, piled the loosened fill dirt onto a canvas. By the time she dragged the tree around back, her hair was matted to her head and beads of perspiration trickled down her chest. She added leaf mold from Rose's compost heap and turned on the hose, heart thumping against her ribs as fast as Seth's must have during his race.

She wasn't prepared for the article that appeared in the local newspaper a few days later. *Phantom Gardener Strikes Again.* The Rutherfords were quoted on the matter of their pine straw, and Joe Kincaid, who'd left Rose up north yet a while, reported that he'd returned to find a tree planted in his backyard that hadn't been there before.

"The phantom's not malicious, otherwise he wouldn't go around doing people's garden chores," Peggy Rutherford was quoted as saying. "But still it's frightening, thinking he can come and go like that without being seen."

He.

Cora's throat filled with what she couldn't quite identify as embarrassment or amusement or, oddly, a sense of misplaced power.

"The worst thing he ever did to me wasn't physical, it was

what he said," Shirley told the women at the shelter's kitchen table. St. Andrew's Church had sent leftovers from a potluck supper, and Shirley and Cora were lunching with two residents, Lace McLamb and Kenya. Kenya had returned from the safe house with her babies. Her bruises were healed, her hair newly washed, pulled back to accentuate her Oriental features.

"See, before I left him, I worked in a job center. It was social work, really," Shirley said, jabbing the air with her fork. "You weren't supposed to be supervisor without a degree, but finally they offered it to me, the first time they ever picked somebody who didn't go to college."

Shirley speared a forkful of pasta shells and held them aloft. "I was so excited, I could hardly wait for him to get in the door. You know the first thing he said? He said they probably only asked you because they couldn't get nobody else."

Lace McLamb nodded. Shirley popped the pasta into her mouth. "I'll tell you. Even now the worst thing I remember about him, it's how he made me think there wasn't nothing good about me anybody could want."

To the board of directors Shirley often said, "The reason so many of them go back is because even though he beats her, he makes her feel like she doesn't deserve any better. What we try to do is make her feel like she deserves."

Kenya lifted her plate and, with exaggerated slowness, moved toward the sink. After the initial fear, there was often this sleepwalking quality to the women, an eerie calm as if they were walking on cotton or floating. Surprised and numb and shocked.

Indeed, the whole shelter was oddly sleepy. No late-night calls to the crisis line for a week, no broken bones, no belligerent men. Cora didn't know whether to credit the after-Christmas lull or the fact that the community was poised for a more distant, less personal war in the Persian Gulf.

Still in slow motion, Kenya scraped her leftovers into the garbage. Some shelters wouldn't take women like her after a man had pursued them there, but Shirley had convinced the board that theirs should. "If you don't, then you're holding her accountable for what he does to her. That's one more reason it's hard for her to leave."

Maybe, for the first time, Kenya felt safe. Most men didn't come back to the shelter once their women had been sent away. They assumed the women were gone for good. Since Kenya's return, she'd been out to apply for food stamps, see about public housing, take the children to the well-baby clinic.

Kenya turned on the tap and rinsed her plate. The beep-beep of children's TV drifted down the hall from the play-room, where both her children were asleep.

"Sometimes you wish you could do him like he done you," Lace McLamb said, watching Kenya. "Just once."

Shirley shook her head a vigorous no, though Cora knew that once, when Shirley's husband came in bragging about his other women, Shirley had chased him out with the knife she'd been using to cut onions, and shattered his windshield with the blade.

"He's always going to be stronger than you, some ways," Shirley said to Lace. "You can't use his weapons. You have to fight him with your own."

In Jason's open desk drawer, Cora found a bodybuilding magazine, three unfiltered Camels and a package of condoms. Even without that, she would have known what had happened.

"I might go study at Brian's," he said when she came downstairs. "If Leah calls, take a message."

"I thought you liked me to give her Brian's number."

"Naah. Just tell her I'm out."

His heartlessness contrasted with a younger, less secure Jason she remembered suddenly, running his first cross country races, always outpaced by another boy. "If I don't beat Todd I'm going to kill myself!" he'd roared then.

"I don't ever want to hear you talk like that! Killing yourself over a race! It's just a sport!" she'd screamed.

What she remembered was this: how Seth had scoffed at her agitation. "In a way," he'd said, "everything's a sport."

In those terms, how did one define Leah? Teammate?

Opponent? Or the equivalent of the soccer ball, waiting to be kicked?

A song blared from Jason's tape deck, not his usual rock but loud, raucous country. A taunt. "Hey there, Saddam. . . " The words followed her into the laundry room. "We're not really afraid. . . of your starving armies and all your wore-out tanks." He turned it even louder. "Don't give us a reason. . . "

"For heaven's sake, Jason!"

"To come gunning for you!" the singer rasped.

"Turn that down!"

More instructions to Saddam. "Take your poisoned gas and stick it up your. . . .

"Jason!"

". . . sassafrass."

She came out of the laundry room, into the den. "I mean it Jason. Turn it down. Don't give me a reason."

The volunteer who donated the shelter's laundry detergent had switched to the new space-saving containers of extra-strength powder.

"How could you go through a whole box of this in a day and a half?" Cora asked Kenya while Shirley was away. "Only six people live here right now, and I know half of them didn't do laundry yesterday. This stuff is supposed to do forty-two loads."

"How it gonna do forty-two loads, a box this size?"

"It's that new kind of detergent. You're only supposed to put in this one little scoop." Cora lifted it from the box.

"I don't care what they say, that ain't gonna do no forty-two loads of dirty laundry. Not baby laundry with spit-up and all."

Kenya put her hands to her slim hips and stood firm with conviction. The gesture seemed foreign to her, but so fitting that Cora almost smiled. She made a mental note to tell the volunteer to go back to the old kind of detergent.

The war was on! Desert Shield had become Desert Storm. During prime time, too! In the family room, Seth wielded the remote like a weapon, NBC to CBS to ABC and finally to CNN. Cora brought in dessert and coffee. They studied maps of the Persian Gulf. Heard commentary from Atlanta. Strategy from the Pentagon. On-site reporting from the Al Rasheed Hotel in downtown Baghdad. Imagine reporting from the heart of enemy territory! Imagine tracer bullets. Antiaircraft bursts. Explosions lighting up the darkness.

"You think incoming and outgoing sound the same until the first time you actually feel incoming," Seth said, switching channels again, color high. Jason's face echoed his father's.

The next night they all came home early, to watch again. They hadn't had such togetherness in years.

The correspondent in Jerusalem was frightened. He'd been reporting since the air raid sirens sounded. He wore his gas mask and wandered around the office. A cameraman filmed messy desks and a dark sky out the window.

When the all-clear sounded, he took his gas mask off. Did his hours of airlessness hit him? His sleepless night? His face went pale, he ran his hands nervously through his hair, he looked like he was going to pass out.

Another newscaster joined him, a woman. She took over while he stood aside. "We'll switch to Richard in Tel Aviv now," she said. "For an update by phone."

"Let me ask Richard something before you sign off," the nervous reporter said. He shuffled his feet, fingered his hair.

"Calm down, buddy," Jason told the TV, popping open a Coke.

"He's lost it," Seth added.

"I feel sorry for him," Cora said. "He spent half the night in a gas mask. He hasn't had any sleep."

"That's what he's getting paid for."

"Larry has a question for you," the woman said to Richard in Tel Aviv.

"See, maybe he's getting it together."

But first, a break to the states.

Some strategic question, perhaps? A political matter? Cut to the Pentagon. To Atlanta. Back to Jerusalem. To the crucial question.

"What did you want to ask him?" the woman said.

"Uh—Richard. How are you all doing there in Tel Aviv?"

"*That* was the question?" Seth asked.

"I don't think this speaks well for his career," Jason said.

"I think he's on the next plane out of there," Seth added.

"You have to feel sorry for him," Cora told them.

"For screwing up?" said Seth. "Why?"

Cora and Shirley had driven an hour in the dark, coming back from a workshop on shelter management. They'd left Shirley's car in the shelter parking lot so Cora could drive; it made no sense for both of them to. When they pulled into the lot it was nearly midnight, cold and so clear that the stars were bright hard specks on a black inverted bowl.

"You should have seen her," Cora said. "So *incensed* that I'd question how much soap they were using. Hands on her hips. . . ."

They both laughed. They were tired and not wary, talking about Kenya Washington. Shirley opened the door.

A figure moved out of the shadows so swift and silent that before they had time to register danger, he'd grabbed Shirley's arm, wrenched it behind her, and pressed a gun to the side of her neck. Shirley's coat gaped open, her blouse pressed tight against her overlarge breasts. Cora's first stupid emotion was embarrassment, at seeing her friend so ungainly and exposed.

"You get out, too, or she gets it," the man told Cora. Fear bloomed sharp in her nostrils, like the scent of something burning. In the space of a second she considered leaning on the horn, stepping on the gas, shifting to reverse and charging backwards toward the street. Finally, obedient, she cut the ignition and let herself out into a frigid slice of air.

The man, she saw, was Howard Washington.

"Now we're gonna go inside, and I'm gonna talk to my wife," he said, low. He pushed Shirley toward the shelter's back door as he spoke, twisting Shirley's arm until her face grew taut and expressionless with the effort of not showing pain.

"Get the key," he said to Cora.

She did. Her fingers were shaking; her mind went flat.

They stood close in the doorway, the mellow waxy odor of Howard Washington heating the air, a combination of hair dressing and sweat and anger. But no liquor, no glassy cocaine high. Just a nervous, calculated sobriety.

The back door led into the kitchen, a sudden whoosh of heat. A night light glowed over the sink and into the empty silence of a sleeping house. Howard held Shirley a little tighter. "I know you got Kenya here," he said, caressing the pistol with his thumb. "Now we're all going to go upstairs and get her." He nodded toward Cora. "You show us the way and your friend walks right here with me."

The refrigerator motor switched on as he propelled them into the hall. No question of getting to a phone. The panic button was twenty feet in front of them, on the front wall, hardly inconspicuous. Shirley said nothing. Howard Washington pressed his thin frame against her wide back. He played the pistol up and down her neck.

What was wrong with this picture?

"We'll just bring her down here, and nobody has to get hurt," he said. A trio in slow motion now, inching down the hall toward the stairway. Did she hear movement upstairs? Maybe not.

Ten feet from the alarm. Five. She'd have to lift her hand to press it. Not possible.

If they don't shoot at once, Seth always said, they probably aren't going to shoot at all. She slowed down.

"Keep your ass moving lady, or your friend here gets it."

"We better, Cora," Shirley whispered urgently. Her blouse was bright, electric orange, a power color. A Christmas gift from her children.

Howard Washington, Cora saw, was hardly older than Jason.

"You expect us to go up and get her with you pointing that gun? Is that how you want her to see you?" she asked. Buying a few seconds to study him. If the blood would stop rushing through her ears, she could think.

"I ain't gonna tell you twice," he said, reeling Shirley in. Shirley's eyes were black marbles, circles of fear.

Cora moved down the hallway, toward the stairs. She thought she saw a woman appear at the top, then shy away. He was at the wrong angle to see her.

What he saw was the red knob protruding from the wall, the panic button.

"Move away from that thing, bitch." He pointed the gun at Cora.

You can't use his weapons to fight him.

She moved away. Up the stairs. Slowly. Slowly.

"Freeze!"

He turned, startled, clutching Shirley tight. Two police were poised at the bottom of the stairs, weapons drawn. The women upstairs must have called them. Howard Washington was the only one surprised to see them.

"You come any closer, I'll blow her away," he said. Shirley wore no expression at all; she might have been standing at attention. At the end-point of terror. Having escaped a brutal husband, to meet her end at the hands of a teenager. Cora thought she finally understood the meaning of the term, *beaten*.

She remembered Kenya, with her hands on her hips, sure of something.

Howard pulled Shirley into him, the gun pointed toward her head for everyone to see.

That's when Cora knew all she needed to about weapons.

"It's a toy," she whispered. And then louder to the men at the bottom of the stairs. "The gun's a toy."

The police moved then. It took Shirley a second to register freedom, but then she leaped away with more grace than you'd credit in a woman her size, and in thirty seconds it was over.

They couldn't sleep, not after all that. Cora didn't get home until two-thirty, having called Seth earlier to give him a brief outline. To her surprise, he arrived at the shelter while the police were taking their report. Cora stood with Seth's hand

on her shoulder, watching Kenya and Shirley give their state-
ments, each dazed and almost cushioned—Shirley by her
size, Kenya by her gaunt beauty—and yet, in contrast to
Cora's coupled state, each entirely alone. When Seth followed
her home in his car, unasked, the gesture seemed wholly an
act of love. Later they lay in bed stretched out flat in the darkness, hands behind their heads, rehashing the evening.

"How did you know the gun wasn't real?" Seth asked.

"I told you—Jason."

"I don't know how you could be so sure." He looked up at
the dark ceiling, unmoving.

"Remember how Jason used to have all those guns when
he was little? When the bullies were after him? And how you
used to say they didn't look like the real thing?"

"Nowadays they do," he said. "People rob stores with toy
guns. They rob banks. The weapons look completely
authentic."

"This one didn't."

"You could have been wrong." He sat up and turned on
the bedside lamp so as to impress her with the force of his
gaze.

A tremor began in her neck, then melted away. Too late to
be frightened. She smoothed the crease of worry that formed
between Seth's brows. "No," she said. "I knew."

Still bathed in his concern, she turned out the light and slid
closer, running her hand along his mottled skin and touching
the paunches at his sides. This made her try to pull her own
stomach in, not with much success. Unaccountably, she
wanted to laugh. What squeezed her stomach so ineffectively
was not muscle mass but old age, she supposed—hers, and
his, too. Then Seth pulled her toward him with such urgency
that it seemed not to matter. In spite of temptations like Trish,
he was not likely to leave her, or she him. They would probably spend their next twenty years together exploring their
mutual and advancing flab.

She forgot herself then—because what worse could she
think of than mutual and advancing flab?—and the touching
was better. As if, in some way, even though one system was

shutting down, another was taking over.

Jason sat on the deck in shorts and T-shirt, attached by earphones to his radio, goosebumps dotting his bulging arms against one of those warm spells that briefly graced the Southern winter. Today wasn't as warm as it looked. A few feet from him in the yard, admiring her bounteous blooming camellias, Cora hugged herself into her windbreaker.

"You ought to put some clothes on," she called, forcing Jason to lift his headphone away from his ear to hear her.

"I'm all right. I need some color."

"What? A red nose from from the cold you'll get?"

"A gorgeous February tan." He extended an arm, flexed the bicep, studied it lovingly. She hated his recent swaggering attitude, and this gesture didn't endear him to her. The condoms in his drawer had been supplemented by others (until Seth spoke to him about it) in the glove compartment of the car. At the same time, he'd started going to parties with other boys instead of Leah, and bragging about flirting with Leah's friends. In Cora's view, Leah was being nicer than he deserved. Her notes had taken on a sort of pathetic dignity.

I've given you something I can never give anyone else. I'm not sorry. I've learned more from you than I have from anyone. I've learned how to study and apply myself. But I'll tell you this honestly: I don't want to lose you.

Still preening, Jason looked down at his chest muscles, visible through his too-tight shirt. He'd taken to wearing smaller shirts to accent his bulk. Cora pointed toward the yard next door, where the Rutherford's four-year-old was swinging.

"If you ask nicely," she said, "maybe you can borrow some shirts from *him*."

"Very funny, Mom." Jason snapped the earphones back to his head and closed his eyes against Cora's sourness. The more he fell in love with himself, the more he felt entitled to ignore her. She extracted a pruning shears from her pocket, turned from the camellias, and began cutting what might have been deadwood (but was hard to tell now, in the dormant season) from her roses.

Head back, eyes closed, the wispy beginnings of whiskers dotting his upraised chin, Jason offered his face to the light. Seth opened the screen and soft-shoed around him. "He's sunning the body beautiful, I see," he said to Cora.

"Working on a case of pneumonia," she replied. Jason's radio was so loud that they could hear a faint beep wafting out from the earphones. He might have been on another planet.

Seth lugged a chair off the deck and into the yard. Cora dropped down beside him as he plucked a few strands of bristly grass. "I did a damned fool thing the other day," he said.

"What?"

"I went to Army headquarters to see if they needed any middle-aged ex-officers to help out while they've got so many guys in the Gulf."

"I didn't know you were interested in doing that."

"Neither did I."

Embarrassed, they both stared ahead of them, at sun on the brown grass, at the glossy camellia leaves, the show of pink blossoms.

"The upshot is, they don't really need you if you've been out twenty years," he said.

She didn't know how to reply. It seemed an enormous confession.

"You've got your business, anyway," she managed finally. "You couldn't really leave."

He shrugged and flicked the strands of grass away from him. "What really makes you feel like a jerk, though, is doing something to try to relive your youth. When you know damn well that's impossible."

A garden center had sent its unsold flower bulbs to the shelter, nearly a hundred altogether. The bare sunny spot behind the building cried out for flowers, but whenever a volunteer offered to plant them, it rained. The box sat in the corner of Shirley's office, untouched and accusatory. "What we need is that phantom gardener," Shirley said one day.

A pure jolt of adrenaline shot through Cora's veins.

They were sitting on the floor at the time, paperwork for the new budget spread out all around them, Cora juggling figures on a calculator. She felt her face go red as if from a hot flash.

"We got all this mess to bother with," Shirley said, indicating the papers. "So you'd think some guy that likes to garden so much would come down here and help us out."

"Maybe he's out of business," Cora managed. "I don't think he's done anything lately."

Her back ached from sitting too long on the floor. Funding from two different grants was being cut.

"What I don't understand is why he picks a neighborhood like yours instead of coming down here where we need it," Shirley joked.

Cora set down the calculator and tried to straighten her back. The heat really *was* a hot flash. She stood and fanned herself, coming face to face with her reflection in the mirror over the couch. Beads of sweat had formed above her upper lip, but her cheeks were not flushed, her ears not red, none of the great visible upheaval she had expected. She said to Shirley lightly, "Maybe he's racist. Maybe he just doesn't like women."

Sortie. She hadn't even known the word three months ago. Sorties in the air and operations on the ground. Death by friendly fire. Iraqis surrendering by the dozen. Seth claimed he was tired of CNN, but as soon as he switched channels, he always switched back.

Cora heard the news dimly in the distance as she pulled laundry out of the dryer. The war had begun to remind her of the year her high school football team always won by forty points. No question of the outcome, more like a struggle put on for show. A game.

Was there such a thing as an unimportant war?

In the kitchen, Jason talked on the phone in low and serious tones. When he was finished he trailed Cora to the washing machine. "I broke it off," he said.

"With Leah, you mean?"

"It's better, isn't it? I never really liked her that much. I mean, it wasn't really fair."

Cora did not say, you mean not fair to screw her and not care about her? She folded a towel.

"Also, she was getting so attached. Scott Newman wanted to date her. You know Scott. But he couldn't, with me around."

"Scott Newman likes her?"

"When I told her I wanted to break it off, she asked me if I meant we should only go out sometimes," Jason said. "But I said I thought we shouldn't go out at all. That's better, isn't it? A clean break?" He looked earnestly troubled. He leaned against the door jamb. He looked younger than he had.

"I always thought a clean break was easier in the long run," she said. His distress charged the heated room. She knew the helplessness of not being able to love someone back. The fierceness of repulsion. She hadn't married till thirty, after all. She'd once left a date in the middle of a restaurant because she couldn't bear to be with him a moment longer.

Had she really done such a thing? Yes.

But still she didn't forgive Jason.

I never thought I'd have a child, she wanted to say. She picked up a pile of towels and headed for the linen closet. I was thirty-five. Old, in those days, to be a first-time mother.

He followed her.

I thought you were entirely precious, she thought.

"When you get older," she told him, "you'll learn the value of kindness."

Later, out in her garden, by the slant of light that drifted from the den, she cut camellias from each bush—not so many that the loss would show—and filled an empty laundry basket.

There was no longer such a thing as bomber's moon, the reporters said. Moonlight made the planes visible to antiaircraft gunners. No, a pitch-black night was better for sorties these days, when infrared and laser-guided bombs could hit targets through inky darkness.

There was no moon as she drove to Leah's house with the laundry basket in her trunk. No light at all after she cut her headlights. The blossoms, as she scattered them across the yard, spelled out, she hoped, the name of Leah's admirer, Scott.

In time, she would tell Shirley. On a day when things were dismal, when a woman like Kenya went back to the man who beat her, when Shirley was repeating statistics in consternation: "It makes no sense that she leaves five to seven times before she stays away." Cora would keep the secret till then. I'm the phantom gardener, she would say.

Oh, right, Shirley would reply.

I am.

Cora, you're a crazy woman.

Yes, probably.

They would laugh.

She came back to Seth at the TV and Jason on the phone again, telling a friend about the breakup. Bragging? In the den, the screen showed clips of beige tanks on beige desert, the desolation of sand.

"Cold out there?" Seth asked.

"Not if you move around."

Jason hung up. Restless, he bounded up the stairs. And down again. Refrigerator opening. Closing. Up the steps.

"I look at him and you know what I don't see?" she asked Seth.

"What?"

"I don't see the skinny six-year-old who got beat up on the bus. I don't see the kid who couldn't quite win a race and wanted to so much. What I see now is a kid who has sex with girls and then dumps them."

He put his hand over hers. "I think he was just scared. He won't be that way forever. He'll be all right." In the dim light his skin seemed smooth, a little puffy around the wedding ring but not yet marred with veins.

Jason filled the doorway, can of Pepsi in one hand, bag of chips in the other. He came in, plunked down in front of the newscast without a word. Apparently he had no one left to call. Cora was sticky under her shirt, hot from strewing blossoms. Cut to the Pentagon. The White House. Seth and Jason focused on the screen, so intent and passive that the sight of them made her sad. "I'm going to take a shower," she said finally—loving them perhaps more than she had, but grateful, too, that theirs was a distant war and hers so close that neither youth nor age could reduce her to watching it on television.

A NOTE ABOUT THE AUTHOR

Ellyn Bache is the author of three books: a non-fiction book, *Culture Clash* (Intercultural Press, 1982); and two novels, *Safe Passage* (Crown, 1988; Literary Guild and Doubleday Book Club Selection; English edition, Judith Piatkus Books, 1989), and *Festival in Fire Season* (August House, 1992, also a Literary Guild Selection). Her stories have appeared in *O. Henry Festival Stories, Ascent, The MacGuffin, Crazyquilt,* the North Carolina Fiction Syndicate, and others. She lives in Wilmington, North Carolina.